# BREAK
# THESE
# CHAINS

## Kirsteen
## Stewart

First published in 2020 by whitefox

Copyright © Kirsteen Stewart 2020

ISBN 978-1-912892-76-1

Also available as an ebook
ISBN 978-1-912892-77-8

Typeset by seagulls.net
Cover design by Heike Schuessler
Project management by whitefox
Printed and bound by Clays

*To Achara, Luke and Theo*

# Prologue

## March 1966

Here she was, at twenty-one, back on the Solway Firth, back where it all began. The fractured childhood, the missing father – "missing, presumed dead". The mother who couldn't love her, who had run away along the river, red hair streaming behind her, with the horse-trader, the rabbit man and then the Rumanian waiter with the violin. Her grandmother, Eveline, appearing out of the mist that unforgiving night, a majestic figure in tweeds and cashmere and a little felt hat, directing operations with her walking stick and taking her away to London wrapped in a blanket in a black Humber. The adored but undemonstrative Eveline, whose silk blouses must not be stained with her tears, whose standards wrought in war and austerity could not adjust to London's new glitter and sexual freedom, whose loving disapproval in life was followed by a strange challenge in death.

Ten years old, trudging home from school along the same track beside the Solway Firth. It was November then – the beginning of the black months. She was cold. She had lost one of her mittens and her chilblains ached and itched. Her kilt was too short and the slits in her old wellington boots let in the water. She needed new clothes, but she'd have to wait for the next parcel from her grandmother. She pulled down her jersey, her precious striped jersey, all the colours of the rainbow, made up from the odds and ends of wool left over from socks and gloves. This was no casual hand-me-down from one of her favoured cousins. This had been knitted by her grandmother especially for her, a sign that she loved her.

In the distance she could see figures strung out along the dunes. Only a disaster brought a crowd of people on to the shore – a lost boat, a suspected drowning. Her heart contracted. Her shoulders tightened like chicken wings. Something terrible must have happened. The sort of thing she dreaded every time her mother fell in love.

Then she remembered. The neighbouring farmer had lost his new bull, a beautiful toffee-coloured creature, a young Charolais mix, bought with a loan and the reckless notion of making his fortune in stud fees. It wasn't her mother they were searching for. But surely the bull would not have strayed off the sedge. Cattle were naturally wary of marshland. Everyone knew that. Still, it took them time to adjust to new terrain and the young bull had only just arrived from somewhere green and sunny.

A flock of Canada geese flew over from the Scottish side of the estuary, in their perfect V formation, their familiar honking filling the air. She stopped to watch as they swept low on the darkening water. Something caught her eye. Something in the mud beside the decaying piles that used to be a jetty when the shrimp boats went out. There was an iron ring in the mud. That wasn't surprising. The quicksands claimed every sort of object. But this was moving slightly. Lydia picked her way towards it, ten feet out from the bank, into the danger area she'd so often been warned about, intent now, sinking into the slime, the muddy water seeping over the tops of her boots. The ring was attached to a pair of unmistakeable pink nostrils, opening and shutting like clam shells, a few inches above the mud.

Lydia stopped and stared. But only for a moment. The incoming tide sucked at the mudflats. Very soon the mud-coloured nose would disappear under the mud-coloured water. She shouted and waved at the figures in the distance. No one took any notice of her. She had to warn them. She tore off her precious sweater and laid it on the bank to mark the spot where the ring could be seen.

Panting, dressed only in her liberty bodice, she ran up to the farmer.

"Whatever're you doing, wee Lydia, got up like an orphan child?"

They brought the tractor and attached a rope to the ring in the bull's nose. Because he was young his nose was delicate, and Lydia feared they would hurt him. But they pulled very slowly, very carefully, shouting instructions to each other in the November dusk, a race against the tide, keeping his nostrils just above the incoming water. The sinking sun caught their faces, blinding them for precious moments. Then the bull was halfway out and suddenly he lurched forward on to the bank with a leap and a squelch. She marvelled at the sight. He was alive, he was unhurt, spattered with mud up to his beautiful blond eyelashes. He shook himself, chastened but triumphant, and pawed the ground, digging her striped sweater into the quicksands. Lydia reached down to save it, and the young bull turned on her, swarthy and rippling, massive shoulders, thick neck, head lowered, horns swishing through the air like torn silk. Dangerous and beautiful. The farmer shouted and jerked his head away and now the bull's huge testicles swung towards her, more monstrous than anything she had ever seen in the childhood farmyard.

"That mother of hers," sneered one of the men, "away after something like that. Rather than cooking her tea."

Half understanding, Lydia was silent.

"It's not right, so it's not," said the farmer. "You've saved my bull – saved him and me. You're a good lass, daughter of Rio. You'll win through. You can be like him." The farmer was the only person who referred to Rio Renfrew, her father, who had been swallowed up by The War a few months before she was born. Lydia had no way of knowing how she might be like him, and only half-formed ideas of what her mother was and shouldn't be, and what she too might become. "Will you go home and get yourself warm? Will you be all right on your own? The waiter this time, is it? The Rumanian from the Silloth Hotel?"

She nodded, eyes on the ground, knowing that they all judged her mother for leaving her on her own, for prowling after men in the dark.

"Well, he's moving on, that waiter, so's I've heard. Can't be too soon. Him and his whole caboodle. His caravan and his horse and his violin under his chin."

He meant it to be reassuring.

Now Lydia was frightened. They all moved on – the horse-trader with the Kendal Fair, the rabbit man back to his wife. Leaving her mother howling after them. She didn't prowl, her mother, she chased desperately, deaf to Lydia's pleas. It would be worse with the blue-eyed Rumanian. He'd stayed longer. Flora might have thought he would stay for ever.

Then she would stay on the track, cold as she was, and she would catch up with the Rumanian in his departing caravan, take hold of the horse's bridle and turn it round and bring him back for her mother.

A straw-coloured moon disappeared behind the clouds. She knew the track, every bend and pothole and tussock. But things looked different in the dark. Surely this was where the caravan should be? The flattened grass and the post where he tied his horse. A huge white owl swooped down, cross and mysterious, peering at her. Lydia screamed. A barn owl signified death. She ran faster.

She shouted for her now. "Flora. Flora. I'm coming." It didn't seem right to shout "Mother" – she was the one who must do the protecting. Her voice echoed over water. It was quite close to her now. She could hear it hissing – water in front of her as well as beside her. It shouldn't be ahead of her. Could she have taken a wrong turning in the dark? She looked around her. There was water behind her too. There was no track.

Like all the estuary children, she could interpret the moods and movements of the tide. It was rising fast when she found the young bull, so it was nearly high now. That was dangerous here. "Mother. Mother. Where are you?" Her voice was squeezed by panic, a sound like a lamenting bird. The Solway Firth creeping in around her, visibly, inch by inch, like a hungry creature. She shouted out again, desperately now. "Mother. Mother. Help me. Help me."

The only escape was to her left, over the shifting sands. Sinking in with each step, over and into her wellington boots, too heavy to pull out her legs, too slow to outrun the tide. She splashed on a few steps, sobbing with fear. She was cold, cold. The water was up to her knees.

The moon came out again, surrounding her with a black and silver world, out of an evil fairy tale. To her right, the shape of something, a hunk of wood, one of those old shrimp boats, disused now, rocking on the tide. Lydia splashed through the deepening water and threw herself over the gunwale and on to the curving boards inside, wailing, "Mother. Mother. Come and find me."

\* \* \*

More than ten years she'd been away, away in London. Today it was noisy and bright on the Solway Firth, a shrill March wind in her ears, gulls and terns screeching a few feet above her shorn head. Her hair felt sparse and bristly, like the backs of pigs. She still wasn't sure how she had managed to cut off so much, the long black curls that Marvin would never again wind around his fingers. The memory of his hands on her body filled her with loss and longing.

They told her that she had grabbed hold of the clippers he used to shear the sheep, and taken them to her hair, leaving an anti-halo. They thought it was an act of deranged, unmanageable grief. But there was penitence in it too, for not understanding, for her failure to make it all fit together – the love affair that drew her away from her grandmother, the wide-open opportunities of London and the glitter she couldn't resist. In the moments before she was fully awake, before she remembered, it was all just a bad dream, a film that could be rewound. Then bits of clarity stabbed her, like shards of glass piercing bare feet, the pain taking her breath away.

Forty Tamworth pigs were following her along the shore in a placid pied-piper trail, snuffling in the mud. As a child she loved the pigs. When the warmth of human beings was missing she had hugged animals, proper animals, working sheepdogs and untrained Labradors, horses of various sizes and unpredictable temperaments, even one or two favoured pigs, cheek against bristles, breathing their heated scent. The pigs were unchanged. It was she who had deserted them for London. And now she was back, stumbling about in a sorrow that threatened to suck her down like the quicksands of the estuary.

The sedge smelt of wild thyme and crab shells, as it always had. The tide was out now, a ribbon in the distance, glazed by the sinking sun, innocent and beautiful. But turn your back and the sea came in over the mudflats. You had to keep alert. She watched the black clouds humping over the horizon. The dusk was sudden in the winter months. She must round up the pigs and bring them safely back to their pens. This was all her mother would trust her to do. The mother who had preferred her lovers, the mother who'd never behaved like a mother, was looking after her now. And it was her own actions that were threatening to suck her down.

# Chapter 1

## 1965: A year earlier

It was in January of Lydia's third year at university that a student she'd never met invited her to his birthday party. One of a group who fancied themselves as cool operators, entitled to send invitations to girls who were talked about or considered pretty or likely to be lured easily into bed. Lydia wondered which of these she was supposed to be. It was billed as a starry event. Nothing suitable to wear. A black lace petticoat bought from a cheap shop in Queen Street and a few extra frills sewn on. The long string of fake pearls and her *Breakfast at Tiffany's* cigarette holder. No need to buy cigarettes. Everyone's reaction was to offer her theirs. Dry Martinis were new to her. An icy transfusion of self-confidence. She had wandered about, making remarks to strangers, peering at them over the rim of her cocktail glass. Twisting to Chubby Checker on a tabletop. Dancing as a way to be free. With each swivel of her bare feet, the black lace floated out in a bewitching curve. Again and again.

A girl strode up to the table, snarling.

Her partner took Lydia's hand and they jumped down together to the floor.

"Ah, Camilla," he said, quite casually, as though it were natural to be dancing on a table with someone not his girlfriend. "Meet the lovely Lydia Renfrew."

Camilla's angry little eyes glittered and she sprang towards Lydia.

"Of course. Lydia Renfrew, the daughter of the nymphomaniac pig farmer…"

"I'm sorry? What did you say?" How could someone in Oxford know about her mother? Something exploded inside her. "Take that back this minute."

A clearing opened up around them, like a boxing ring.

"A slut from the Solway Firth. Like mother, like daughter. You need teaching a lesson." Camilla grabbed hold of Lydia's pearl necklace and pulled.

The cheap thread broke and fifty fake pearls cascaded on to the floor and bounced away under the tables. Thudding around the silenced bar. People gasped. People were horrified. People scrabbled to pick them up.

"You bitch. You filthy bitch." Lydia had only ever used the word 'bitch' to describe a farm animal.

Lydia leapt upon Camilla and punched her gloating face. They scratched and fought each other in a way Lydia hadn't done since primary school. The blood was pounding in her ears and it was exciting to want to hurt her. She sank her teeth into Camilla's hot pink cheek and it was exhilarating to hear her cry out and the blood on her own lip was the nectar of the gods, and a startling scarlet stream trickled down the satin of Camilla's shirt like a Jackson Pollock painting.

\* \* \*

"This is Constable Fryer from the Oxford police, Miss Renfrew."

Lydia faced the principal of her college with a hangover laced with shame and anxiety. The room tilted. The violent-patterned carpet was alive under her feet. The gas fire hissed venomously. Sunlight streamed brutally past inadequate curtains.

The principal sat upright in a stiff armchair, a tall grey-haired woman, so austere and shy that she stared at her shoes when she spoke. She was rumoured to care more about the French Cistercian monks than college students or worldly affairs.

"Er ... This is Constable Fryer, Miss Renfrew. He tells me that last night he was called to a ... place in the town I don't have the privilege of knowing ... called, I think, La Roma. Have I got that right? It seems you were involved in an incident ... A fight between girls. An entirely new concept as far as I'm concerned."

The principal made an effort to raise her eyes as high as Lydia's knees to emphasise her determination to confront this intrusion from the non-academic jungle.

"Unfortunate provocation ... taken into consideration ... not making any charges ... hoping to keep the Proctors out of this ... but very bad for the reputation of the college, Miss Renfrew, a women's college especially ... required to have unblemished standards of behaviour ... you understand this, I'm sure ... a number of college rules broken too ... out of college after midnight without a pass."

She seemed to be musing, wondering whether there was anything else she should have taken into consideration, uncertain where to take the matter next. Then she pulled herself together, straightened her back, and ratcheted her gaze upwards so that she was staring at Lydia's throat.

Lydia kept very still, the headache waiting in the wings.

"Constable Fryer will not be pursuing this matter because we're suspending you from the college. We are not sending you down; we do not wish to ruin your academic chances. Your work is very good. We think it best if you take a year off and sort yourself out, Miss Renfrew, and if things settle down, you should certainly come back and finish your degree course. Think of it as retaking your third year. I would go as far as to say we hope you will come back to us. Ah, and Constable Fryer has these for you."

She handed Lydia a brown envelope filled with the huge fake pearls that had been scattered over the floor of the bar. Lydia looked at it and nodded very carefully. She hadn't said a word throughout the interview.

"We ... that is, I, have had a word with your tutor and I ... we ... have a suggestion for you. One of our former students is working at the Department of Education and Science in London. Researchers needed ... temporary arrangement ... new Labour government ... new education policies ... the end of the eleven-plus ... new universities ... I'm not so sure about that idea, but still, that's what they are planning ... You know about this sort of thing, I expect."

Lydia tried to concentrate. Very little national news percolated out to her from the free copies of *The Times* piling up beside the gas fire in her little bedroom. But she followed the new Labour government over the rims of coffee mugs in colleges and cafes.

"We can vouch for your intellectual standards. Go to London, Miss Renfrew, that's my advice to you. I don't go there myself. My research takes me to the north of England, as you will know. But there are all sorts of opportunities for a clever girl nowadays. We will have a word. Chance to wipe the slate clean. Sort yourself out, d'you see? And come back and retake your final year in October."

Lydia wanted to cry, to say she was sorry, to throw her arms around the principal. But all coherent thought was snuffed out. What a suitable word – hangover. The past was hanging over her. Her life snagged around the very thing she wanted to free herself from, like a skirt caught on barbed wire, and the more she tried to pull away, the worse the damage.

The principal stood up very straight, hands clasped in front of her.

"A serious moment in your life. We are going out of our way to help you because you have exhibited considerable potential. Don't waste this chance. And now, Miss Renfrew, I must ask you to pack up your possessions and leave this college."

\* \* \*

Lydia Renfrew sidled over to the fireplace.

"Sit down, Lydia, for goodness' sake," said her grandmother. "This is not a social call. We are having one of our serious talks."

This was her beloved grandmother, Eveline Ashfield, former society beauty, with eyes the colour of the North Sea and a huge, well-managed bosom, here on home ground, in her elegant drawing room in Chelsea, surrounded by glass-fronted bookcases and small circular tables covered with photographs: a handsome young pilot clothed in hope and uniform, eyes on the horizon; her sepia second husband with moustache, Panama hat and submissive spaniel, confident in some grand portico. Son Edmund, as a schoolboy, in one of those V-neck cricketing sweaters and white flannel trousers, eyes downcast, unable to look at the camera. Edmund's three children, Lydia's cousins, the perfect blond grandchildren. Lydia herself at seventeen, tidied up for a professional photographer, almost unrecognisable. But no Flora. Lydia's mother, Flora, the daughter who had disgraced Eveline, exiled to a farm on the Solway Firth, was erased from polite society, her space usurped by an elderly aunt with a grim expression and lace up to her chin. No wild-looking creature with a haunted expression for a visitor to ask questions about. Her grandmother making a point.

Lydia knew the price to be paid for her suspension. Live in Aunt Patience's studio, a neat little bed-sitting room in direct line of sight of the main house. Check in with Eveline. Create a sensible London existence. "Settle down." She hugged her grandmother and dropped into the familiar armchair. Tugging at her short skirt and hiding behind a curtain of hair, those untidy black curls that must have come from her missing father. They were all silky redheads on Eveline's side of the family.

Today, Lydia was intimidated by the mahogany furniture and the small silver objects and the china figurines. She felt imprisoned by these crowded surfaces and serried memories. A tall maple tree tapped on the windowpane, leafless and forlorn. A single lemon-coloured leaf still hung on the fig tree in the pot on the balcony, as though there were something to be covered up. A shaft of sunlight slid past the brocade curtains, briefly lightening the late afternoon gloom. Then the clouds closed in.

Eveline filled two little crystal glasses with Tio Pepe, the pale, dry sherry that she always dispensed to visitors. It jangled Lydia's nerve endings. It sat on a tray too small to hold a decent-sized bottle of university mainstay Algerian red and was served in glasses too easy to shatter.

"Tio Pepe is best sipped, my dear, not gulped down like that. Surely they teach you that sort of thing at university. They must have sherry parties at Oxford." Eveline sighed. She gathered her voluminous clothing around her comfortable behind and sat down.

"So tell me the news."

"The Americans are bombing civilians in North Vietnam. It's criminal, don't you think?"

"I mean *your* news, Lydia. Is that how they talk at university? When communism is the real threat to everything we stand for." Eveline always spoke of "university" as though it were a criminal offence. "I was proud that you did so well at that school I sent you to, but I should never have let you go to Oxford."

"But Grandmama, my heart was set on it."

"Yes. Yes. That's why I gave in. Against my better judgement." Eveline shook her head sadly. "I've heard that university girls wear dirty knickers, Lydia. They don't bother to change them. Alice Dryfesdale told me. A friend of her daughter's came to stay, she was from Oxford University, like you, from a good family too, so no excuses, she should have known better. A nice house. A maid unpacking her suitcase. She had no change of undies and her nightgown wasn't even clean. The shame of it. She's lost respect for how she was brought up."

Lydia giggled. A hint of a smile flickered over Eveline's features, but she smothered it ruthlessly.

"But Grandmama, that's the whole point. To break away from the stuffy old standards of the past. Knickers don't matter. Nuclear disarmament does."

"It is best for girls of your age and background to get married when they leave school. And if, these days, they really must go to university, they should at least get engaged to someone suitable while they are there. If they want a year or two to see the world before they settle down, why, there's Florence or Rome, even a secretarial course, or a nice little job at Sotheby's or Christie's, like your cousin Griselda. Look what happened to you at university. We need to get you back on the straight and narrow."

"I've already got a job." In fact, Lydia had an interview for the researcher job in the Department of Education tomorrow. It didn't do to show Eveline even a chink of uncertainty.

"You've found a job by yourself, Lydia?"

"In a government department – the Department of Education, no less."

Eveline patted her silver-grey curls, a characteristic gesture whenever she felt outpaced by the changing world.

"My goodness. I didn't know people like you could do that sort of thing. I've never heard of anyone working there. How unfeminine and stuffy. The Department of Education – it even *sounds* depressing. You don't want to be labelled 'a career girl', Lydia. Nice young men will find it off-putting."

Lydia shifted in her chair, trying to relax. She didn't want to listen to this. Eveline's 'nice young men' had corduroy jackets and flannel trousers and places in the country.

"But I'll be working for the new Labour government. Think of that."

"Dear me, I'm not sure that's what we want for you, Lydia. Out of those university libraries and into a dusty office with a lot of people who live in the suburbs? It is bad for your health, as well as your eyesight. I do want you to see the light of day. I could still have a word with someone at Sotheby's."

Eveline picked one of her pairs of spectacles off her bosom and looked Lydia up and down.

"And, dear, there's another thing. All that black stuff round your eyes and that horrid pale lipstick. It makes you look like a woman of the streets."

Lydia averted her smudged eyes and ran anxious fingers through the tangle of hair.

"Oh, Lydia, I do want you to be a social success. You could be so lovely. You have that thing your cousin Griselda doesn't have, good-looking though she is. Allure. What we called 'It' in my day. I've watched you, walking along the street, bus conductors whistling. You must take all that stuff off your beautiful eyes and go to that nice woman at the Elizabeth Arden counter at Harrods. You must keep up appearances, especially you, because ... because of ... you know ... the example of your mother."

Lydia took a gulp of Tio Pepe and spluttered. Her mother – the constant shadow. She glanced automatically at the pastel portrait in the far corner of the room, half hidden by a bowl of chrysanthemums – young Flora, red-haired, blue-eyed, a heart-rending hopeful expression on her face. Before anything had gone wrong. Lydia's shoulders stiffened, like a tortoise shell, a protective mechanism. "My mother ... Was she always ...?"

Eveline clutched the collar of her pleated blouse, eyes glittering with something that could have been tears. The moment passed. She straightened her back and shook her index finger. Her rings clinked.

"That's enough, Lydia. We won't talk about all that. Just try to be more like your cousin Griselda."

Could Eveline really want her to be more like Cousin Griselda, with her tweed skirts, her expensive little sweaters, and her cultured pearl necklace, her teenage refrain of "I must, I must, increase my bust", and her admonitions about not kissing anyone before your third date, nor getting into a taxi alone with a man?

Eveline tapped her ringed fingers on the table beside her.

"Did you hear what I said, Lydia? I'm over seventy. I won't last for ever. Promise me that you'll find yourself a nice young man before I die."

Eveline said it sadly, no doubt remembering the simplicity of her own conquests. Her sea-blue eyes flashed in her powdery face. Fierce and severe though she was, Eveline had tears in her eyes.

Lydia was crying too. "Don't say that, Grandmama. You have to live for ages. You know I can't do without you."

She jumped out of her chair and flung her arms around her grandmother, giving her an awkward sort of hug, instead of a promise she knew she couldn't keep. She knocked over her glass and a stream of pale dry sherry ran off the shiny mahogany surface and on to the Persian rug, like a tiny waterfall of tears.

# Chapter 2

They stood together outside a tall, imposing building.

"I'm terrified of this interview. You know about the world, Poet dear. Give me some advice."

The Poet was Lydia's only friend in London, a link to her mother whom she had seen so little after her grandmother took her away. The Poet had always adored Flora. He was her godson, or something less formal than that, an arrangement set up by his parents, who lived and then died suddenly in an inaccessible part of Wester Ross. For a week of every school summer holiday, Eveline had packed Lydia off on the night train to Inverness, where Flora and the Poet would be waiting for her on the platform. Eveline decided that it would be good for Lydia to keep in touch with her mother in a controlled setting under a responsible roof and far away from the Solway Firth.

The Poet's name, Maelrubha, after the local Celtic saint, was difficult to pronounce and impossible to spell, which was why they called him 'the Poet'. In his teenage years his poems were full of tragedy and mourning. Nowadays he wrote and recited poetry in London, in basement rooms and cafes, sometimes accompanied by long-haired musicians. The poems were still about love and death, a sort of Scottish Johnny Cash or Roy Orbison. Or so Lydia described them. He was tall and hunched, with a slight limp from a bullet injury during National Service. He looked battered but spiritual, standing up there in front of close-packed admiring audiences, sparse reddish curls and a cigarette stuck to his lip. She loved him like an elder brother.

"Why are you asking me, Lydia? Of all people."

"You're all I have. I know nothing about jobs. At least you actually have one. At that advertising agency. Imagine either my mother or grandmother having a job. What will the civil service think of me? Suspended from university and in disgrace?"

"You'll be fine," he said. "Just be yourself."

"But I'm unsuitable, aren't I?"

He looked her up and down.

"You like being unsuitable, Lydia. It's part of your personality. Still, that's a weird-looking skirt, even by your standards."

"Aunt Patience gave it to me for Christmas. So I had something suitable for her country friends. I hate corduroy but I thought, well, best not to turn up in a miniskirt."

Lydia knew that the Poet had even less idea what you should wear to a civil service interview than she did, but she liked the way he nodded wisely.

"Take a pen with you. It looks serious. And just brush your hair, Lydia. They won't be used to wild Pre-Raphaelite tresses. And I'll buy you a Cinzano afterwards to celebrate."

"Honestly. You're hopeless. Poets can't drink Cinzano. It has to be absinthe."

There were more people in the interview room than she'd expected. Five of them, all men, ranged around a semicircular table, and she sitting opposite them like a trapped animal, but with her back straight and her hair clamped down in a barrage of kirby grips.

A grey-haired man in a dark suit asked her why she was interested in working for the Department of Education. She was enthusiastic about that. She wanted to work on things that mattered, reforms, to change things for the better. Then she wondered if she'd been too enthusiastic. Civil servants weren't meant to have passionate views; they had to weigh up the evidence and give neutral advice.

The weasel-like one beside him suggested that she tell them how she saw the next few years of her life. "You understand," he said, "that this isn't the graduate entry. There's a special entrance exam for the higher level of the civil service, which is indeed open to women applicants. Not many of them succeed, of course, but we welcome them. This job we are interviewing you for is a temporary arrangement." This was tricky. She was intending to go back to Oxford next year to get her degree. And then, who knows? On the other hand, she needed to sound serious.

"I'm planning to take the civil service entrance exam next year, during my final year at university. I'm hoping to use this opportunity to learn a lot about it. And, you know, contribute something."

With twisted lips, he smiled or grimaced. She wasn't sure which.

"A girl like you," he said, looking her up and down, "can we assume that you are thinking of a long-term career? Suppose you got married?"

Lydia wasn't thinking long term. She had been told that you could only take three months off in the civil service, even if you had a child. It seemed unthinkable, but irrelevant at this stage of her life. She wasn't thinking more than three months ahead anyway.

"I'm committed to a serious career," she said grimly.

Someone off to her right addressed her. "Well, Miss Renfrew, you are studying history at university, I believe. Tell me, then, what historical character would you most like to have dinner with?"

Lydia turned to him in delight. What a wonderful question. "Oh, if I could only sit next to Bismarck for a whole evening – ask him, did he have any idea of the repercussions of the unification of Germany, how it would lead, in my view anyway, directly to the outbreak of the First World War? Did he see that he was changing the balance of power in Europe for ever? Did he set out to humiliate the proud French? Reduce them to eating the animals from the zoo during the siege of Paris?"

He interrupted her with a laugh, an ordinary human sound in that high-ceilinged room.

"Thank you very much, Miss Renfrew. You have persuaded me. And now my colleague has a question for you."

The rest of the interview was fine and they told her she had the job – the temporary but serious job, a grown-up job, in the hallowed civil service, under a Labour government that she believed in. Lydia longed to rush round and share her new prospects with her grandmother, convince her that she wasn't the only girl of twenty who wanted to work on things that mattered, reforms, changing things for the better. But Eveline was already disappointed by this one safe piece of Lydia's life – eight hours a day and five days per week in the grip of recognised routines and principles, the steady backdrop to her determination to recreate herself on the glittering London streets and in the cafes and in clubs, in the city where people had moved on from self-conscious university-style pride in discovering The Beatles to the more dangerous delights of Mick Jagger. Lydia longed to confide her hopes and fears in Eveline. Ask her whether she must cast aside miniskirts for knee-length corduroy in order to be taken seriously? Whether she would be able to weave her way safely through the drugs and casual sex, she who may have inherited the weakness from her mother, the unbalanced response to passion, the nymphomaniac gene? But she couldn't. And there would only be Tio Pepe anyway. So it would have to be Cinzano with the Poet, who wasn't very interested in the civil service.

* * *

Lydia asked for a day off in the very first week of her civil service job. She sidled out of Aunt Patience's flat into the side street. The sky was slate grey and an east wind whistled round her legs. As though the weather was frowning on her escapade. But the bus conductor didn't draw back in horror when she asked for a ticket to Wormwood Scrubs. Could it be that the buses that went along Du Cane Road were always filled with passengers visiting the prison? That it was a perfectly normal thing to do?

Wormwood Scrubs didn't seem much like a prison. You approached through a courtyard where ordinary-looking people were arriving at offices, and cars were haphazardly parked. There was nothing punitive about it. No forbidding noticeboards, no policemen patrolling with guns, although the spy George Blake and violent criminals were known to be imprisoned within those walls. The building reminded Lydia of Oxford colleges, but with a satisfying contrast between the brickwork and the white stone facings. And slightly less intimidating. From a distance it could even be a large church, from which a well-behaved congregation would emerge. But that didn't make this a respectable day out.

Here were two men, lounging against the prison wall, eye-catchingly cool, long limbs sketched out in jeans and denim jackets, silhouetted fingers, smoking under a No Smoking sign. You could tell immediately that neither was what her grandmother would call 'nice young men'; neither would own corduroy jackets and flannel trousers and places in the country. Were they here for Fred too? Both turned towards her. One was very tall, with prominent eyebrows, short dark hair and suntanned skin. The other was what her grandmother would call a 'matinee idol', regular features, soft brown hair curling behind his ears, smooth skin, and a shifty blue glance. They looked her up and down and returned to their conversation. They ground out their cigarettes in unison and lit new ones. Lydia wished she had a cigarette too.

She wondered how you were supposed to welcome a newly released prisoner back into the outside world. She hadn't come across anything like this before. Was there a ritual or procedure? Could you celebrate it, like a wedding or a birthday? Ironically, alone of her family it was her disgraced mother, Flora, who would accept imprisonment as one of the inevitable staging posts on life's journey, like desertion and betrayal, tragedy and death. Lydia felt superstitious about the idea of celebration, fearing that it would tempt malevolent Providence. Her instinct was to drag Fred into a nearby church and, unreligious as she was, pour holy water over him to keep him safe.

The wooden doors opened, inch by inch. There was something almost biblical about it. Lydia had expected him to be spat out of a side door. There was a solemn creaking noise and a levering of a massive structure to release one prisoner back into the outside world. Dramatic recognition that he had paid his debt to society. She liked that.

And there was Fred, a stick figure under the arch, hesitating, blinking in the light, gathering momentum, bustling towards her, swaggering a little too much, a grin perhaps too wide, hat in hand, acting as though he were coming out of a fashionable resort hotel. Then the hesitation, the telltale sign of uncertainty, the left hand passing rapidly over his face, from forehead to chin, as though removing a sticky cobweb.

He flung his arms around her.

What a pair they were, she thought – barely into their twenties, she on a sort of probation, forced to live under the gaze of her Aunt Patience, and he actually sent to prison. Fred had been her friend in her first year at Oxford. At that stage he only stole flowers, presenting them to his women friends, romantic gestures as a cover for his secret preference for men. Camellias from front gardens in small Oxford side streets. Bunches of purple and white lilac broken off over walls. Lydia had been complicit, accepting a rare orchid plucked from the world-famous Botanic Garden, proffered on one knee on the pavement in the High Street. Fred lingered outside florists, sweeping up armfuls of cut flowers, selecting only the rare and exotic, rejecting red roses and gladioli as banal, hovering for heart-stopping moments over deep purple irises and white gypsophila, trying out the most beautiful combinations. But when he went to London he graduated, you might say, to stealing pictures, and the police caught up with him. He was starved without beauty, he explained to Lydia; he only stole pictures from people who could afford to lose them and were incapable of appreciating them. Lydia had always felt protective of him. She too believed in the need to reinvent yourself. But Fred was sinking in too far. The thing she feared.

"Darling Lydia, so good to see you. But your clothes. Such a disappointment. I told the screws that I was being met by a Russian princess. Ah. If only I could have dressed you myself. For such an occasion as this. My re-entry into an expectant world. Release from dire and undeserved incarceration. Famished eyes and starved imagination. You know how important beauty is to me, Lydia. A proper tableau. An emerald necklace painted on to your beautiful neck. A hat with ostrich feathers reaching to the ground. Purple shoes. To set off those sad violet eyes. Where oh where are your purple shoes?"

The two men came forward. Fred shook hands with them. Lydia could see that he was pleased to see them and at the same time uncertain of them. The matinee idol pulled him aside at once and started talking to him in a low voice. How predictable, Lydia thought. Just how it happens in books. You make all these criminal connections in prison. They meet you at the gates with urgent information about a heist.

The tall man turned towards her.

Lydia had learnt to interpret people by looking at their eyes and their bodies, the result of a childhood spent watching. Touch had been missing. A mother who kept a distance. No father. Understanding men by watching them, anticipating how they might treat her from the look in their eyes and the arrangement of their bodies. Guessing what theirs would feel like against hers.

She examined him carefully. He had brown eyes, the colour of ploughed earth in October, with flecks of truth in them; one of the prominent eyebrows was slightly misshapen by a scar. He held out his hand.

"I'm Marvin. Who are you?"

Who was she indeed? It was too soon to say.

The matinee idol, introduced as "the famous Dave Perry", packed them into a taxi and took them off to the Café Matisse in the King's Road, the famous coffee bar where, according to Aunt Patience, "nice girls don't go".

Bronzed arms stretched out towards Dave Perry like the tentacles of an octopus. Fred was greeted with delighted cries. Finn Caradoc, the wild Irish boy, saluted him. Marvin seemed to know them all, models, photographers and even film stars. But Lydia noticed he kept aloof from them, guarding her, making sure she had somewhere to sit among the throng. Softly, against the noise and laughter and the scraping backwards of chairs, he told her that he was a mechanic. He looked after the engines of sports cars, owned by the rich and famous, the people here, names that Lydia had read in the gossip columns.

"Are there enough sports cars around to make a living?"

"Of course there are. Haven't you noticed them? Everywhere. Low on the road. Open tops. Gleaming paintwork. Here, racing along the King's Road. Parked all over London. People driving to work in Sunbeam Alpines and Triumph Spitfires. Property people with blondes in E-Type Jaguars. It's the thing."

"Not where I come from, it isn't. On the Solway Firth people get by in dusty old Standard Vanguards. And in Oxford everyone rides bicycles."

She was laughing at him. The Solway Firth felt such a long way away that it seemed safe to invoke it.

"Whose side are you on, little girl from the North? Out of London, I agree it's different. Where I came from, too, they think there's still a war on. But here it's the new world. The boys have jobs and money. The sons of people who died in the war, who never really knew the Blitz, they have the money to spend on fast cars."

"Don't you think that's wrong?" Lydia didn't want him just to accept this. "Isn't it disrespectful of the older generation, who suffered so much? Such hardship, losing their husbands and sons in the war, austerity and rationing, and now watching the younger generation having enough to eat and fast cars as well."

"These people don't see it like that. They expect to die young too. Nuclear war or some other catastrophe. So they drive dangerously. They don't want to grow old."

"You too?"

"I earn a living. Repairing the latest models when they crash them. Replacing them when they write them off. Have you ever really looked at the bodywork of a brand new sports car, Lydia? The insides of the engines? They are the new works of art. Better than that stuff in museums." He paused, giving her a long, undecipherable, brown-eyed look, which came from somewhere not urban at all. From somewhere deep in a forest.

"They're my friends. I don't judge them. Why would I? It's the cars I mind about. The boys like to have me around. On tap. To keep their cars in working order, tuned up and ready for long continental journeys. Finn Caradoc, over there. He comes and goes. Each time with a new car. Take Dave," – Dave Perry, with his indulgent curls and soft red lips – "speeding along the Corniches on the Côte d'Azure, with a long-legged girl in the passenger seat. That's his life."

There was Dave Perry himself, following Fred out into the King's Road. "I'm off with the five finger discount merchant," he said. "And you? You've not let this bird out of your sight all day, Marv. Not exactly your type, is she?"

"Watch it, Dave."

"No offence intended. She's cool. Race for pinks."

Lydia was silent. What was "race for pinks"? Who was this stranger with golden hairs on his hands and long mechanic's fingers?

# Chapter 3

Eveline Ashfield felt personally affronted. She pursed her lips, straightened her aching shoulders and marched out of the foyer into the street.

"The times are out of joint." Who said that? To think that the Aldwych Theatre, where she had seen so many delightful drawing-room comedies, should have staged something so shocking. It was another example of an institution that could no longer be trusted, falling from grace one after another like a row of dominoes. To think that she had lived to see this. It disturbed her more than all the other changes taking place around her. The Victorian grandeur, the high dome, the circle of gold-painted seats, the decoration that promised familiar entertainment, the setting you thought you could rely on, had spewed this empty immorality out on to the stage.

Even the language was offensive. So raw and unpolished. No doubt there were people who behaved and talked like that, but why rub the audience's noses in it? You didn't want to be faced with ugly and depressing things on a night out. To dwell on what was normally swept under the carpet. Why would a West End theatre audience pay money to watch this and, good heavens, applaud it so enthusiastically? What goes on behind the bedroom door was better kept there. You knew it had to be faced but you didn't want it flaunted in your face at the theatre.

She wished her friend Alice was with her. She felt sure she would agree. Those ugly words belonged to building sites, not polite company. There were witty ways of turning arguments into dialogue without lashing out at each other. Why dwell on hopeless lives when there were so many pleasant and entertaining subjects?

Outside on the pavement, Eveline felt quite faint. Her car and driver didn't seem to have arrived. She leant unsteadily against the theatre wall and dug about in her handbag for the sal volatile to calm her nerves. She was on her own. Alice had been rushed into hospital that morning.

Their theatre choices were made by word of mouth. They rarely bothered to read the reviews. This month they'd left it to Alice's daughter, an aspiring actress who recommended this as the most interesting play on in London. Eveline had simply rung up Mr Lashmar, her theatre agent at the Prowse Ticket Agency, and it was all arranged. She'd sold off the second ticket and set out on her own. She had felt delightfully intrepid. And when she'd arrived she had been glad to be free of the garrulous old friend who struggled to get up the stairs. She suddenly felt like the eighteen-year-old who turned heads as she entered the theatre on her father's arm.

But now she was upset. And where was her car? She and Alice usually shared a taxi. Now she was all alone. She became aware of a young man, not far away, pretending to read from the posters outside the theatre. He turned and walked up the road towards the neighbouring theatre and studied the notices there. They were showing another of these modern plays. They seemed to be popping up everywhere.

Then he came back towards her. He was quite close to her now. He seemed to reread the notice he had already read. He was the sort of person she would be frightened to meet in a dark alley. Black hair. Pale skin. Haunted, bleak-looking. Violent, even. And if it hadn't been for the theatre and the brightly lit street, she would have retreated into the foyer.

He was quite close now. Long white fingers, clenching and unclenching. No proper suit, of course. She sighed. Narrow trousers, the sort of skimpy jacket that barely covered his waist. He could either be homeless or fashionable. How could you tell these days?

Lean and hungry, she thought. Take Shakespeare. His characters were violent and immoral too, but it was different when it was expressed in poetic language by actors dressed to emphasise their distance from today's world. You couldn't imagine Shakespeare's words in today's clothing.

He was looking directly at her now – dark eyes glittering in the street lights, wild, disturbed.

"What's the matter with you, young man? You look as though you have seen a ghost."

"Excuse me. I didn't realise you were there."

When he spoke his voice was gentle, with a slight accent, which of course she couldn't place. He looked at her again, registering that she was not of an age or class to be on the street at this time of night.

"Are you waiting for someone? Can I help you?"

Eveline realised how late it was. She must have been here for some time, preoccupied with her thoughts. The post-theatre crowds had evaporated, the jostling disentangling itself, threading away along lamplit pavements.

Her car wasn't going to come. Well, she wasn't going to panic. "Yes, you can, young man. Tell me this, do you often go to new plays like this?"

"I write them."

"My goodness. How… well, I mean, how very clever of you. What did you say your name was?"

"It won't mean anything to you. I'm doing something else now."

"What a pity. You're just the person I need to explain to me why these new plays have to be so raw and ugly, rubbing your nose into things you don't want to think about. They bother me so much. Don't misunderstand me," she added, "I'm not prudish about violence. I've lived through wars. I enjoy the violence in Shakespeare. *Titus Andronicus* is one of my favourite plays."

For a moment he just stared at her. Then he must have realised that she really wanted an answer.

He turned towards her and looked at her.

"As I see it, people want something real nowadays. That they can identify with, that's like their own lives. About things that affect their families and themselves. They aren't interested in cocktail cabinets and tasselled dressing gowns. No one has tasselled dressing gowns these days. Young… er … I mean people I know, they're interested in different things."

He used his hands expressively when he spoke.

She laughed.

"But I like a nice tasselled dressing gown myself."

Now Eveline looked at him properly. She decided he must be one of those young men she'd read about, who grew up in bleak northern towns, who before the war and through the years of austerity would have stayed up there and worked at a local mine or factory. And somehow now, twenty years after the war, by some process she didn't fully understand, had been released from that sort of confinement, had lost most of his accent and settled into London, like a migrant bird. A process that was apparently much admired. But must be quite difficult.

She knew it would be rude to put on her spectacles, but she inspected him as though he were a specimen of natural history. Evidently this young man had prospects here in London. Yet to her he was a sort of curiosity. She didn't often meet people outside her social circle. There was her housekeeper, of course, and gamekeepers on the moors in Scotland, and the nice man at MacFisheries in the King's Road, but she thought of them as simple souls without awkward aspirations.

She sighed. There was so much in life to be re-examined before it was too late.

"I'm waiting for my car to arrive."

"Are you all right?" He held out his hand. "Would you like to sit down? Wait inside where it's warmer? We could go to that bar over there."

\* \* \*

Eveline stared round her at the array of different-coloured bottles, the row of men on the bar stools, the fog of cigarette smoke hovering over their heads like deranged halos. Fascinated, she peered at the grime on the floor and the splashes of beer on the counters. She pulled off her gloves and let out her breath.

"I've never been anywhere like this before. How clever of you to find it."

"I know this area pretty well."

"Thank you for bringing me here. It's so... so exotic."

He seemed to be smiling.

"I almost feel as though I am in one of those plays. Now please tell me your name and explain to me what that playwright was trying to do? I go to some of these new plays and I don't really understand what they are getting at. I suppose you have seen *The Birthday Party* which we went to last year?"

"My name is Arthur Shortcross. I don't suppose you've heard of me. I ... Well, yes. I take quite an interest."

Just then a black Humber drew up across the road and a man with a cap got out, looking frantically about him.

Eveline sighed.

"There's my driver over there. I suppose I'll have to go."

She was taken aback by her disappointment. She didn't want to lose this interesting stranger. She really wanted to stay longer in this atmospheric place. An idea developing in her head was in danger of being strangled at birth. She wasn't used to that.

"I don't suppose I should keep the driver waiting, but it seems a pity to say goodbye, Mr... er... Shortcross, when we've only just met. I'm going to Chelsea. Can I give you a lift home in my car and you explain to me what was going on in that play?"

\* \* \*

A nearly full moon competed with the streetlamps at Hyde Park Corner. The familiar landscape seemed different tonight and filled with hidden incident. It occurred to her that this encounter might seem as strange to the young man as it was to her. A foolish, talkative old woman, unlike anyone he'd met before.

"And what does *this* mean, Mr Shortcross? Turning the Royal Court Theatre into a private members' club? What will happen? Will actors show their bodies on stage? Do rude things to each other in my local theatre? Will I still be able to get tickets?"

The playwright laughed at her, but not unkindly. He had a nice merry laugh, at odds with his solemn appearance.

"You will be able to get tickets if you become a member. But the stuff they put on. It might be quite racy."

He explained that the Royal Court was planning to cheat the censor by turning itself into a private club in order to be able to show John Osborne's *A Patriot for Me*.

"Oh, so you know all about it. You are one of those Angry Young Men yourself, I suppose."

Yet she noticed how he leant back against the soft leather seats of the Humber, how the luxury seemed to reassure and relax him. Her idea was taking shape now.

Then suddenly he began to talk.

"It's like twisting a knife in my heart, passing the Royal Court, Mrs Ashfield. Only a year ago my play was a sell-out there. 'Thirteen Years'. I don't suppose you saw it."

"I'm sorry to say that my friend Alice and I decided not to see it because it was critical of the government. We're Tories, you know. Not really our idea of entertainment. But people talked about it a lot."

Eveline felt a tiny shift in the tectonic plates of her certainties.

"But how clever of you to write that sort of thing." She peered at him with increasing interest. A specimen of something. She wasn't sure what.

"But I can't write any more. That's what has happened to me. A few years of public success. Then nothing." He leant forwards, covering his eyes with his hands. "I don't know why I'm telling you all this."

"If you can do something like that, just do it again, even if it is not to the taste of people like me."

"But I *can't* do it any more. It's called writer's block. It's not something you can really talk about. Famous writers have suffered from it, but they only ever talk about it in the past tense. Afterwards, it's tossed out in conversation. Glibly. But if you suffer from it, you keep it quiet. Dead quiet. It's unbearable – to suffer from it in the daytime and talk about it in the evening."

It distressed her to hear the cracking of the joints in his fingers as he clenched his fists. She wanted to stretch out a comforting hand.

"As darkness falls" – he spoke in a low voice so her driver couldn't hear, a low, thrilling voice – "I slink out into the West End, trailing around the theatres, reading and rereading the posters about *other* playwrights' successes, the congratulatory snippets of reviews. Every night. I do the rounds of every West End theatre. Anything connected with modern plays. Who are the directors and actors? The words used by the critics to describe them. Rival playwrights' successes. I'm not interested in anything else. Food. Drink. Women. The dogs. Imagine it, if you can, Mrs Ashfield."

This was a bit more than Eveline had bargained for. Yet how fascinating. No one told her their secrets any more, not since Lydia had gone to university. No one had ever talked to her quite like this.

"Good heavens, Mr Shortcross, you playwrights speak so dramatically. It's as though your own life were one long piece of theatre."

"I'm sorry. Am I boring you?"

"Not at all. Not in the least. Please go on."

He sighed.

She couldn't stop herself patting his arm.

"Write something entirely different, I say to myself. Don't even try to reflect on the human condition. It's too difficult. Try something light. A straightforward narrative. Just tell a story. A history play. History is littered with unexploited stories. Shakespeare left lots of unused English kings. William Rufus. Stephen and Matilda. Get out the *Oxford History of England*. Run your finger down the indexes of history books…"

"I love a good historical play," murmured Eveline.

"And I'm a master of plots. Or used to be. Read what the critics said. Stop trying to say something significant. Turn your back on the terrible unscalable mountain of meaning. That glittering unreachable prize."

"My dear young man," said Eveline, "I had no idea that writing plays was so soul-searching. How thoughtless of me to imagine… to imagine that it all flowed out like a stream."

"But it did! Exactly like that. I don't know where the words used to come from. The stuff just poured out. Then it stopped, like a dried-up reservoir. The voice that had been speaking through me, the muse, wandered off to one of my rivals."

"Mr Shortcross, we are at your door. In fact, we have been here for some time. It is quite late now, and I do pray that you will sleep calmly tonight. My recipe for troubled nights is charcoal biscuits, but I suppose that may seem rather old-fashioned to you. But then I am rather an old-fashioned person."

He shook her hand. He bent his head, to hide some emotion. She hoped he couldn't see that there were tears in her own eyes. She seemed to be moved to tears so often these days.

# Chapter 4

In Marvin's basement in Kensington Park Road, Auriol Wedderburn stood out. Stern and aloof, she leant against the door, surveying the roomful of young and beautiful bodies. Pale blue eyes, carelessly cut caramel-coloured hair, dressed in dark colours. She disdained the latest fashions spilling out into the King's Road, yet she had a distinctive style and an unintended elegance. Lydia thought of her as having a low centre of gravity, like a dangerous siege engine. She made sharp throwaway comments. Sometimes she seemed to be barely suppressing some anger or anguish.

One of Marvin's mysterious friendships. "We go back a long way, Auriol and I." In the casual careless circle that drifted around the dazzling Finn Caradoc, Marvin and Auriol were fiercely protective of each other. "Unlike the rest of us, she's interested in politics. Things stir her up."

One cold evening, when a vicious frost covered the puddles on the pavement outside, Lydia was struggling to open the fastenings of her winter coat with icy fingers. She expected Auriol to watch her, sceptical, possibly an eyebrow raised, but she came over to her, pushed her hands away, and undid the little black buttons for her, one by one. She put her hands on Lydia's shoulders under her coat. Then she kissed her on the lips. It was difficult to tell whether this was meant to be aggressive or a sign of special attention.

"What's it like, Miss Civil Servant, being manacled to a government department?"

Lydia started to answer.

"Where did Marvin find you, anyway? You're a bit different from the rest of them."

Did she mean the people in their circle? Or Marvin's string of previous girlfriends?

"The world's gone crazy, hasn't it? Operation Rolling Thunder. Bombing Vietnamese children. I'm going to America to join the student protests. Track down Martin Luther King too, if I have a chance. Take care of Marvin, Lydia Renfrew. Or I'll kill you."

Then she pushed Lydia away and resumed her role of gatekeeper to this world that Lydia entered with apprehension.

Marvin's basement room was filled with smoke, bodies leaning on cushions, propped up against the walls. Very young, very pretty girls, doing a bit of modelling, slender doe-eyed creatures, smoky eyelashes, being but unspeaking, like glittering insects. Long-haired Jean Shrimpton look-alikes with elegantly folded limbs and patent leather boots. The men, cool and undifferentiated, short jackets and expensive shirts, mainly pink, often frilled. Talking cool talk, in short sentences. Suddenly Lydia felt lonely, missing the slouchy attention-seekers of university parties, and even the crinkly-haired public schoolboys in corduroy trousers and the frowning bespectacled pipe-smokers. And the hallowed bottles of Algerian wine. This, here, was the grown-up world. Here, where gin bottles came and were emptied, food appeared mysteriously and erratically, and joints were prepared and passed from hand to hand in unholy sacrament.

She leant against Marvin's shoulder, lured and scared by his unfamiliar world, a world that felt like a river in which you might lose your footing.

"Have a drag, darling. It's not so scary." Marvin pulled her towards him and kissed her neck. "It's my mission to corrupt you. To save you from being a serious person."

"I'm high enough already from the haze."

"Stop thinking about it. Just do it. It won't do you any harm. You want to. I can see it in your eyes."

She looked up at Marvin, trying to interpret what was going on in *his* head. She couldn't confide in him, not yet anyway, confess her fear that if she started smoking hash she wouldn't be able to stop, that she would become addicted to that, to his lifestyle, and most of all to the casual sex of it, in one huge disastrous downfall.

He put the spliff to her lips. She shook her head. He smiled down at her, the smile that crumbled her bone structure. She leant against him, taming the jolt of desire by counting the hours till she had to be back at her desk, guarded by reports and statistics. Dull, reassuring, yes, but less disturbing than this casual, gold-dusted world.

"I have to go, Marvin. It's three in the morning. I have to work tomorrow. Unlike all these people here."

He shook his head sadly, smiled and got to his feet. He grabbed his car keys and folded his long legs into the Mini Cooper. He turned the key, the engine roaring into life, a souped-up yellow object streaking through the deserted London streets as though they were his private race track. Lydia held her breath, scared and exhilarated. Somewhere in Kensington he took a final drag of the spliff and crushed it out in the ashtray.

"Aren't you worried about the police? What if they stopped you?"

"The fuzz? No chance. I drive more carefully when I'm high. It's good to go fast. A Mini Cooper driving sedately is suspicious. Don't worry so much."

"At university we thought you had to be criminal to get drugs."

"That's why it's better to live in London." He put a long arm around her and held her against him as he accelerated westward along the King's Road. He leant over and kissed her, his right hand spinning the steering wheel as they turned sharp left. "I'd do anything for you, darling honey, but I wouldn't have to drive across London if you'd spend the nights with me."

They sat in the car outside her flat. Now she had dragged him away she didn't want to let him go.

"Please understand. It's a life saver, my job. It has to be made to last."

"Like sucking a sweet slowly?" He laughed, but stroked her hair. "I used to spend my sweet ration on sherbet lemons. And my dad always said to slow down. 'Don't chew them like that. There'll be no more till next week.' It's no good taking things slowly. There's no time to lose. You have to take risks or you'll miss what's happening all around you."

"But I need to earn money."

"It isn't the only job in the world."

"After what happened at university, I was lucky to get it. It's a chance to prove myself. I have to save enough to escape Aunt Patience. I have to seem like a steady person." She laughed. "And look at me now."

"You look pretty good to me." He tucked a curl behind her ear. "Only a little pale and anxious."

"You sound like my grandmother. She says I'm pale because of long hours in neon-lit rooms, flicking through dusty files."

He laughed. "Is that what you actually do? I thought you went out and built schools."

"My job's research. I have to find out information from dusty old files and send it to the people making policy, with a neat little summary and a recommendation."

"Jesus. I had no idea people had to do that sort of thing."

"Oh, Marvin, don't you see, I want to be up all night with you. But it's not that sort of job. You don't know what it's like. If a civil servant, even a junior one, makes a serious mistake, the minister resigns. Imagine that."

Now she was almost in tears.

He was probably too high to take in what she was saying. He certainly wouldn't see the point of it. Nor could she, at that moment. He looked thoughtful, though, tracing each one of her fingers with his, slowly, stroking the gaps between them, none of the familiar student scrabbling to reach under her skirt, just stroking her with his fingers until she ached to feel them running over her body. She buried her face in his shoulder.

"That's no life for someone like you, darling honey."

Someone like her. Who was she? A serious civil servant trying to enter a man's world with dancing in her heart? The reluctant bearer of her grandmother's standards in a glittering drug-filled basement? Inevitable inheritor of her mother's disgraceful ways?

* * *

Her head ached. She said good morning to the three colleagues who shared her office, their desks face to face, in a block of four, in the middle of their room on the third floor, separated by tiers of wooden in-trays, stacks of documents and telephones.

Pinched Miss Fletcher nodded and pursed her lips.

"'Morning, milady," said Gavin. "Honoured that you've deigned to come in." She laughed. He was the best of them.

"A rough night, was it? Randy boyfriend?" This was Howard. She didn't know how to handle his relentless barrage of salacious remarks. It was something to do with her university education, inglorious though it was, and her temporary status outside the rigid hierarchies of entry levels. Or maybe he treated all women like this.

She lit a cigarette and studied her in-tray. Files of rustling papers, all in date order, held together with little string ties, asking her for information. If it was 'urgent' it was marked with a little red flag; less urgent, pink, or routine pale blue for something without a deadline.

Another file with a red tag was delivered to her desk. She had hoped for a quiet morning. Would she please find out when the first technical schools were introduced, what specific goals they were intended to achieve and how many existed now? As soon as possible. For a speech being given to a conference by one of the ministers.

She had to requisition files that would answer the questions. They were not available in the registry across the corridor. It might take days for them to come from somewhere deep in the basement of the building, or from another building far away up the Northern Underground line. Everything was supposed to be recorded somewhere. If files went "missing" or got lost on the way, there was an outcry. But mostly they arrived eventually. Mostly the stories they told were interesting. When she had all the information she needed she would write out her summary, drawing attention to important documents with little flags on them and address it to the minister's office. To a man – almost always a man. Policymaking seemed to be a man's world.

Trolleys stacked with files went up and down the long lino-covered corridors. Today, after too little sleep, it seemed to her that there were more trolleys than usual, like a flock of strange animals in a slow-motion stampede. Twice a day they were joined by a different type of trolley, delivering coffee and tea and small stale cakes and bleak biscuits to people in the offices on this floor. You queued up with your mug. If you missed the moment – suppose you'd popped up to the fourth floor of the huge building, where the Secretary of State and the ministers had their rooms, and their private secretaries and their other sort of secretaries, as she'd had to this morning – that was that.

"Bad luck. Just missed the trolley," said the hated Howard, elbow on his desk, sucking the stem of his pipe with his wet pink lips. Lydia sighed. An entire morning without coffee. She really needed coffee. She considered running down to the second floor to see if their trolley was there. You weren't really meant to get coffee on other people's territory. The refreshment trolleys were all driven by women, and the file trolleys by men. That was weird, she thought. Did someone think women couldn't be trusted with documents? Mind you, she wasn't sure she herself could be trusted with documents today. Especially this urgent query about the technical schools. She lit her second cigarette of the day. Poor Miss Fletcher didn't smoke.

"Oh, Marvin," Lydia murmured. "Don't you understand. I want to be up all night with you. But I have to be able to concentrate. I mustn't make mistakes."

\* \* \*

It was one of those cloudless March days that pretend spring has arrived. There were snowdrops under the trees, crocuses in the parks and wood anemones in the woods. There were no imperfections, no sinister cloud formations, just a brilliant blue backdrop rustled up by a film company for the day.

"We're off to the seaside," said Marvin.

"I thought you had to be seen in the King's Road on Saturdays."

"I want to be alone with you today. Just the two of us."

No Dave Perry in the passenger seat. No hawk-eyed Auriol Wedderburn. No hangers-on.

Lydia had never been to the south coast and didn't know what to expect. The only beaches she knew were on the Solway Firth, the dangerous tidal marsh-strewn tongues of water that you must interpret like runes, watch carefully or you would drown. And the neat little villages of Southwold and Walberswick, on holiday with her cousins. West Wittering sounded wild and exotic. She imagined it would be something like the posters of Deauville, one of the glamorous destinations favoured by Marvin's circle of friends. Models in bikinis and striped deckchairs.

Instead it was very simple, wide open, windswept and almost deserted. The wind blew in from the south-west, chucking waves in furrows on to miles of ochre beach, whipping up sand on to anything laid on the ground. Marvin set up a windbreak, a blue canvas thing that Lydia secretly associated with postcards of Blackpool or Scarborough. She stood and watched. He took trouble to get the angle right, spread out a thick rug, out of the wind, sheltered from the sandstorm, as though it were a daily routine.

There was crusty bread and a rough sort of pâté she'd never eaten before, and olives, and apples and chocolate. Proper coffee, of course, from a little blue thermos. For Marvin, no day was worth living without proper Italian coffee. Not at all like the usual seaside day out. It was a revelation to her that a picnic could be an exotic and sensual experience. Lunch on the beach with Aunt Patience consisted of cold salmon and sandy lettuce in round buns with fizzy lemonade. Picnics in Wester Ross with the Poet took place under rugs, to keep the rain off the Spam and the sausage rolls.

"Come here," he said, lying down and holding out his arms to her. "It's all right. I'm not going to rape you. I just want to hold you."

They lay together in his little haven, arms round each other. This felt ordinary and reassuring, the sort of thing any pair of lovers might do anywhere. It didn't feel dangerous, it didn't seem to be infected by his bohemian circle, in which people slept with each other carelessly, took drugs and didn't have jobs, and spent freely from unmentionable sources of income. With them, Lydia felt like a ridiculous lonely figure, paralysed on the brink. Here, on the sand, in Marvin's long denim arms, she was surprised to feel that this was where she was intended to be, that his windbreak would protect her from disaster. It was one of the most intimate things that had ever happened to her. She felt like a snail coming out of its shell.

He seemed to divine her thoughts.

"Relax your stiff little body, darling honey. It's all right. I'm not like Dave Perry." He curled a strand of her hair around his finger. "My family are very ordinary people – not like Finn and Auriol and all the rest of them. My father breeds pigeons. My mother worked in a cotton mill before … before she died."

He turned away from her and looked out to sea.

"I can't read or write very well, Lydia. Please listen to what I'm saying." His eyes were still on the horizon. "It's quite difficult to say it, even to you. I can't read a book all the way through. I can do anything with an engine but not from manuals and instruction books. I'm not like you. If you need that, I'm no good to you. So it's a contest, the Department of Education and me. And you're better off with me."

Lydia laughed. His real rival was the shadow of the Solway Firth. She wasn't quite ready to explain.

He looked fondly at the little row of hand-rolled cigarettes under the band of elastic in his tortoiseshell cigarette box. He took one out and put it to his lips. And another, and passed it to her, as he always did. He lit them both. He sucked in slowly, tipping his head towards the sky and blowing out the smoke.

"It's lovely being with you," she murmured into the rough wool of his shoulder, "and I've never known a man who could make a picnic."

He shook his head.

"You've lived a very sheltered life."

Lydia moved closer to him, then stopped.

"This isn't a Woodbine, is it? It's hash."

He laughed and laughed.

"You knew, Marvin. You did it deliberately. How could you?"

"What's the fuss about? I'm only trying to relax you."

She turned away from him, got to her feet and strode off along the shore. The sand was cold between her toes and the wind blew her scarf away over the dunes. He reached it before she did and wrapped it tenderly round her throat, making her look at him.

"Don't be upset with me today, Lydia. It's my birthday."

On the way back they stopped in Chichester, a very south-of-England sort of town, and there Lydia bought Marvin a fountain pen from a shop that was just closing.

"You could write a few words to me with this. Those times when you go away. Tell me where you are. Keep in touch."

The Parker 45 lay slender and fragile in his mechanic's hand.

"No one ever gave me anything like this. I've never written a love letter in my life."

# Chapter 5

"A nice little piece of chicken pie for your dinner, Mrs Ashfield?"

"Ah. Something lighter would be better today, Mrs Clutton. An omelette or a fish cake, if you wouldn't mind. I'm lunching out."

Eveline had never learnt to cook. She prided herself on not being able to boil an egg. Mrs Clutton, 'nice Mrs Clutton', lived in, serving her meals, making her bed, caring for her clothes, and supervising the tasks entailed in the smooth running of the St Leonard's Terrace flat that had been her home since her second husband died.

Thank goodness for Mrs Clutton, she said to herself, there is so much to think about.

Her days were not difficult to fill. She read a lot, light novels, poetry, occasionally a newspaper, but preferred to keep up with what was going on in the outside world by listening to the news on the Home Service at 10 p.m. Then, nearly upright on a pile of lacy pillows, she would ponder the state of the world and her family before she fell asleep. Especially now, especially Lydia.

On that spring morning, Eveline felt restless. Perhaps she needed some Andrews liver salts. Perhaps she needed to take the air. She sailed out of the flat into the Chelsea Pensioners' gardens. She didn't exactly have a right to walk there, but felt entitled by her age and long residence in the area.

Then she had lunch at Searcys in Sloane Street with a dear friend, the one who gossiped about Lydia's friends. She'd been looking forward to it but today she found her conversation predictable and irritating.

She was set in her ways, intolerant of the changes happening around her. Eveline surprised herself. Since when had it become boring to listen to sensible conservative opinions?

Afterwards, she visited Truslove and Hanson, where each week she asked the advice of the young man behind the counter for a suitable new book. Often he considered the latest publishing sensation too explicit for her taste. He had steered her away from D.H. Lawrence – not just *Lady Chatterley's Lover*, but *Sons and Lovers* and *The Rainbow* too. She was usually happy to be guided back to one of the classics, or to read a new edition of the poetry of her girlhood, Tennyson and John Masefield and especially Walter de la Mare, to whom she could claim to be distantly related.

"No. Not that. I'm not interested in poetry today. Do you, I wonder, stock printed copies of those 'modern plays' that are all the rage nowadays?"

She found what she had been looking for.

"If I may be so bold, Mrs Ashfield, I don't believe that will be quite to your taste. It's a bit…"

"Risqué?" asked Eveline cheerfully.

"Explicit, yes, and politically radical."

Eveline was impatient to get back to her flat with her outrageous purchase, but she had to go to Peter Jones in Sloane Square, where they kept her intimate measurements. She commandeered a shop assistant and ordered three new vests, and half a dozen pairs of identical pink silk knickers.

"Post them to me, will you," she insisted, although she lived barely a quarter of a mile away. She didn't want to stand here waiting while they parcelled them up. "Or deliver them, if you prefer."

Enough undergarments to see her through, she thought.

\* \* \*

She read *The Millstone* straight through at a sitting. Afterwards, she stared out of the window at the bare branches of the maple tree, washed in the spring rain, tiny buds glistening. Then she sent Arthur Shortcross a note asking him if he would care to call on her one afternoon, if he had time, if she wasn't interrupting his writing. She was grateful to him for coming to her rescue the other night. She didn't say this, but she wanted to have another conversation with him.

And here he was, two days later, entering her drawing room, settling into the armchair that Lydia always sat in, placing his strange-looking suede shoes on her Persian carpet. She felt excited and a little shaky.

"Is it all right if I smoke?"

"Of course. Everyone smokes these days. My granddaughter Lydia has taken to rolling her own with a horrible little device that looks like a piece of unmentionable medical equipment. She uses Woodbine tobacco too, like a working man. Making some sort of statement, I suppose. Now yours – I don't know what they are – but they smell exotic and delicious." They reminded her of something long ago.

They were Sobranie Russian. She couldn't know that he had smoked Woodbines himself as a teenager and only developed a taste for the Sobranie in his successful days. And that now he felt he had lost a finger without one.

There was tea on a silver tray, in her pretty blue-and-white teapot, tiny cucumber sandwiches cut into triangles and a Fuller's walnut cake with coffee icing. Arthur glanced hungrily at the cake. He looked starving. But she didn't think it was only food that he needed.

Eveline held up her copy of *The Millstone*, expectant as a schoolgirl who has done her homework.

"This. What about this then?"

His eyes lit up.

"What do you think of it? Did you like it? Is it too bleak for you?"

"It's … er … very expressive, I must say. Yes. Very vivid." She chose her words carefully. She didn't want him to think that she was prudish or timid. "I can see exactly what their lives are like. But I can't quite identify with the characters. Or perhaps I just don't understand them."

"It was very successful at the time – 'Breaking new ground', 'Arthur Shortcross shines the spotlight on private greed', 'Heart-rending portrayal of the innocent victims of the closure of the Lancashire cloth mills.'"

He paused, obviously trying to control his emotions. She fixed her sea-blue gaze upon him to reassure him.

"*Thirteen Years*, the first one, was even better received. 'Politically on the button', 'Savage indictment of the Macmillan government', 'Post-war promises broken', 'A playwright of rare vision and original-ity'. And so on."

Arthur leant forward, pushing a hank of black hair away from his face. His eyes glittered. His pale hand fluttered. "Pathetic, isn't it? Still quoting the old words of praise."

Eveline sat with her ringed fingers heavy in her lap while the strange dark playwright told her about the last terrible year. He looked much younger in daylight. How old would he be, she wondered? Somewhere in his mid-twenties? It was so difficult to tell with young people nowadays.

"Have some more cake, Mr Shortcross. All Fuller's cakes are excel-lent, but I find the walnut one especially comforting."

Listening to him, she felt as though she were in one of these plays. Allowed into a world that had been hidden from her.

Arthur Shortcross was not predictable, that failing of her ageing friends. He wasn't family, so she didn't have to worry about him. She realised that she hadn't listened enough in her life; she'd been so preoccupied in making sure that people were paying attention, that she kept things going, that standards were maintained. Now, so late, she didn't want him to stop telling her about the things she didn't know. When he hesitated, she fixed him with her searchlight gaze, and nodded encouragingly.

"The beautiful early blossom that promises a plentiful crop. But yields only withered apples. The tiny withered social life. The drying up of the stream of long-haired girls who used to beat a path to my door when my name was in the gossip columns."

"How terrible for you." He didn't say it in so many words, but she thought he was perhaps hinting at a sexual impotence that must have hideously mimicked the inability to write. Reticent herself about that sort of thing, judged to be prudish even, Eveline felt liberated by Arthur, free to talk about anything with him. It excited her.

"I don't know why I'm going on like this," he said. "I'm usually quite a shy sort of person."

Eveline wanted to comfort him. Offer him her strange admiration. Some protective cloak. Some financial help.

These days, you could no longer tell from their clothes what sort of family they came from. She could see that Arthur's suit wasn't Savile Row. His trousers too tight and black, his jacket with a high collar and no comforting lapels, his pale pink shirt with an unmanly frill down the front. He reminded her of some dull-coloured creature with one garish feature, a bird with a shockingly bright beak like a puffin, or a monkey in a zoo with a coloured behind. Well, what did she expect? He wasn't a stockbroker. He was a playwright.

"Clothes. Even in my young days there was room for subtle variation round the edges of what was proper. For my poor daughter, Flora, sadly there was the war, the shortages, the clothing coupons, one good frock designed to last and cleverly adapted by the dressmaker with pins in her teeth and a mournful expression on her face. No room for individuality then. But now it's gone too far the other way. I see all these little shops, quite close by, up and down the King's Road, piles of clothes flung together, all alike, and so cheap that young people can buy a new frock every week. Nothing designed to last."

She hesitated, thinking her remark might be offensive, he with his background in Burnley. She generally didn't much care if she offended people, but she certainly did not want to upset *him*.

"But it's wonderful," he said. "Class divisions disappearing from clothes. It's really happening."

"Well. It's disconcerting to someone like me, I can tell you. My beloved Lydia in tiny dresses with no waists and boots up to her knees. No womanly curves. Smudged eye make-up and pale lips. So unbecoming. Only a few years ago, she and her cousin Griselda were dressed alike. Now they have nothing in common."

"Clothes are personalities nowadays, Mrs Ashfield. Our clothes are more important than our bodies. We can... rewrite ourselves."

"I wonder, Mr Shortcross, do you ever rewrite things?"

"I hardly changed a word of my first two plays. They came out almost exactly as I wanted them, spilling out on to the page. The third was more difficult, squeezed out like pellets. And now they hardly come out at all. Like constipation."

She laughed. "That's wonderfully graphic."

Eveline thought of the charcoal biscuits by her bed and the senna pods soaking in a glass on the bathroom shelf.

He twisted his long slender cigarette in his long slender fingers and stubbed it out in her ashtray. He was preparing to get to his feet, picking up the packet of Sobranie, patting his pocket for his precious lighter, smoothing it down. Precise preparations for departure, which Eveline sought to delay.

"I ought to be going. Thank you for inviting me here. I am very pleased to have seen you again."

Eveline stared out of the window. It was still raining. It looked as if it might never stop. She didn't want him to go.

"I was just wondering, Mrs Ashfield, whether ... you see, I have complimentary tickets to the opening of *The Last Stand*. A week on

Wednesday. With your interest in these new plays, and your friend in hospital, I was wondering whether... whether you would care to come with me as my guest."

# Chapter 6

"I'm back." Marvin was revving up the Mini Cooper in the street outside, Aunt Patience's neighbours tut-tutting over tiny, well-tended London gardens. "Aren't you pleased to see me?" Elbow on the window, beckoning finger, one eyebrow raised. His eyebrows, straight lines across his brow sketched in charcoal, dark and fierce, leaving Lydia unprepared for the laughter in his eyes. And the twist of her heart.

He unfolded himself from the driving seat. Why did such a tall man insist on driving a Mini, and tiny, tight little sports cars? She threw her arms round him, hugging him, cheek pressed against a button of his denim jacket. She feared he had given her up because she wouldn't jump into bed with him. Because she was too serious. Because she worked the wrong hours. Because she hesitated on the sidelines of his decadent world. Because she was scared of her immoderate attraction to it and him. All of it jumbled in her head, the steep downhill slide.

She breathed in slowly.

"Where have you been all this time?"

"A bit of sunshine and sea. Finn Caradoc's idea of a birthday celebration. Southern Spain. We raced down the road from Ronda to Marbella, Dave, me and a couple of the others, in the fastest cars we could lay hands on. Finn drove a brand-new Lotus Elan off the edge of a cliff on the way down, somersaulting through the scrub. He's fine, but that model he's seeing was injured."

"How terrible. Is she all right?"

"Concussion. Broken leg and collar bone. That sort of thing. Still in hospital. She'll survive. Imagine it, Lydia. The hairpin bends, the sheer drops, the sun in our eyes, the far distant view of the sea. Breaking all known records on an unsurfaced road. You should have been with me, darling."

"Is that all you ever think about? The thrill of fast cars?"

"What else do you want me to think about?"

"The girl who was hurt. Her life, maybe changed for ever. Her family."

"Come on, Lydia. She chose to be in his car. It's what they all do. The wantonness of wealth."

Death in a fighter plane. Death in the Blitz. Death by nuclear explosion. Death in a sports car. Rich people who didn't have to struggle, assuming they would die young and had the right to grab their chances of pleasure while they could.

"I didn't know where you were. You just disappeared. Didn't you think that I might want you to come back safe?"

"What are you fussing about? No one plans ahead. I'm here now, aren't I? Come on. It's the weekend. Even you can't be working. We're off down the King's Road."

Marvin took Lydia by the hand. "What a tiny wrist you have. I can reach round it with my thumb and finger. How easy it would be to crush it."

"Not much use compared with yours. All I have to do is hold a pen. And smoke a cigarette."

The golden hairs on his hand and his long fingers filled her with lust and longing.

She looked up at him. Yards of sun-bleached denim, shades in his top pocket, eyes alight. Marvin was the only person who really smiled. Her colleagues at work looked askance at her, Aunt Patience pursed thin scarlet lips, and even her beloved grandmother's expression was sad and disappointed nowadays. An air of melancholy suited the Poet, of course. The haunted half-smile of her faraway mother was no more than a faded photograph.

They turned into the King's Road, alive with its Saturday crowd. Lydia's eyes were open now to the sports cars. How many there were – sparkling in the chilly sunlight, open-topped, sheepskin-muffled, blond-haired drivers hooting and waving to passers-by. Like some crazy, non-military parade.

"There's the new Sunbeam Alpine … That's Piers' brother destroying the gearbox … Ah. See the beauty of that bodywork." As though he were judging racehorses in the collecting ring before a race.

"You find cars more beautiful than people, don't you?"

"Some of them. Sure. But not on the King's Road. Everyone here is young and beautiful. Human versions of sports cars."

A throng of people threaded and unthreaded and dallied under blustery blue skies. Heavy clouds gathered on the horizon. Anyone brought up on a farm, like Lydia, with the slightest eye for meteorological conditions, could see that you could not depend on sunshine that day. But there was blossom on cherry trees and pale green leaves on the beeches in the squares. The air sparkled and fizzed, catching your breath, and lime trees scattered pollen like stardust on the light-headed. The young peacocks had thrown off their winter plumage, their frogged velvet and their customised peacoats, and strutted along the King's Road, displaying their Saturday sexual magnificence in outrageous fashions, sipping Italian coffee as though from ornate bird baths. They were beautiful and invincible.

She and Marvin sauntered past newly opened cafes and small glittering clothes shops. They didn't have a destination. They were looking about them, hand in hand, soaking up the atmosphere, at the same time merging into the crowd, adding something to the melee of short skirts and slim-legged, loud-checked trousers on the pavements. People turned to stare at Marvin, his height, his Levi's and his recently acquired Paco Rabanne shades, and Lydia, beside him, floated in a force field of delight, caught up in a web of rapture.

"Look. Over there. That would suit you."

Marvin pointed to a tiny dress with a scallop-edged hem and long scallop-edged sleeves in the window of a new boutique. He led her into a half-dark emporium at the back, cordoned off with a curtain, lit by a tilting standard lamp and cluttered with beautiful girls in various stages of undress, girls with short, straight fringes and kohl-blackened eyes, and their boyfriends and hangers-on lounging about on velvet cushions. There were piles of tiny discarded frocks on the floor and a male assistant conducting the chaos in a French accent.

It seemed to Lydia that she had stumbled into Aladdin's cave. For her, there had been two extremes of clothes shopping. Dragged along after Aunt Patience into the changing rooms of Harvey Nichols, where prim shop assistants showed Cousin Griselda outfits for cocktail parties and long weekends in the country. Piles of tissue paper and taffeta and expensive tweed. Aunt Patience suddenly remembering Lydia and insisting on buying her a good corduroy skirt. And at university there had been nothing except making your own clothes and Millets. Millets, filled with rows of military greatcoats and jeans, but bleak-lit and unadorned.

Marvin watched her undress. Secretly, Lydia was shocked. Teenaged Cousin Griselda had laid down rules about boyfriends, what you could and couldn't do, insisting that the arts of dressing and make-up should be kept a secret from them. Lydia had long ago rejected Griselda's advice on everything, but she hadn't managed to blot it out completely.

Marvin stood back to study her, apologising to a girl in brassiere and suspender belt behind him, whose naked toe he trod on. He tweaked Lydia's dress a little and shook his head. He went out to examine the rails. Eventually they agreed on a pink and black sheath with tight little buttons up the front. Marvin paid for it. Lydia could hear her grandmother saying "kept woman". But she wore it out into the street, tossing her discarded wool dress into a heedless rubbish bin.

"I'm not trying to seduce you, Lydia," said Marvin, as though he knew what she was thinking. "Not yet. I'm giving you time."

She scarcely noticed the stately figure in a Persian fur coat. A woman of a certain age threading her way along the pavement with a faintly affronted dignity, protected from the contagion of fashion by her elaborate stitching and pleats, her flowing silks and her little felt hat, looking steadily ahead of her and ignoring the wild patterned tights and the short geometric dresses in the glittering shop fronts she passed.

When they were almost abreast of each other, the two worlds collided. It was only surprising that it hadn't happened before. People of Eveline's class and age had always lived in flats and houses in this part of Chelsea. Until that moment, it hadn't occurred to Lydia that they might have as great a claim to the King's Road as the young invaders.

"Grandmama. Hello. It's me, Lydia."

For once, Eveline Ashfield seemed at a loss. She looked them up and down, speechless. She picked on one of the pairs of spectacles tethered to her ample bosom, and examined the length of Lydia's dress and the tightly buttoned crotch of Marvin's Levi's.

Marvin, with the effortlessness of someone for whom the situation had no complexity, bent down and picked up the glove that Eveline let fall on the pavement. Lovingly, he patted it clean. "What a beautiful little thing. So perfectly made. The colour of pigeons' wings." He stroked it once or twice before handing it back to her. "How nice to meet one of Lydia's family. We're on our way to Solange's for breakfast. Won't you join us?"

Eveline blinked, once, twice. She pursed her lips. She seemed to hesitate. Then she straightened her back, laid her spectacles back down on her chest and adjusted her hat.

"I breakfast at eight, thank you very much, and I'm already late for my appointment. Come and see me, Lydia, on Monday."

\* \* \*

It had been a long day: meetings with deputations from local education authorities complaining that the schools in their areas could not
be turned into comprehensives without purpose-built new buildings.
The head of Architects and Buildings Branch sat there listening to
them and explained that there was no money because of the state of
the economy. Yes. Of course Swedish comprehensives were purpose-
built. But if the government was going to introduce them in England,
they would have to be made up of former grammar schools linked to
nearby secondary moderns and pupils be distributed between them.
'Thirteen years of Tory misrule', a lot to answer for, thought Lydia,
taking notes of the discussions. Still, Tony Crosland was going to
see it through. One chief education officer ordered her to fetch an
ashtray. To do him justice, her colleague explained that she was a
researcher on the team and that an ashtray would be provided when
coffee was brought in. A long day in dark brown rooms, lit only by
the spark of reform.

Eveline received her in her bedroom. Like entering the past.

The high box-spring bed was piled with coverlets, silky and pink.
Even the curtains were fluid in this room. It should have signalled a
special intimacy. The little chair Lydia was directed to sit on was ornate
and pretty, pale grey woodwork and damask upholstery, probably
French, certainly valuable, but its seat was scratchy against the back of
her stockings.

Lydia knew that Eveline had been shocked to see her wrapped in
Marvin's arms, 'half naked' in a public place, in what Eveline thought
of as her part of London, on a street where her old friends trotted along
the pavement to MacFisheries or Boots. Today, Lydia happened to be
wearing one of the outfits she thought of as suitable for the office. But
she knew Eveline would disapprove of that too, thinking it 'unbecoming'. More decent but hardly more to her taste than the King's Road
pink and black sheath. How vividly Lydia's clothes reflected the ill-
fitting pieces of her life.

"Why can't you wear a nice tweed suit? Like Cousin Griselda. And the pearls I gave you. You'd look so nice. Oh, Lydia, when I was your age I had all these wonderful frocks, even though it was wartime, silks and chiffons and cotton lawn. It makes me sad to see your clothes. To think that you will never wear anything truly beautiful. All the expensive things I wanted to leave to you."

Lydia wriggled in the stiff little chair, trying to relax. She turned to look out of the window, letting her hair slide over her face to protect her from Eveline's gimlet gaze, the defence mechanism she knew was pathetic.

Eveline opened a drawer in her dressing table, slowly and theatrically, watching Lydia out of the corner of her eye. Nests of expensive gloves in various colours and lengths, like the one Marvin had picked up for her.

"So important, gloves, Lydia dear. You can't have too many. Each for a different occasion."

Eveline took out a pair of pale elbow-length calfskin opera gloves with an opening in the middle – like the slit you made in the stomach of a brown trout to clean it, Lydia thought, and tiny pearl buttons to close it when it was on your arm. Lydia had learnt to clean a fish with the Poet at Gairloch. There was something brutal about the slits in the soft white skin.

"The uses of gloves, Lydia. The mystery, the seduction, the slow unbuttoning, the uncovering bit by bit of an arm or a hand. More suggestive than unlacing your corsets," Eveline mused. "In fact, I tend to prefer the glove stage of a relationship myself."

Lydia laughed.

"Putting them on can be powerful too. A toss of your head. A sign of disapproval, a barrier against too forward a flirtation, a line drawn at the end of an assignation. All that and more, expressed through a pair of gloves. You young things nowadays don't have any of this to fall back on. Everything proceeds so quickly."

Of course it was true. Lydia was still catching her breath.

"Sharing backgrounds and interests. These days, young people are throwing that idea to the winds. Thinking they can pick someone from any part of society on a whim. Such a risk, that, Lydia. That's why you must find the right sort of person."

"I have a boyfriend already." Lydia stared at her hands.

"Oh. So he *is* your young man, is he? Very tall, isn't he? I've always thought very tall men are better seen from a distance. Like castles. Too much to take in close up."

Eveline sighed, putting the glove firmly back with its pair in the drawer, as though it had been tempted to stray from its partner and had to be brought into line. She patted her perfectly ordered silvery curls and turned her sea-blue gaze on to Lydia. "Well then, I suppose you'd better tell me about 'this person'."

"He's got a name, Grandmama. He's called Marvin Brewer."

"Marvin? What sort of Christian name is that? I don't think I've ever heard it before. A family name, I suppose. Where does he come from? Who are his people?"

"Um. Well. His mother died when he was a child. He doesn't talk about her. I'm not really sure what his father's job is but his real interest is breeding pigeons."

"Homing pigeons? Like the royal family? Like in the war, when they were used to send messages to the battle front?"

"Not like the royal family, I don't think. But you know, like people who breed pigeons in their back gardens. He lives on the edge of open country – it sounds lovely – and he has rows of pigeon lofts, you know, somewhere in Yorkshire. Or do I mean Lancashire? I haven't been there yet."

Eveline digested this without comment.

"So where did you meet him?"

Lydia crumpled a little further into the chair. She thought of Marvin leaning against the wall at Wormwood Scrubs, his first brown-eyed scrutiny, the long denim leg that ground out the stub of a cigarette, the tilt of his head as he lit a new one, and the thick gold hairs on his wrist that brought saliva to her mouth. She thought of Marvin, rapt, untouchable, head under a newly sprayed bonnet, the hairs on his arms matted with grease.

"He... um... works with sports cars and racing cars. You know, those sleek cars with open tops and fancy engines. I don't know much about them myself but he and his friends are obsessed with them. They own a business, in Bayswater, he and Finn Caradoc. You know who he is, of course. He's friends with people like Auriol Wedderburn." Lydia thought that this would go down well.

Eveline nodded.

"The Wedderburns. Yes. Very good Northumberland family. Beautiful house. But you know, dear, I've heard that Auriol has behaved very badly recently, criticising her father in the newspapers, of all things. And falling in with some unsuitable people. I hope those aren't the people you spend your time with."

The elegant bedroom felt stifling. Lydia was silent. For Eveline, the concept of marriage must have obscured the idea of going to bed with her husbands. Now it was the other way round. The idea of marriage was disappearing behind a veil of sexual experimentation.

Eveline sighed. "Hmm. Well, child, I don't like the sound of it at all. We can't have you getting involved with the wrong sort of people. This is my second lecture to you, isn't it, in a very short time? I don't want there to be a third."

# Chapter 7

"Are you *still* not sleeping with Marvin?"

"For heaven's sake, Auriol," said Lydia.

Auriol Wedderburn was waiting for her at the door of the French Club.

Auriol had come up to her in Marvin's basement. "I was there, Lydia. I was actually there. When the students marched on Washington. Joan Baez was there. You can't imagine what it was like. Thousands and thousands of us. It's such a let-down being back. But it's my birthday, and I might as well celebrate. Lunch tomorrow. Chez Solange at three."

"You know I can't do that. I get an hour for lunch. You just don't get it, do you? You don't understand working lives."

Lydia threw out an invitation of her own.

"The French Club in St James's Place. One-fifteen. But only for an hour."

Unused to receiving instructions, Auriol agreed.

"So, what is this French Club anyway?" she asked, as they climbed the stairs of the narrow building in St James's Place. "I've never heard of it."

The tables were small and covered with red and white gingham. The food was decidedly French.

"It's a nice mix of people, don't you think?" said Lydia. "Labour government advisers come here. Look over there. That's Lord Balogh at the corner table with the men in dark suits hanging on his every word.

They'll be talking about the balance of payments. Borrowing from the IMF. I like that about it. Ideas swirling in the air and exciting discussions going on around you."

"Lord Balogh? The Hungarian who advises the Chancellor of the Exchequer? You mean he has lunch here?"

"Yes. He's a member. And so are those long-haired men in poloneck sweaters over there. They will be working in TV or that advertising agency in Berkeley Square. There's always a few of those too. And even one or two writers. That's why I like it. And I love the food."

"The food. I thought you were so puritanical."

"You can't live on sardine sandwiches alone."

Lydia supposed her love of food must have come from her father. Her grandmother rose above such sensual delights. Her mother ignored it. Thank God taste was a sense that could be indulged without danger.

"I didn't think clubs accepted women," said Auriol.

"Most of them don't. It's outrageous, isn't it? Women should be able to go to clubs too, shouldn't they? There's that University Women's Club. Women only. Disapproval in long tweed skirts. I guess the French Club has always accepted women. It was set up by French freedom fighters in London with General de Gaulle before the liberation of France. There was more equality in the war. Anyway, it was set up by a woman. I suppose your father takes you to places like Boodle's?"

Lydia didn't like reminding herself that she didn't have a father. "The Poet proposed me and lined up some of his advertising friends to second me."

"The Poet?"

"Maelrubha MacKenzie. You know who I mean?"

"Well. You *are* a surprise, Lydia. I didn't know you did anything interesting – apart from being Marvin's girlfriend, of course. So this is where ministers come to talk about government secrets? Really?"

"I don't know about ministers. But their advisers, yes."

"Tell me this, Lydia. Who makes all the bad decisions? Is it the advisers? Or the civil servants who work in government departments, like you? Or the politicians? Who?"

Lydia wasn't sure what Auriol was getting at. She seemed very agitated and angry.

"You know how government works. I thought everyone at Sussex studied politics!"

"I went to Sussex to annoy my parents. And studied literature. I want to understand who's to blame?"

"Advisers like Balogh are really influential. But it's the politicians who decide. In theory anyway. They try to change things. That's what the new Labour government is trying to do. That's why it's exciting working at the Department of Education. Tony Crosland getting rid of the grammar schools. End of the unfair eleven-plus. Opportunities for all."

But Auriol wasn't interested in education policy. Like most people Lydia met.

"But why are the streets of Birmingham full of barefoot children? Twenty years after the war. That's what I want to know."

"It's not Labour's fault. Give them a chance. Thirteen years of Tory misrule. And they've only got a tiny majority. At least Harold Wilson is refusing to support the Americans in Vietnam. You must be pleased about that."

They picked up the menus. Auriol had thin, hesitant fingers, quite at odds with her tough demeanour. Perhaps she was musical or more sensitive than she appeared. She kept glancing round the room with a thoughtful expression on her face.

Their boudin noir arrived. Boudin and a few green beans, crisp, covered in butter, and neat little sautéed potatoes. And a small carafe of red wine.

"So are you *still* not sleeping with him, Lydia?" asked Auriol, curling her long tongue lasciviously round her first slice of boudin.

"For Christ's sake, Auriol, what's it to you? It's no one's business but ours."

That same old subject. All people ever wanted to talk about was who was sleeping with who. Why couldn't they forget it for a while and discuss something serious? The trades unions. Communism and the Iron Curtain. Nuclear disarmament. Any of those. She knew that Auriol was interested in politics. Yet who was sleeping with who was forever more fascinating. Apparently, even who *wasn't* sleeping with who was of sufficient interest to sustain a conversation.

"Are you frigid or something? What are you so frightened of? Did someone leap out at you from the bushes when you were a child?"

"I thought better of you, Auriol. I thought we might have a serious conversation."

"Don't you feel desire for him?"

Lydia put down her own forkful of glistening sausage.

"What's desire got to do with anything? Of course I want to sleep with Marvin. Who wouldn't? It's sort of torture holding back. But I'm not going to do it just because everyone else is. It has to be more than that. I've been desiring men since the bricklayer when I was eleven years old. Sitting on his knee, on his motorbike, reading *Titbits*. The first male body up close. But you can't let the desire thing dominate your whole life." She wasn't going to explain herself to Auriol, how she could be overtaken by desire for the weirdest and most unsuitable of men, about her mother.

Auriol sat up, eyes alight. She put down her knife and fork. "Wow. That's quite a statement, Lydia. Still, isn't that the point nowadays? You can sleep with the bricklayer, and anyone else you feel like. All in the same week."

"That's just patronising. The Pill is still illegal unless you are married. It's only well-connected people like you and Finn Caradoc who know doctors who will oblige. Ordinary doctors don't prescribe contraceptives, didn't you know that? And the shame of getting pregnant. Think what that's like for most people. Who can *they* turn to? They have to live with their mistakes. Or go to back-street abortionists. I suppose you got fitted up by a doctor friend of Daddy's."

Auriol blushed. "Something like that. You mean that you won't sleep with Marvin till there's free contraception for all."

"Stop it. That's *not* what I'm saying. Maybe I'm frightened. Frightened of getting involved in something that's too much for me. Frightened of myself. Had you thought of that? Sleeping with people seems quite complicated to me."

Lydia paused, her knife and fork suspended in the air. She dropped them on to her plate with a slight clatter. Lord Balogh and his companions turned to look at them.

"Lust is fine on its own. Falling in love is just about manageable. But putting the two together might be too much. I don't think I can trust myself with that. I might be swept away or something. And once I start sleeping with people, I might never stop." Long ago, she had constructed a concept of 'falling in passion' to explain what had destroyed her mother. And might not that happen to her too?

She thought Auriol would laugh.

"I'm sorry, Lydia." Auriol took hold of Lydia's hands across the table. "It was crass of me. I don't want to spoil our lunch. Mind you, we seem to be giving Lord Balogh a thrill."

Lydia looked at them out of the corner of her eye and laughed.

"I agree with you really," said Auriol. "Sleeping around is a luxury. Like all the luxuries, it falls into the laps of the rich and well connected. But you and Marvin. I still don't see why *you* don't sleep with *Marvin*. Since you love each other."

"I told you. I'm frightened of falling off the edge of things. Falling in too deep. And never coming up again." She'd had enough of trying to explain it. "And you, Auriol, who are you sleeping with then?"

"I'm not sleeping with anyone. I'm giving all that a rest. And concentrating on politics at the moment."

"Then why are you bullying *me* to do it?"

"I'm not bullying you. I like you, Lydia. And more than anything else I want Marvin to have a nice time. While he can."

"What do you mean, while he can?"

The waiter arrived with the bill. Lord Balogh and his hangers-on scraped back their chairs and got to their feet, picking up briefcases, coats, a scarf from under the table.

"We're all going to die young, aren't we?" said Auriol. "Our generation. Burn out or something. We have to take our pleasure while we can."

\* \* \*

"Nice long lunch hour, Miss Renfrew? Your colleague said you went out at one o'clock."

Michael Suffolk looked at his watch. He had summoned her to see him. He was sitting behind his government-issue desk, man and desk equally stiff and commanding. He was a small man who knew he looked more impressive sitting down. In his fifties, probably, considering his rank in the Department of Education. She guessed that he must have looked much the same in his twenties. Unhealthy dark hair, sparsely set out as though transplanted from another, smaller head, shiny skin and pale, heavy-lidded eyes.

His seniority entitled him to a room of his own.

He tapped his fingers on the surface of his desk, a nearly empty in-tray and an impressively piled-up out-tray signifying the speed and efficiency with which he dispatched the papers that were delivered to him for decision.

Lydia felt his gaze rove up and down her body. She was not sensibly dressed. She had quickly learnt that women in the Department of Education – the women in the hierarchy, that is, the secretaries had more room for manoeuvre – wore sensible coats and skirts teamed with brown stockings and lace-up shoes, or a wool twinset in a muted colour with a loosely pleated skirt if they were being courageously casual. So she had gone out to Derry & Toms and reluctantly spent hard-earned money on two outfits that she could just about bear to put on in the morning, and might pass as suitable at an office meeting. Today's short turquoise skirt and frilly white blouse was not one of them. It was chosen for lunch with Auriol and the waiter had told her it was saucy.

Nervously, she pulled at her skimpy little skirt.

"I called you, Miss Renfrew, because the Minister requires some information. The Minister, no less. And urgently. For a debate in the House of Commons. A bad show, you not being at your desk."

"Wasn't Roger around?"

Roger Maybury was the senior researcher. The research team consisted only of him and a couple of very old part-time archivists in a room full of files called 'the registry'; Lydia, on a temporary contract, was hived off at a spare desk in the less friendly room across the corridor. Roger was kind and shy and walked sideways along the corridors with small hesitant footsteps, as though ashamed to be taking up space. He was a Fellow of All Souls, it was explained to her in hushed tones, and probably the cleverest person in the whole department.

Why then was he not at the very top of this grade-dominated world? Why was Michael Suffolk senior to him? The civil service was full of mysteries. Lydia came to the conclusion that Roger Maybury must have made a mistake at some point in his career. Mistakes were a big deal in the civil service. People got to the top because they hadn't made any mistakes, not because they had done something new or remarkable. New and remarkable were bad marks. A 'safe pair of hands' was what counted.

She looked down at her own hands. Twig-like fingers. Crushable hands. She might never qualify. She had been employed on the personal recommendation of the university tutor who sympathised with her over her suspension. It was a temporary job. "It might turn into something more", they said. She was lucky to get it.

"Roger Maybury is off sick," said Mr Suffolk, "So it is for you to step up to the plate. We need facts and figures about the comprehensive schools in Sweden. The Minister leaves for the House of Commons at five o'clock. We must get the information to his Private Office before then. Can I depend on you?"

"Of course."

Lydia got up to go.

"One moment, Miss Renfrew. Sit down, please. Your job ... Personnel Department is asking ... we must be thinking about your future, mustn't we? ... only a temporary post, isn't it? ... a lot depends on it, I believe. You've done very well on the whole ... the right moment to be considering your future ... putting you forward for transfer to the permanent ranks of this department ... the senior grades ... even sit the examination to the administrative grade."

Lydia opened her mouth to speak.

Michael Suffolk, thoughtful, soft spoken, speculative, rose to his feet.

"Of course, my recommendation would be influential."

He stood looking at her.

"Yes. You've made something of the job in quite a short time."

He walked round the side of the desk.

"Systematic and perceptive, Roger Maybury says. Not bad. No. Not bad at all."

He strolled up and down the room, hands behind his back.

"On the whole, I would say that we are quite pleased with your work."

He moved up behind her chair, where she couldn't see him, like a teacher looking at her exercise book over her shoulder.

"A few concerns here and there. Punctuality issues. A certain frivolity of appearance, perhaps."

He was disconcertingly close behind her.

"You're young, of course. Have to prove that you are serious, my dear. In for the long haul."

The heat of his body, a stale smell of cloth, much too close.

"Not many young women are taken on for these jobs. Have to be able to cope with the pressure. Very much a man's world, you know..."

Suddenly, she realised that his erect penis was pressing against her shoulder, through the material of her jacket, unmistakable. Oh Lord. Lydia froze.

"Good reference from Roger, of course. Certainly. But the Board will be swayed by *my* recommendation."

Lydia didn't move a muscle. She held her breath.

At last he moved away to the window and looked out of it thoughtfully. "Yes. Yes indeed."

She muttered something and scuttled from the room.

Was this what it would always be like? Sex lurking behind every door? She shut herself up in the grim, high-ceilinged departmental toilets to get away from it all for a while, blowing her nose on the stiff government lavatory paper, coming to terms with the demands of working in a man's world.

It wasn't the Swedish comprehensive school figures that were the problem. Within minutes she was engrossed.

Lydia left the huge concrete building in Curzon Street and walked away through the little streets of Shepherd Market, the reputed haunt of upmarket prostitutes. It was not the shortest way back to the number 19 bus stop, but it was usually lively and diverting. Today it seemed discordant and shallow. And London felt rootless and loose.

# Chapter 8

"I expected to be so pleased when Griselda got engaged to Henry Sturridge, Mr Shortcross. Yes. Yes. A nephew of an old friend of mine. I've known the family all my life. Very well set up."

Arthur told her that he had seen photographs of Griselda Ashfield attending the sort of events that featured in the social pages of *Queen* and *Tatler*, escorted by men with double-barrelled names, or "sharing a joke". He told her that he had been invited to those parties himself when his name was in lights, even temporarily flattered by the attention of girls like her. He didn't say that she was always in a group of identical-looking girls, dressed like their mothers. He didn't say that he preferred the idea of Lydia.

Eveline was accepting her friends' congratulations with haughty grace. But privately she had her doubts. She wasn't used to doubts. She had a reputation for knowing her own opinion and not hesitating to express it.

"But I can confess to you, Mr Shortcross, that when he was sitting there on the sofa, I felt uncertain. Of course he is suitable. My daughter-in-law, Patience, made sure of that. She practically interviewed the young men Griselda was permitted to go out with. And Griselda does what is expected of her.

"They've hardly had time to get to know each other. But that isn't necessarily a bad thing. You don't need to *know* your fiancé, of course. I hardly knew my first husband when I walked down the aisle with him." How well she remembered those flirtatious little conversations and her fluttery hands on his manly chest. "We thought there would be plenty of time to get to know each other later. But there wasn't. I'm not sure I ever really knew him at all." The first eye-opening glimpse of a male body on her honeymoon in Monte Carlo, almost traumatic; a few awkward, white-bodied weeks. "Then he went back to war – the First World War, I've lived through two of them, you know." So soon after they married, and she, a young red-haired beauty, evacuated to his family home in Cheshire, exiled in the country among his younger brothers, who all fell in love with her and presented her with roses behind the box hedge in the walled garden. She created a memory of Cecil, clothed him in family photographs, and filled out his personality with anecdotes passed on by his grieving mother and doting siblings. He lived on in her mind as a sort of unblemished hero.

Her second marriage was different from the start.

"There were fewer men about, after the Great War. I was admired for getting another husband. Bertram may have disappointed me in some ways, yes." She didn't talk about 'the bedroom side of things', even to the playwright. Perhaps, she thought, I have preferred the dance of courtship to the untidy business of love.

"But we kept up appearances. Many couples did in those days – the husbands went away for years, they were both changed by the war and had almost nothing in common when they came back. It is making it work that counts. Sharing backgrounds and interests. These days, young people are throwing that idea to the winds. Thinking they can pick someone from any part of society on a whim. Such a risk, that.

"My son, Edmund, outwardly conforms. He made a sensible marriage. And that's what Griselda seems to be doing. Lydia's mother, my daughter, Flora – oh, a different matter altogether." She shook her head. Then patted her hair. "No. I can't bear to talk about that."

She sighed.

"So there's nothing wrong in principle with Henry Sturridge…"

Eveline faltered. She could not imagine Lydia sitting on her sofa, holding hands with someone like Henry Sturridge. How could she doubt the very process she was pressing Lydia to conform to?

Eveline had grown hungry for the company of Arthur Shortcross. For years, her surroundings had been enough to make her feel safe. But now invisible uncertainties lurked, like woodworm in the mahogany antiques. Bit by bit she convinced herself that it was all right to confide in him. Fears and dilemmas were a playwright's stock in trade, weren't they? She hadn't told anyone about the day she had bumped into Lydia and the man called Marvin in the King's Road, dressed in their disturbing finery. How Marvin had dusted the dirt of the street off her glove. She was surprised how easy it was to describe its complexities to Arthur.

"I don't spend much time thinking about my own children. I haven't done very well with either Edmund or Flora. And it's too late now. So it's my grandchildren I'm anxious about. How will they fare in this topsy-turvy world? How can I keep them safe? I won't live much longer. I want to gather them all up and hold them close to me." She picked a crumb of ginger shortbread off her knee and put it on her plate. "Could I, I wonder, call you Arthur? Surnames seem to be a bit formal for this sort of conversation, don't you think? And I could be Eveline to you."

She could see that he was pleased.

"Have another sandwich, Arthur, you always look hungry." She knew that he wanted some more ginger shortbread too. "I sometimes wonder whether you eat anything at home."

"I starve for days on end till I come to tea with you, Mrs… Eveline." He laughed. "It's a lovely name, Eveline."

"You don't know what it's like, Arthur. Every day of the war, steeling yourself for the telegram that tells you or one of your friends that your husband or son has been killed, the daily destruction, the friend of a friend crushed in the bombed-out remains of her London house. We welcomed the austerity after the war, people like me. We thought it seemed appropriate. It takes time to unfreeze. And just when you feel things may be all right again, the future brighter, you look out at the world around you and it's changed. The new generation, throwing convention to the winds, questioning everything, risking everything that we kept together for them – standards, morals, property, savings – frittering it away on sports cars and outrageous clothes... Lydia. A 'blue stocking', a 'working girl', a 'socialist'!"

Her hand fluttered to her hair, adjusted her spectacles, twisted the rings on her fingers.

"Griselda will be all right. She's launched now ... like a sailing ship. But it's so hard, Arthur, minding so much about Lydia ... breaking all the rules."

"You mustn't worry so much. It's what people like Lydia *should* be doing. Tearing up the scripts the older generations have written for them and writing themselves new parts. In blood, if necessary! Rules are made for breaking. Look around. In art and music and theatre. Creative demolition."

'Creative demolition' indeed. What an expression. She could see that Arthur really meant what he said. That he'd thought about it. That he must have done something like that himself, and that for all his conviction, life wasn't easy for Arthur. There was demolition of hope in *The Millstone*. Suddenly she wondered about Arthur's family. She didn't know whether it would be intrusive to ask. It only occurred to her much later, too late really, how her confidences might affect Arthur, that Arthur might begin to soak it all up, and members of her family begin to take root in the spaces in his barren world, like flowers in a desert after a rainstorm.

Creative indeed. Was what Lydia was involved in 'creative'? She hadn't strayed all that far socially from Eveline's own world, simply fallen in with a degenerate version of it. Eveline had done her research. Finn Caradoc had wrecked the life of the daughter of a good family, might as well have killed her; Finn Caradoc, who had been page boy to the Queen. That David Perry was said to be friends with the Kray brothers. Auriol Wedderburn, former debutante, the granddaughter of a school friend, publicly insulted her family in the pages of an evening paper. Was rumoured to be a socialist and or even an anarchist, whatever that meant. What was so creative about them? No one knew anything about Marvin. He'd simply appeared in that tarnished golden circle, with his strange appearance and his Lancashire accent and his talent for building cars.

Eveline patted her hair and fixed Arthur in her blue-eyed gaze.

"I don't usually complain, Arthur. But I feel so worried about Lydia. She's living just for the present, no glimmer of an orderly future, of children, of being settled. I can't possibly approve of Marvin's unsavoury world, him taking her away from her background, away from me and everything I stand for. Oh dear, I don't know what to think. I've lived too long."

"Why must you doubt her? I don't think you should see it like that. It's exciting. It's like the beginning of something. The prologue to something new. Lydia's wonderful."

"What do you mean, Arthur? You don't know Lydia."

"You talk about her all the time. I can picture her exactly. I do character notes in my head. You know, like the bit at the beginning of *The Millstone*: 'Fred, twenty-one. Tall. Skinny. Crooked teeth. Loose pink underlip.' It's fun writing them. It used to be, anyway..."

"But she hasn't been to see me for two weeks in a row."

Summer rain poured slowly down the windowpanes, like tears.

"I used to think that my experiences and beliefs would be useful to my grandchildren. But now, suddenly, at the end of my life, I'm not so sure about anything. You're the playwright, Arthur. If you're so creative, write me a play where it all comes out right. Could you do that? That would be beyond price. I would give anything for that. Anything, Arthur, anything..."

# Chapter 9

Arthur had missed the dogs during his self-imposed isolation.

They went back a long way, he and Reg, bunking off grammar school, taking the bus to the Belle Vue Stadium in Manchester. Reg was nowadays teaching maths somewhere in the East End. There he was, familiar, stocky, square-shouldered, a packet of Embassy tipped, the dregs of a pint of bitter and a copy of the *Greyhound Star* balanced on the ledge of the viewing window at White City.

"Glad you haven't stood me up again," said Reg. "Beginning to think that the dogs were too downmarket for the famous playwright."

Arthur could take it from Reg.

"How's things, Arth? Gone a bit quiet lately, haven't you? Nothing about you in the gossip columns these days."

"Let's get a drink. The usual?"

They added two pints of bitter and two double whisky chasers to the items on the ledge.

The stadium was filling up around them. Men in dark coats and caps, cigarettes and pipes and cheroots, the rustle of newspaper and the discussions of form. A few serious women too, aficionados with spectacles. The behind-the-hand whispered tips. In the distance the intrusion of upper-class voices, a group of people in their twenties, with clean blond hair and sludge-coloured corduroys.

"Friends of yours, Arth, slumming it at White City? At least you don't dress like them."

Arthur raised his elbows from the ash-covered ledge and dusted them down. He was wearing a donkey jacket, but an expensive version bought when he had money to spend. He looked at Reg's jacket and tie.

"I know. I know," said Reg. "Came straight from school."

"How's it in Leytonstone then?"

"Oh, you know. Gruelling. Now we're worried about these fancy comprehensives."

"I thought they were supposed to be a good thing? An end to the sheep and goats thing at eleven?"

"That's all very well. Half those Labour MPs in Parliament owe their success to the grammar schools. And where would *you* be without that English teacher? Speckles? Or Freckles? Whatever was he called?"

"Where indeed. But I thought the idea was that the comprehensives would do that for everybody."

"What's up, Arth? I'm your best friend, aren't I?"

Arthur laughed. He was glad, now, that he'd come. He found himself telling Reg about writer's block. Describing it in its full horror for the second time in as many weeks. It was much easier this time. He could turn it into a performance now. An actor delivering the lines. He had Eveline to thank for that.

"The sleeplessness. The tossing about, the pillow too hard, the wrong sort of pillow. The voices starting up in his head. The characters, the choreography, the 'exits and the entrances'. All crowding in, making speeches, offering suggestions, jostling the pallid playwright from his rest.

"Awake, he tries to get it all down. The cast that gabbled away to him in the middle of the night, they clap their hands over their sly little mouths at dawn and refuse to speak. The significance is lost.

"The treacherous little flicker of faith that today will somehow be different. That lasts through the first two cups of coffee. All the remembered words. All that he wants to say. The long day in front of the typewriter. Sheets of white paper staring up at him, malevolent, one useless little scribbled line after another, cast up like little pools of half-digested vomit on the page. The screwed-up piles around the wastepaper basket. The sigh of the cleaning woman as she enters the room on tiptoe so as not to interrupt the 'muse'. The terrible moment, the disappearance of another wasted day."

What must old Mrs Ashfield have thought of him? She must have been frightened when she saw him prowling along the street like a vagrant. Listening to him raving in her Humber. How brave she was. Even his old friend looked slightly bemused.

"Crikey. It can't be much fun. I thought it was all so easy for you."

"It was. But now it isn't. Nothing pouring out on to the page. No money coming in."

"Can't you get a job? Sorry. I mean another sort of job. To tide you over?"

"I do a bit of work at an advertising agency. The famous Martel and Tillotson. They employ playwrights and poets, people who are supposed to be good with words. Earns quite well too. Word for word." He laughed.

"There you are then. Lucky you."

"But it's a world where even the poets are posh. Educated at Oxford University. Savile Row suits, gold cufflinks and Sunbeam Alpines parked in the street outside. In-talk. Their social wavelengths. Their financial safety nets. Always something to fall back on. Unlike the Burnley boy from the council house. There are some of them over there, by the way, in that group at the other end of the bar."

Reg examined them from a distance.

"Hah. Come across, do they, know what I mean? Those girls with the long clean hair? Wouldn't say no to a bit of that."

"Some of them. Yes." Some of them certainly had when his name was in lights.

"Time to study the form, Arth. Take *Sporting Life* and I'll check the *Gazette*. I'm developing a system, you see. Win every time. Hang around, mate, and you'll be flush."

Arthur laughed.

"So grammar school wasn't wasted on you either. All that swotting. Just as well we broke with the Park Street boys."

In fact, Arthur always regretted that. The eleven-plus parting of the ways.

"I'm serious now. Using statistics and probability. I'll explain when I've perfected it. You should come regularly, man. It's the English Greyhound Derby next week. Just do what I say. Concentrate. Put your money on Pimpernel in this race."

A few minutes later the traps rose, six grey shadows streaked past in front of them and the race was over. Forty seconds flat.

"I'd forgotten how fast it is. Fair takes your breath away."

"Magic, isn't it? Pure bloody magic. Well done, Pimpernel. Now we put double the winnings on the next. And double the whisky with the next half and half."

Arthur felt himself unfreezing inside. Walking beside Reg, he allowed himself a bit of a swagger.

There were forty or fifty booths, and people jostling around them. He lost Reg in the crowd but queued up at the nearest window to place his next bet as instructed. On his way back to the viewing area he caught sight of Maelrubha MacKenzie, the poet whose company reconciled him to working at the advertising agency.

"Want a tip, Poet?" he asked cheerfully. "I didn't know you came to the dogs."

"I'm out of my depth, honestly, Arthur. My friends insisted. Come and say hello."

Maelrubha pointed to the group Arthur and Reg had spotted earlier, crowded round the far end of the bar. He recognised a couple of other people from Martel and Tillotson. The rest Arthur didn't know. He wavered.

"Who's the girl with the long black hair?" he asked.

"In the outrageous pink dress? She's lovely, isn't she? A family friend. Lydia Renfrew. Come and be introduced."

Arthur's heart missed a beat. So that was Lydia. Crazy black hair falling over slender shoulders. Pale face. Long, thin legs. Knock-kneed. Fragile-looking. He heard his mother's voice in his head: "Uppity sparrowy little tart." He couldn't see her expression. Or the colour of her eyes. Was he writing character notes? He was overwhelmed.

"I won't now, thank you. I'm with a friend who's developing a foolproof system for winning."

"Something I could do with," said the Poet, walking off with his slight limp. "See you at the office."

The next race. The flaps open. The mechanical hare streaking off ahead of them. The stretched-out dogs skimming over the sandy track. All over in seconds again. The winner, the brown-grey face, wise eyes, pricked ears, long tongue hanging out. Though it won a tidy sum of money for him, Arthur couldn't afterwards remember much about it.

But he couldn't forget Lydia.

# Chapter 10

A low-slung dark green sports car sat outside Lydia's government offices at six o'clock, engine idling, parked in the place reserved for ministerial transport. Lydia, emerging, stopped on the top step of the exit. The doorman crushed his cigarette end under his toe and lumbered slowly towards the car. Marvin jumped out, pulled Lydia down the last few steps, folded her into the tiny space behind the front seats and accelerated away towards Westminster Bridge. He didn't say a word until they reached the Old Kent Road.

"Delivery job. Came up suddenly. We're off to Menton. Catch some rays."

His friend Dave Perry turned round from the passenger seat.

"We're taking you along for the ride, Lydia. Your horizons need broadening. You're the sort of girl who has to be kidnapped."

"But..."

"Tell them you've got tonsillitis," said Dave. "Standard practice to give you a week off work for tonsillitis."

"How would you know, Dave?" said Lydia. "You've never done a day's work in your life."

"Impertinent, your bird, Marvin. Shall we abandon her by the roadside?"

"I don't even have a doctor."

"No problem," said Dave. "The bloke in the top flat in Kensington Park Road. A medic of some kind. He owes me a favour or two."

"What about Aunt Patience? She checks up on me all the time."

"For Christ's sake, Lydia, be a bit inventive," said Dave. "Tell her someone's mother has invited you to go away with her. Do whatever your friends do when they go off with their lovers."

Lydia said nothing more for a while.

\* \* \*

In northern France, it poured with rain. Marvin drove silently and fast. Suddenly, in the black and silver dark, the car plunged into a pool of floodwater, indistinguishable from the wet road. It planed out of control, swerved and zigzagged, nearly skidding into the ditch. Lydia was thrown against the side window. She must have fallen asleep. She caught sight of Marvin's face in the mirror. His eyes were hooded, his lips set. This is what he looked like when he really concentrated on something.

"Hairy," said Dave. "Close run thing. Burnt a bit of rubber there, demon driver."

Marvin drove on more slowly, then stopped.

"I'm not happy about the engine. It's not firing on all cylinders. Water, probably…"

He made them climb out of the car. It was no longer raining, but very dark. Lydia had no idea where they were. It was a single track road, long and straight, stretching like wet ribbon towards a cream-coloured moon.

"Look. Those trees. A moonlit avenue."

"Never been to France before, obviously."

Why, she wondered, was Marvin so determinedly fond of Dave? The word 'louche' seemed to describe him perfectly. Lydia, so easily seduced by Marvin's world, so hungry for wild adventure, found him objectionable and immoral. She turned away from him and started walking along the road.

They were surrounded by black countryside. There were no cars, no houses, no lights. A dilapidated sign on a dirt track led to a sleeping quail farm. A quail farm – she hadn't known such a thing existed. It seemed impossibly exotic, a set of buildings crouching around runs of little birds, whose bodies and eggs were sold to sophisticated continental diners. Damp lime leaves whispered in an arch above her head and there was a sudden movement that made her jump. Something flew across the road and settled on a low branch. A pure white barn owl stared down at her with huge accusing eyes. She seemed to be intruding upon its territory. She turned back, slightly alarmed. She would like to tell Marvin about it, ask him if he believed that an owl hooting at night predicted death, as her friend the Poet claimed. But she wasn't risking Dave's scorn.

Back in the car they were eating real Russian caviar on white sliced bread. It was that sort of trip.

"White bread because it doesn't produce crumbs," said Marvin. "Take care, you two. This car's got to be in perfect condition when I deliver it."

"Where do you get this caviar from? What is it, actually, this car?" asked Lydia.

She had never heard of a Facel Vega. She didn't know that they were legendary.

"Did they say you could take us along for the ride?"

"It's like any other delivery job, Lydia," said Marvin. "If you're paid to take a sailing boat from Portsmouth to the West Indies, you can take along a crew. A long-distance lorry driver takes his kid or picks up a hitch-hiker. All that matters is the condition of the car when it arrives. Town car really. I don't know why they chose this for the Côte d'Azure."

Marvin drove on southwards across France, through the night, silently, another landmark passed, another sensual stroke of the steering wheel, another winding down of the window to run his fingers over the gleaming paintwork. Lydia stopped herself from reaching out and stroking the back of his neck.

Forbidden to drive, not allowed near the controls, Dave had been put in charge of changing the 45s on a record player wedged into the glove box. Dave Brubeck mostly, because Marvin insisted, and after all he was driving. Mixed with Otis Redding.

"C'mon, Marvin, we've got to have *King of the Road*. We haven't had it for at least two hours," said Dave.

On this, Dave and she ganged up flirtatiously.

"Yes. It's the only thing Dave and I have in common, our love of Country and Western. You have to encourage us, Marvin."

"Roy Orbison, Johnny Tillotson," said Dave.

"*Pick Me Up on Your Way Down*," said Lydia. "*Smoking Cigarettes and Coffee Blue*."

"*In Dreams. Mean Woman Blues.*"

"Mush. Sentimental rubbish," said Marvin. "It's like taking children for a ride. Dave chronically in need of a South of France fix, my serious little girlfriend giggling in the back seat. I'll turn you both out by the roadside if you go on like this. See how you'd like that."

"Just try it. You know what I'd do with her."

Curled up in the cramped luggage area, Lydia dozed fitfully. They stopped only once more. In a lay-by, early in the morning, somewhere near Lyons. They slept for a couple of hours stretched out on stony ground in the scrub beside the precious car until the cafe opened. The bright morning sunlight burnt them awake and they dived into the car for their shades like a row of eider ducks.

The bar stools in the cafe were filled with French lorry drivers drinking cognac and black coffee out of tiny white cups, eyelids heavy, elbows on the counter and Gauloises stuck to their lips. They looked up briefly when the three of them came in, bristling against the intrusion but deciding it was too early in the morning for a confrontation. They returned to the rows of little glasses and the sports pages of the local paper.

"Can't take you to Menton looking like a civil servant," said Marvin. "Take off those clothes or I'll have to undress you myself." He handed her a parcel. She edged past the row of navy-blue backs in the urinoir, wondering if she was using the wrong cubicle. The automatic light went off several times while she struggled to change in the tiny toilet. But when she emerged in a yellow gingham dress and a pair of white slave-girl sandals, the men at the bar turned round and applauded.

Marvin stuffed her office clothes into a municipal rubbish bin outside.

Lydia laughed. The sunlight scoured away her lingering notions of duty and responsibility. This was an adventure. She had travelled very little in her life – a month in Paris to learn French and a weird couple of weeks ferry-hopping in the archipelago off Stockholm with some university friends. When other students set off to Greece or Italy in the summer vacations, to work in Canada or to cross the US in a Greyhound bus, she had gone off to Scotland with her mother, strictly speaking to watch over her. Distant minibus and motorbike destinations required more freedom than she had.

Somewhere too close to Ventimiglia and the Italian border, they were stopped by the police. Marvin behind the wheel, enormous sunglasses, pink sleeveless vest on his mechanic's torso, and Dave beside him, custom-made shirt and jeans that looked as though he had just bought them rather than slept in a field in them. Lydia herself, tousle-haired and sleepy, bare knees and a frill of yellow gingham.

The Italian border policeman seemed to like what he saw – the car, the young English – or the sun was out and he was having a good day. He directed them to a villa on the hillside a kilometre or two back in the direction of Menton.

Marvin relinquished the car reluctantly to the over-indulged blond-haired son of a hospitable parent with well-coiffed grey hair, a peach-coloured linen jacket and a wandering eye. Marvin patted the bonnet as though he were sending a beloved child out into the grown-up world. Then he transferred his attention to Lydia, guiding her through the evening, through a haze of expensive white wine and cigarette smoke, Gauloises and Disque Bleu, nothing illegal with the older generation present.

The three of them stayed on that night, sleeping beneath the umbrella pines at the far end of the sprawling garden, under the stars, a night of pine needles and crickets and droning mosquitoes landing in a perfectly synchronised aerial bombardment. Dave was aggrieved and sulky, expecting to be installed in a guest bedroom in the villa. In the morning he waved goodbye, walking off towards a white Mini Cooper, brown hair curling down his neck like an Italian film star and his arm around the shoulder of a girl in a green sundress, the prettiest of a group of house guests, whose blonde hair stretched like cobwebs down her sun-browned back.

Lydia and Marvin took off together in a taxi westwards along the corniche, so overwhelmingly beautiful to Lydia that she could hardly breathe. The office seemed far away.

"Never seen an umbrella pine before? Oh, darling honey, what a sheltered life you've led."

Marvin was perfectly at home here, pointing out familiar landmarks, beaches and cafes and markets, eventually directing the taxi driver off the main road into the hills in his easy colloquial French.

"Where are we going? How do you know all of this?"

"I'm often here. Delivering cars to the South of France. At least this time I can show you a place that I love."

They gained height slowly, windows wide open, twisting and turning among violent green pines and red rocks covered in flowers, pink convolvulus, scabious, orchids and white daisies. Cicadas buzzed in competition with the taxi radio.

Lydia felt her heart turn over, stop and start again in a different key at a different rate. She longed to lay her skin against this earth, the shallow yellow-white stones scattered over the fields, the strips of dark red earth slipping down the sides of the road, the earth on the terraces, the rich brown soil between the sprouting knuckles of the grape vines. All this had been hidden from her northern-restricted years, waiting for her to discover it. And it was Marvin who was conjuring it up for her.

The taxi dropped them off. At first Lydia thought they'd made a mistake, that they had stopped at someone's private house, but behind a low wall she made out a few cast iron tables. Scarlet bougainvillea spilled out over a trellis and there were pots of rosemary and verbena on the low white wall. She and Marvin sat by a tumbling stream, holding hands.

The owner shook out a tablecloth the colour of the pine trees with the grace of an ancient fisherman casting his net. There was only one item on the menu – fresh trout from the river. That and a wild boar pâté, a baguette and a tomato salad that tasted of sunshine. Lydia felt dizzy. She had never eaten anything like this before. She'd had trout for breakfast often enough, freshly caught, carrying within its flesh the icy peat-brown Scottish water. But these little trout, the same breed of brown trout as far as she could tell, fried in olive oil, they were the dish of the gods and by eating them she felt herself bewitched.

Now she was ready to drown in her wine glass, wishing for nothing more. She raised it to Marvin, to drink to him, or them, or something impulsive and infatuated, but he had gone. In that peculiar way that is mysterious and incongruous in large men, Marvin could move very silently, lope suddenly out of sight in London shops and streets. She looked round for him. There he was, at the entrance of the cafe, enfolding a woman in the hug that Lydia had dared to think he saved for her.

"Lydia, this is Laure. This is Pierre. This is my ... Lydia."

Marvin explained that Laure was a former girlfriend – Laure laughed – and a very successful composer of classical music. She was self-deprecating. She was taking time off from Paris, living in St Tropez with Pierre, a Pied-Noir Algerian, a psychoanalyst. Laure seemed to Lydia to epitomise everything out of reach about French sex appeal and sophistication. Short dark hair, green-grey eyes, simple sleeveless dress in dazzling fuchsia. Pierre was dark-skinned, brown-eyed, black-haired and intense. Both were neat and small, Marvin towering over them. Lydia felt ungainly.

"How pretty, this English girl!" said Laure. "What a lovely dress."

It was all right after that. They drew up two more chairs, and after lunch and little cups of black coffee, Laure and Pierre insisted on putting Marvin and Lydia into the open back of their Deux Chevaux and spiriting them away to Laure's little white villa on the shore outside St Tropez.

"Laure's got lots of money," said Marvin when they were alone. "She's been very successful in Paris. It's nothing to her to buy a little place down here. It's outta sight."

"So cool," Lydia sighed. "How did you meet her?"

Lydia still found it difficult to ask Marvin direct questions – how long had Laure been his girlfriend, what had it been like for him, why they weren't together now? Of course he must have slept with her.

"Travelling with Auriol. Done a lot of that. French châteaux. Staying with some old lady with a huge house near Blois. One of her fancy Catholic relations. Picked up Laure in a cafe. Laure playing in some local group. Laure aged twenty-three in a pale blue smock and bare feet."

He paused, a slight narrowing of his brown eyes, which she tried to interpret.

Lydia wanted to ask Marvin more questions. Were they attracted to each other immediately? Did they go straight to her flat or whatever it was and jump into bed? Imagining it agitated her.

But Laure made it impossible to be jealous. They talked about art and architecture and Lydia even managed to discuss psychoanalysis with Pierre in her rusty French.

Later, in the whitewashed bedroom with the blue-green shutters and the blue-green sheets, Marvin pulled Lydia towards him.

"Laure won't understand that we are not sleeping together. So we'll just have to pretend that we are. It makes it easier." He ran his hands down her back and drew her towards him. Then stopped.

Lydia felt a whole new level of inadequacy. French women seemed to have a sort of confident sexuality that existed long before these so-called liberating times. There was something seamless about it that Lydia envied. Marvin's sophisticated friends jumped in and out of bed with each other without hesitation or repercussion, lived bohemian and sometimes criminal lives. Being with him felt like being in the eye of the storm, the quiet centre of a whirl of colour, flamboyance and drama, temptation and lascivious glamour. It was all there just waiting for her. The longed for, much feared freedom.

You couldn't shelter in the eye of a storm for long.

Marvin sensed what she was thinking.

"I'm not like Dave, you know. One bird after another. One more willowy creature with long blonde hairpieces and legs like a thorough-bred. Like sleeping with tadpoles."

\* \* \*

Marvin and Laure took her next morning to a boutique so small and glittery that Lydia had to steel herself to enter. She loitered uncertainly in the doorway. They spotted Brigitte Bardot on the pavement outside. Then they chose a pink bikini for her, and she could see that it secured her membership of the world of draped bodies on colourful beach towels. And as the sand of the rich and privileged pressed between her toes, she felt a surge of hunger to be like them.

But then suddenly there was something unbearable about it all, the colour, the beauty, the effortless entitlement and sophistication. The umbrella pines, the blinding sunlight, the ice-gold sand, the violent strips of bikinis slashed across the beautiful brown bodies, and the tumbling ink-blue sea. It was all too much for her and she longed to be back in Silloth, on the grim Solway Firth, bleak, windswept Silloth, with its sullen grey-brown sea, the sand whipped up in her eyes, clad in her navy school swimsuit, the scratchy unflattering woolly material a sort of protection from the cold. And from temptation.

She thought of her mother, all that she hadn't had, that one jaunty photograph of her, a forties'-style glamour girl sitting on Rimini beach in a blue-striped two-piece swimsuit. That must have been before her world collapsed in on itself.

Lydia's heart twisted inside her. She cried out.

Marvin pulled her to her feet and wrapped his arms around her.

"Time to get you something to eat. In your heart of hearts you're a pleasure seeker, Lydia, just like me," he whispered in her ear.

# Chapter 11

"Are you serious, Lydia? Back to the reports and statistics." Marvin stopped walking, stood still on the pavement and took hold of her hands, pushing her a little away from him, and looking her up and down. "It's summer. Look around you. All the exciting things are happening out on the streets and you look so beautiful. You could do anything you want."

"But I want to do *this job*. I think it's ... you know ... worthwhile."

"But what sort of life is it, darling honey? It's dangerous to spend your time on that sort of thing. It'll kill your spirit. I don't understand this about you. Fighting for a chance to do something boring. Most of us have come to London *to get away* from boring things."

He pulled her back towards him and hugged her. He put a long arm around her shoulders as they walked on.

"When everyone else is doing new things, breaking down barriers, you are putting them up. What is it that you are so frightened of?"

"But Marvin, it isn't boring. It's about breaking down barriers too. Between success and failure for eleven-year-old children."

It was no good saying that a different education system might have changed his life. His life suited him perfectly.

"Time for a cup of coffee. Black gold. More precious by far than any metal. Can you remember what coffee was like before the Italians arrived?"

"Coffee meant Nescafé at university. And in the Department, it's even worse. Thin and grey and disapproving. I don't know how they make it like that. You've introduced me to a new and better world, Mr Brewer."

Was it normal, Lydia wondered, to be filled with desire for someone because of the way he worshipped coffee? For his weird little likes and dislikes, rather than something more dramatic or momentous? To be stirred with lust by a raised dark-haired eyebrow? Saliva came into her mouth as he struck his Zippo lighter with his long fingers, as he lit his cigarette and leant backwards in his chair and let the smoke drift up towards the ceiling.

While she was flicking through musty papers at the Department, Marvin was building an Aston Martin from a sort of kit, for one of his friends. She couldn't even imagine how you would do a thing like that. But she had seen the intent expression, the narrowing of his eyes and the movement of his fingers on the bits of interconnected machinery. She glanced at his hands; there was oil under one of his fingernails. Her fingers strayed to his thigh under the table. She ought to stop herself from doing what she didn't yet know how to do. Distract herself from the idea of unbuttoning the flies of his sun-faded Levi's under the chic little table in the Café Matisse. Think about reports and statistics again.

"You want to be free *and* safe, you crazy bird."

Marvin closed his eyes, lashes long and dark on his skin as though sketched in charcoal. She could tell that he was hiding something from her.

"What's going on? I know – you're driving away to Marbella tonight."

"No. No. It's Finn Caradoc going away for a few weeks. That car crash and the model. Complications. Running away from the press. And I'm moving into the Belgravia pad. Come and stay. It's time you started sleeping with me, Lydia Renfrew. You can't keep up this puritan stuff in summertime." He unwound his long legs from under the table to show that the conversation was finished. "Bring the clothes you wear

to the office. I want to watch you get dressed in the morning. Change
from a princess into a frog. I'll even drive you to the office."

"You'd never get up in time." She laughed to cover her confusion.

In London there was no one to talk to about love. For the Poet it
meant only heartache. He'd never got over a love affair with a married
woman in Cyprus during National Service. Most serious subjects
involved heartache for him. But still, it didn't seem fair to burden him.
Cousin Griselda would say that you could allow a little messing about
as soon as you got engaged but to cling on to your virginity till there
was a wedding ring on your finger.

Lydia thought about her university friends, taking their finals now.
How distant they seemed, their first-year conversations about love and
sex, shoulders hunched over mugs of Nescafé, dropping the ash of their
Embassy cigarettes on to their earnest resolutions.

"I promised myself that I wouldn't sleep with my boyfriend until
we were engaged," said Jess.

"Any chance you'll keep to that?"

"That girl at the end of the corridor, Victoria something, the one
with the red hair down her back, she's done it already. She told me at
breakfast. Quite put me off my boiled egg."

"It'll be one after another with her. You can always tell."

Could you tell? Was that sort of thing written in your eyes?

"And Jackie Smith, imagine being sent down in your first term."

"Imagine doing it *in her college bedroom!* She just doesn't care. She
tackled the college doctor too. Imagine the conversation. 'I have to
tell you, Miss Smith, that under university rules you are not allowed
a husband by the university, and by the law of the land I may not
prescribe you contraception unless you are within eight weeks of
getting married.'"

"The trick is to mention a fiancé."

"And wear a wedding ring when you go to the doctor. You can get
them quite cheaply at Woolworths."

"How would you know that, Hattie?"

"My mum would kill me if I got pregnant. Never darken my door again."

"You can't blame them, the parents. One mistake and that was it for them."

"Not much different for us, is it?"

"It's all changing in America, with the Pill."

"There are doctors, though, who will give you something. Some girls are sent by their mothers. To be 'fitted up'."

"Sleazy. With soft pink hands."

"Most girls I know don't have that sort of money and connections."

"My parents *believe* in virginity. I can't even discuss it with them. It'll be the coat hanger in the back street for me."

"Or bicycling over the cobbles in Merton Street."

"What about you and Aidan, Lydia? You're very quiet."

"I don't want to talk about him." Lydia had stabbed a slice of pure white bread with the toasting fork and tortured it against the bars of the gas fire. "Let's have some more toast."

* * *

That evening, Lydia looked round Finn Caradoc's flat suspiciously. It was barely furnished. Pop art covered the whole of one wall and leather sofas and chairs were scattered around a state-of-the-art music centre like an altar. There were oil stains on the thick Turkish carpet.

"We had a whole engine here on the carpet one night." Marvin laughed with delight. "When we were souping up a getaway car for one of the Krays. We got so involved we couldn't bear to stop just because Finn was entertaining the crowd that evening. We brought it over here and went on working on it all night. Finn's wife doesn't come here any more," Marvin added, as though that explained everything.

The same crowd was here tonight, all except Finn. There was Dave Perry, and a number of the usual hangers-on. There was nothing intimate about it. A less congenial version of the Kensington Park Road basement, populated by more arrogant, more expensively clad layabouts. Lydia was dismayed. She had expected them to be alone the night they first slept together. Didn't he think like that?

Joints were passed around in the usual way but tonight the conversation was about heroin.

"Bloke's been found dead of an overdose in the pad I've been living in," said Dave. "The fuzz are asking questions and I have to disappear for a while. Not so inconvenient really. There's always something interesting going on in Cannes."

Dave was flicking off death like a speck of dust from the cuff of his Michael Rainey shirt. To Lydia, this was monstrous. Death being treated so casually. The death of someone their own age. A real death, and they were so cool about it, Dave simply heading off for the sun, in someone else's expensive sports car, without a backward glance.

Lydia stared at him in disgust. "Sex, drugs, criminality. Slippery slope." Aunt Patience was muttering in her head again. Eveline too, shaking her stringy be-ringed finger, their voices clamorous.

"Bit silent, your bird, tonight," said Dave.

"Seems fine to me." Marvin put his arm round her.

"Needs a good going over."

"Watch it, Dave."

"Don't flip your wig, man."

Lydia had never heard Marvin angry before, nor seen Dave look uncomfortable.

Marvin wasn't Dave.

Marvin loved cars for their own sakes, like an artist. Driving them to indulgent locations was the way he earned a living. He was not a vain and thoughtless sybarite. In this London scene Marvin's mechanical skills were his calling card, allowing him to slide in and out of any social setting. Welcomed for his talent among the rich and fashionable. Perhaps he was taken up by them merely because they needed his skills. Perhaps they liked his calm presence in the melee of clothes and parties and self-obsession. They admired the trace of Lancashire accent, congratulating themselves on having a friend from a different section of society. Marvin made his way among them, unspoilt, and with a guarded amusement in his eyes. That's what she believed, anyway.

Eventually, they wandered off into the dawn.

"Thank goodness they've gone. I don't think Dave Perry has any morals at all. Why are you friends with him, Marvin?"

How little she knew about this man she had fallen in love with. How uncertain she felt about some of these friends. And how little she trusted herself with them.

Marvin took her hands and turned them over in his.

She pulled them away and went over to the window.

"Marvin, seriously…"

"Give us a break, Lydia. We go back a long way, Dave and me. I don't want to talk about that. I want to make love to you."

"Why did he have to be here tonight? It's upset me. I'm sorry but I'm sleeping on the sofa after all."

Lydia expected Marvin to be angry. In the familiar liturgy of the Ashfield womenfolk, their privileging of male expectations, she had 'led him on'. He didn't get angry. He got stoned.

He came and stood beside her at the window and unbuttoned his beautiful purple shirt with his long mechanic's fingers. She shivered.

"OK, Lydia. I've brought you here to set you free, not to imprison you. To stop you wasting your life." He stared out at the blood-coloured dawn.

"Red sky in the morning, shepherd's warning," thought Lydia.

"Sleep wherever you like. Leave, if you want to. But you're better off with me than the civil service."

It usually amused her when he said that. Tonight it seemed that it was only a game for him, a parlour game played by people like Dave Perry. That nothing meant more than a joke. It was serious for her. Tonight she wanted Marvin to say that he had brought her here because she was different from the others and because he had begun to love her.

She sat down on the sofa with her back to him, shoulders hunched.

Marvin came over from the window. He didn't confront her. He just sat there behind her. Quite close. Then he began to unfasten the zip on the back of her dress, the dress that they had bought together on that Saturday morning in the King's Road. It had stuck at the top, somewhere under her hair, and it took him time to untangle the little hook without hurting her or the cloth, to free the strands of hair from the teeth of the zip and draw it slowly down. Lydia sat still, hypnotised, his fingers warm on her neck, moving over her vertebrae one by one, warming her skin, stopping time, turning her heart over, and soothing her as you might a frightened animal.

She stood up and at last turned to him, dress dropping to the floor.

"Take off those stockings too, darling, I want to feel all of your skin."

He took her hand and led her to the bed in this gilded promiscuous flat. On Finn Caradoc's satin sheets he held her tightly against him, every bone and sinew of his long limbs lined up against hers, brown eyes opaque and darkening as though he wasn't seeing her any more. Then she abandoned herself to a sightless half stranger, guided by touch alone, touch that she knew so little about, with its power to obliterate all thoughts and fears.

There was shock, at first, as though he was doing something more brutal than it should be, as though something had gone wrong, then a dizzying urgency, and last, oblivion. When he came back into focus, he was laughing at her.

"Why didn't you tell me you were a virgin? I didn't know there were any left. I thought you were stringing me along because I was wicked and dangerous!"

She couldn't explain her feelings to him, but now she could linger over his body.

He lit a cigarette, inhaled once and let out a wisp of smoke, watching her carefully.

He put it to her lips.

She hoped he wouldn't say something about the shared cigarette after sex, something corny that would bring her back to earth.

"Give us a gypsy kiss then, darling? Can you do that?"

Lydia took a deep breath, drew the feathery smoke into her mouth, locked her eyes on to his, pressed her lips firmly against his, and exhaled into his mouth. He inhaled in perfect timing.

They fell back against the pillows. No weed, no need, this was enough.

Marvin slept. His dreams in her hair, his long arms around her.

Lydia lay awake as dawn moved slowly towards the morning of working life. Secure in his arms. Secure and at risk.

# Chapter 12

"Ah, Lydia, at last I've caught you in. I need news. What have you been up to?"

"I've been working very hard."

"The General says" – the General was one of her regular visitors, an 'admirer' and a reference point – "that your Mr Wilson is making a terrible mess of everything. Parliament has no confidence in him. I can't think why you support him. Why does he have to smoke that ghastly pipe?"

Eveline loved to hear Lydia laugh.

"I like the idea of him being 'my Mr Wilson'. He won the vote of no confidence. He's doing as much as he can, Grandmama, with such a small majority. And the terrible mess the Conservative government left behind."

"The country's going to the dogs. His ridiculous policies…"

"They've put an end to prescription charges. Think of that. The difference it'll make to lots of people."

"I suppose the cottage classes will be grateful for that. But how will it be paid for? That's what I'd like to know. But that's enough of that. That's not why I called. What have you been up to?" She decided against questioning Lydia directly over the telephone about the man called Marvin. She couldn't bring herself to say that strange name out loud. "Why haven't you been to see me? Aunt Patience says you turn down the cocktail parties that Griselda invites you to."

"Oh … I've… been to the cinema … and … um … lunch with friends… the Poet…"

"And you went away somewhere." It wasn't a question.

"Yes. A long weekend in France. With a school friend and her mother."

"You didn't tell Aunt Patience."

"You don't need to treat me like a child. I can run my own life."

"Oh, really. It feels like only yesterday that I had to pick you up in a bundle of blankets."

Eveline hesitated. That unforgettable November night.

"I'm sorry to have brought you all the way from London, Mrs A. But it's not right, it isn't. Leaving a ten-year-old alone to look after herself. My husband will take your coat. It's a wonder young Lydia does her homework. If I think of my boys at that age ... And her making her own tea, night after night."

"Thank you very much for contacting me, Mrs Graham. And for looking after Lydia. I'll just take her away with me now."

"Hold on a moment. My husband's making us a nice cup of tea. I just need to finish this row. I believe you knit too, Mrs Ashfield. Wee Lydia's shown me that jersey with the stripes. She's mighty proud of that, you know. You'd think someone would *do* something about it. This isn't the first time. The authorities should get involved. We couldn't stand by."

"We're all very grateful to you for rescuing her..." She was trying to be patient.

"Out along the mud banks, the tide coming in, hunting for her mother. A child. A wee slip of a thing. That mother of hers, prowling along the Solway Firth after a waiter. A waiter! A foreigner at that. With a fancy violin. And all of you from such a good family."

"Thank you again, Mrs Graham. I'm taking Lydia away now. Away from here altogether."

"You know where we found her, Mrs Ashfield?" asked the farmer, still in his old tweed coat, putting a tray of teacups on the table. "In an old shrimping boat. Out on those banks. By rights, she should have drowned. Out all night in only her undies. Wrapped in an old sail-cloth. It's a miracle if she hasn't caught the pneumonia."

"She'll be all right now, I assure you. I've got my car outside."

She'll be all right now. That's what she'd said so confidently ten years ago. There was a catch in Eveline's voice even now, when she remembered the shivering, tearful child. But she tried to disguise it. She wanted to sound stern.

"You are being sensible, aren't you?"

"What about you, Grandmama? How are you? What are you doing?"

"I'm rewriting my will, Lydia."

She meant it to sound just a little ominous.

\* \* \*

Eveline was surrounded by boxes of jewellery when Arthur arrived. "I'm so pleased to see you, Arthur. Just let me get this sorted out."

He seemed visibly shocked. He was staring in dismay at her array of precious stones, sparkling on blue velvet cushions. She had never thought of it as excessive.

"I don't see much point in jewellery."

"It means a lot to me. Most of it came from my mother."

Eveline wondered what sort of jewellery Arthur's mother might have had. She imagined a jet necklace. A cameo brooch. But she didn't know how to ask.

"The diamonds'll have to go to Griselda. That's the only way they'll get an outing. Lydia wouldn't know what to do with them. She'd treat them as though they were ill-gotten gains, lock them up in a vault and worry about them. I'm giving Griselda the garnets too. They're right for her colouring."

"Why would Griselda need all that jewellery? She must have lots of family stuff already. And surely the city slicker will buy her something each time he's unfaithful to her."

"Arthur." His audacity delighted her, but there were limits.

"Leave Lydia something. Please, Eveline. She'll want something you wore."

Of course she intended to do that. She held up a sapphire necklace, dangling it in front of him, like temptation.

"Oh, that's really lovely." He picked it up and held it tenderly. "Perfect for Lydia. Especially the setting. Silver suits her better than gold."

"How do *you* know about what suits Lydia?"

"It's the sort of thing I know." He didn't tell her that he had seen Lydia with the Poet at the greyhounds. "Character notes."

"So you *are* writing again? What would you write about me?"

"That's my secret." He laughed. "I'd start with 'perceptive' and add things later."

She'd never expected to be flattered to be called perceptive. That wasn't how she saw herself at all.

"Your character sketches are perfect, Eveline. You should have written plays yourself."

"I wanted to when I was young. Those evenings at the theatre with my father. Sometimes I came home thinking I could do it better than some of the playwrights themselves. My father loved the theatre. We are all influenced by our fathers, don't you think? After my mother died he would take me with him several times a week. I was quite young then and, well, good-looking, so we got a lot of attention from theatre people, directors and so on. So exciting. We met all the actors. And the actresses. He was very interested in actresses.

"I don't often talk about him." She didn't think that a playwright would be shocked. All families had secrets, didn't they? "I was safely married for the second time before he got into trouble, and my children were too young to understand. It seems so long ago. He set up an actress in a flat and everyone knew he visited her there. There was some sort of scandal." She hesitated. "He left a whole collection of papers and letters. To tell you the truth, I've never had the courage to read them."

She noted the look of interest, flickering across his face.

"Would you like to read them, Arthur? And tell me what I should do with them? I've been thinking about his papers lately … I've left them to Edmund … but I don't think he'd like them …I was just wondering …I do have a couple of secret plans…"

She needed a cover story, an excuse for Arthur to observe her family.

# Chapter 13

Lydia was in her studio bed-sitting room when he rang. The window was open. She could smell the jasmine that climbed the trellis and protected her from direct line of sight of Aunt Patience's fine drawing room. She had been missing him. She wanted to be out somewhere, dancing on the streets.

"No, Lydia. Not St Tropez. I'm in Stockport. My father died."

Marvin had rarely talked about his father. He seemed to float free of family ties, free of almost everything really.

"I'm so sorry. Are you all right? Shall I come?"

He didn't ask her to the funeral. She wasn't even sure that there was a funeral. She'd never been to a funeral. But she cancelled an important meeting with a Senior Inspector of Schools to go up to Stockport.

She felt that it should have been raining, but the sun was shining and a lark sang somewhere high over the moor. Lydia sat on the bank in the back garden of his father's council house. This was a row of ex-miners' houses, the homes of several other pigeon fanciers, winding around the edge of a green hillock. It was at the end of the village on the outskirts of Stockport and the beginning of open countryside. It was neither urban nor exactly rural, but you could see the hills.

When Lydia hugged him, Marvin turned away. He didn't say much but his grief showed itself in the listlessness of his long arms. And there were floaters of agitation in his forest-brown eyes.

"My dad loved these pigeons," he said. "I must get them to good homes. Now. The start of the racing season. It breaks my heart to see them go."

"Does it matter moving them from one place to another?"

"Of course it does. You have to keep them shut in for a while to get used to a new place. Too late to ask my father what else you have to do … that's the worst thing. All those questions I never asked him. When I thought there was still time."

His father bred both racers and breeders, nurtured over forty years.

"He lived for them. Pigeon breeding is obsessive. He really cared more about breeding, though he had a lot of success at racing when he was younger. He kept them all together, cocks and hens. He didn't agree with widowhood."

"Widowhood?"

"Ha. I thought everyone knew about widowhood. What a narrow life you have led."

"But you're the only person I've ever met who breeds pigeons."

Marvin laughed.

"We all grew up with it around here. Main topic of conversation in the pub. Widowhood or keeping them together. Some pigeon fanciers keep the cocks and hens apart after mating. Until they race. Then when you release them, in Peterborough, or Perth, or Barcelona or wherever it is, they are supposed to have more motivation to get back to the lofts. That's what widowhood is. My dad didn't go in for that. He liked them to be together all the time and trusted in the homing training."

She had never seen Marvin bereft.

He had given away the best breeders, the ones his father had been most attached to, delivering them in little carriers to a neighbour. The rest he was advertising through *British Homing World*. He opened and shut every door of the row of empty pigeon lofts, looking inside, checking each one for a trace of his father, perhaps, a piece of memory or the ghost of a prize-winning bird. He cleaned them out, one by one, first with bleach and Jeyes fluid, then with a blowtorch.

She watched as Marvin walked along the row of pigeon lofts, running his fingers over the delicate carvings his father had made on each of the cage doors, the work of hours, each a wild bird, thrushes, wrens and kingfishers, seabirds – curlew and dunlin, every sort of bird except hawks, the enemy of homing pigeons.

"The lofts must be spotless. You put in grit, then reeds. Reeds are better than straw, which can hide lice. Then the nest pans and bowls. For their nests you need dried twigs of clematis, barley straw and a few tobacco stalks. Everything has to be perfect."

He hardly knew she was there. He was talking to himself.

"So many hours of my life doing this. My father was pleased when I grew tall so that I didn't have to stand on a box to reach into the lofts."

He worked with his back to her, but she thought he cried. Marvin was still mostly a mystery to her. It was as though a lens came fleetingly into focus and she could just make out a solitary boy scanning the blue sky for one of the returning pigeons, his watch to record the timing. He had been taught to handle these pigeons with respect, an easy familiarity and a sort of secret joy. And she'd thought of him as dedicated to urban life.

"Why didn't you do it too? Join his business?"

"I was trouble at school. They thought it was because my mother died. But it wasn't just that. I couldn't take exams. So I had to get away. Got a job in a motorbike place. Did well for a bit. Then there was National Service. REME. Do you know what that is? Royal Electrical and Mechanical Engineers. And afterwards I quarrelled with my dad. I wanted to race pigeons, he wanted to breed. So I fancied a bit of greyhound racing instead. Met Finn and Auriol at White City. You know, posh kids slumming it at the dogs. Considered quite groovy in those days. They adopted me."

He came over and sat down beside her on the bank. He put his arm around her.

"You know the rest."

"You're at home in the country, Marvin. I didn't know that. Why don't you give up the car business and go back to the pigeons?"

"I wouldn't mind. It breaks my heart to get rid of those pigeons. But you, would you come with me, Lydia Renfrew? You're stuck in that London job. It's funny really. I introduce you to the delights of swinging London, and now, look at you, it's you who wouldn't leave."

Lydia shook pure white fallen petals of dogwood off her long skirt. Only two options, she had thought. Very short or outrageously long, and she'd chosen long. How vain she had become. How obsessed with clothes. Marvin had opened the doors of those glittery little boutiques along the King's Road and led her inside, and now they were part of her life, she was hungry for them, a counterpoint to the dowdy civil servants of her working hours.

She got up and picked some ox-eye daisies from the grassy slope. Marvin took them from her, gathered some more and laid them one by one on each of the pigeon lofts.

"Moon daisies," he said. "They glow on midsummer's eve. Dad didn't want flowers on his coffin, but he would have liked this. Not rosemary. Daisies. 'There's daisies; that's for remembrance. Pray you, love, remember. And there is pansies; that's for thoughts.' Did you know that moon daisies symbolise patience? Perfect for him and his pigeons."

"You say you learnt nothing at school. Then you quote Hamlet and make it your own! You're always coming out with things like that."

"The Shakespeare is from Auriol. Not everything is learnt at university, darling honey. I do a lot of listening. Auriol's sort of marinated in Shakespeare. You can't travel all over Europe with her and not have some of it rub off on you."

He turned away from the lofts and looked at her.

"I can still quote whole speeches. Does that surprise you? If you can't read very well you get good at memorising. What would you like? Macbeth's 'multitudinous seas incarnadine'? Lear? Auriol likes anything brutal – with death and blood and conflict. I like the songs…"

"What would your father have liked?"

Marvin thought about it.

"Not Shakespeare. A poem about the sea, I think. Walter de la Mare. Or Tennyson. Is it Tennyson – *Crossing the Bar*? He never learnt to swim. Holidays in Whitby or Scarborough, paddling in the sea with his trousers rolled up, but he never went out in a boat. The sea holds a strange allure for lots of people who fear it."

"On the Solway Firth, fishermen don't learn to swim. They say they'd rather not struggle to survive when their boat goes down. What was he like, your father? Tell me about him."

"Sometime, darling honey. But not now. I have to get to the lawyer's office before it closes."

She had learnt a little about Marvin today and she was hungry for more. She felt she'd grown closer. She turned her head away. She shook out her hair, twisted it up and put the comb back in.

"No. Not like that." He undid her hair, ran his fingers through it and re-coiled it, taking a long time about it, stroking her skull with his sensual fingers, surely thinking of something or someone else. He put the comb back in, above her ear, gypsy-like.

"You're changing before my eyes," he said. "When I first met you I thought you must have had a serious illness. Like TB or something. Pale skin and hectic red cheeks. So thin and nervous. But not now. Anyone can see you're thriving. Look how easily I've corrupted you."

He was laughing, holding her away from him to admire her, like a botanical specimen he had cultivated himself.

Lydia wanted to explain that she loved him, that she was like this because of him. That she wasn't scared any longer. She would follow wherever he beckoned her, in or out of bed. She wanted him now, here, by his father's pigeon lofts.

She wished she knew what he was really thinking. The stories he might tell of his father. His mother, who had died when he was a boy. Then she might talk about her own mother. And her missing father. But when she asked about his mother he turned his face away, insisting that he didn't remember what that felt like, only that everything changed. Just shook his head.

"I don't even know how old you are," she said suddenly. Not looking at him, plaiting grasses and plantain together, trying to throw out the remark casually. "I didn't believe what you told me when we met."

"All conversation is lies, Lydia. You know that." He laughed.

His hair was longer now, burnt lighter by the sun. His cheekbones seemed to stretch just under the surface of his skin. His body was all planes, like spliced wood, and she couldn't imagine him wearing anything other than Levi's. His eyes were what had first struck her about him. Flecks of slow thought, sudden sparkles, glittery in anger, darkening and opaque when he was aroused. His straight eyebrows were severe. His skin tanned easily and was rough to her touch.

On the long, slow train journey back to London, stopping at little stations she'd never heard of, Lydia thought a lot about Marvin, the pain in his eyes as he looked at his father's pigeon lofts. She hoped his grief was simple. She wondered if he felt he had neglected his father, had failed to visit him, lost him before refinding him as an adult. She had never known her own father, and there was no knowing her mother. There was only Eveline to worry about.

# Chapter 14

"Please come and see me in my office, Miss Renfrew."

Lydia couldn't believe the timing. There was something uncanny about it. For days on end she ate a hurried lunch in the office canteen, uncertain whether to sit on her own with some papers or ask to join a table with people she hardly knew. For days on end she heard nothing from Michael Suffolk, and today, when he wanted to see her, she was not only late back after lunch but dressed in a short purple shift to avoid depressing the sensitive Poet with one of her dreary office outfits.

Could Mr Suffolk actually be spying on her somehow? Had he been lurking somewhere in the French Club? Lying in wait for her on the days she had lunch with improper people? It was easy to become paranoid working in the civil service. Perhaps she should be in television or advertising after all.

There was nothing Lydia could do to erase the carafe of red wine from her step or lengthen her dress and anxiety built up inside her as she walked the length of lino-covered corridor between her office and his. She knocked hesitantly. The distance between the door and the chair on the far side of his desk seemed interminable; the exposure of too much black-stockinged leg dangerously provocative.

"Ah, Miss Renfrew, I heard you had tonsillitis. All better now, I hope."

Lydia muttered something and coughed.

"I have a proposition to put to you. If you can spare me a moment." His gaze rested on her hemline.

Proposition? What sort of talk was that? Lydia's heart sank.

"As you know, this government is reforming the secondary school system. Not everyone thinks it is a good idea, of course. Getting rid of the grammar schools. But that's not the point for us civil servants, is it? We express our doubts on paper and the Secretary of State considers them, then he decides and we put into practice what he says. That's the system we live with. In July, Mr Crosland will be issuing a circular to all local education authorities requiring them to turn their grammar schools and secondary moderns into all-ability comprehensive schools."

Lydia nodded. She knew about this. She believed in the Labour government's education policies. She believed in this. Not that that was supposed to matter either way.

"The end of the eleven-plus examination across every local education authority in the country. Breaking down the barriers between success and failure. Chances for all."

"Yes, Mr Suffolk. It's one of the reasons I wanted to work in this department."

Mr Suffolk drew back a little, like a cobra before striking.

"Really. Not all of us share your enthusiasm for the change itself. But it is government policy and we, the instrument of government, will put it into practice as best we can."

He paused, tapping his fingers on the desk, its tidiness as usual indicating completed activity rather than idleness. He had a new coffee mug, with patterns on it. Art deco, she thought, and wondered who gave it to him. She couldn't imagine him doing his own shopping.

"Schools Branch has been working on this for some time. As for us, in Information and Research, our job is to contribute to that enterprise. I'm coming to your part in this. As you know, the comprehensive school model has been tried out successfully elsewhere, notably in Scandinavia. You did some research on that, I seem to remember. What is needed now is a summary of all the experience of other countries, the figures, where available, wherever it has taken place. Not forgetting the first few comprehensive schools in this country that were introduced under the previous Conservative government. Their achievements and so on. We need to know about those too." He paused dramatically. "What they will need in the ministers' offices, when the circular is published, is a background briefing document that covers everything. D'you get the picture?"

"Do you mean that I might work on that?"

"What I mean, Miss Renfrew," – he was looking at her intently – "is that this is now a priority for you. You will work on this, and only this, until you have pulled together a report. You will hand over your normal daily research enquiries to the part-time staff. Even, if necessary, to Roger Maybury, who continues of course to have overall responsibility. His experience goes a long way back. Yes indeed. He will have an important contribution to make. But it is you who will be responsible for producing the first draft of the briefing document itself."

He paused.

"And," he said triumphantly, "you will report direct to me."

He was still looking at her. And still sitting safely on the far side of his desk.

"That's the proposition. If you do it well I will recommend that you take the qualifying exam in January, for a permanent job here. It will mean a lot of work. Going where the research takes you. Keeping your eye on the ball. Longer working hours, possibly. I want you to ask yourself whether this assignment is consistent with your, er, with what appears to be your busy social life."

"I think you'll find that I am quite capable of hard work, Mr Suffolk."

"Yes. Yes. We do know that already. And I am here to help you. Keep Roger Maybury in the picture but you will be able to turn to me whenever you want. My door is always open."

Lydia wondered whether he intended that to be reassuring.

"What a project!" he said. "Magnificent opportunity for you."

He hadn't moved from his seat behind his desk but there was a glitter in his eye. Perhaps he was imagining that he would routinely lean over her desk and look at what she was working on. Perhaps he was genuinely pleased for her. Perhaps she had somehow misinterpreted the earlier episode. Perhaps he really believed that a short skirt signalled an invitation.

She knew she would see this through, even if she had to fight off Michael Suffolk on a daily basis. She would show them all that she could somehow combine it with careless-houred nights of love with Marvin.

\* \* \*

"Me? Of all people!" said Auriol, patting Lydia on the shoulder. It was an awkward gesture. Auriol erected an exclusion zone around herself, breached only with trepidation. "Don't you have better people to turn to, Lydia? I'm flattered, but I'm no good at dolly-bird talk."

Auriol fixed her piercing eyes on her. Lydia laughed. She had chosen to confide in the most scornful person she knew. Auriol had a sort of fearless clarity about her. Holding her gaze felt like looking for something in the deep, sunless water of a dangerous pool.

She passed Auriol the note from Marvin, written with the fountain pen she had given him for his birthday. It was the only letter he'd ever written her. And look what it said.

"Bought a sheep farm near Shap. Come and check it out."

Attached to his note was a sketch – a square farm house, two storeys high, with a pitched roof and improbably elegant front windows. A simple structure with a few fancy features and a hint of dilapidation. On the left was a lean-to shed with a corrugated iron roof and a gable end of brick, and beyond it a wooden barn. He conveyed the materials exactly. The words "brick", "flint", "slate" in spidery writing. And behind the farmyard he had drawn a hillside covered with sheep.

"I like the look of that," said Auriol. "Just the thing. I need somewhere to disappear to from time to time."

"What have you been up to? Marvin's been worried about you."

"Here and there with a few Americans friends. Protesting against napalming. They're bombing the Imperial City of Hue. You don't take an interest in anything that's going on in the wide world, do you, Lydia? I had hoped for something better from you. But you're sunk without trace in those comprehensive schools. What about innocent children in Vietnam?"

"Oh, I do notice, Auriol. But you're right. I suppose I am tied up with my work at the moment. I won't be for ever. I just want to feel secure for a bit. But look at his beautiful drawing. I can imagine that house exactly. And I didn't even know he could draw." There was so much she didn't know about Marvin. Was this farm just an impulse buy? Had he bought it because he could? On the proceeds of the sale of his father's pigeon business? "I didn't know he could afford something like that."

"Oh, he makes enough money from the rich boys' cars. And he's spent so much time with them that he's picked up their habits. Go off and live in Greece on a whim. Drop everything and start a new life in a new place. This isn't a big deal by their standards."

"I like that," said Lydia. "And I can imagine him as a sheep farmer. But the Lake District is a long way away. He didn't even talk to me about it. He just disappeared and did it and sends me a card to tell me."

"What d'you expect, Lydia? That's what we all do. Act on impulse. If you think of the consequences all the time, you wouldn't be able to do all these interesting things."

"But I'm ... his girlfriend."

"What's that got to do with anything, Lydia? He's a free person. He's doing it because he wants to and he can. That's what we're all like."

"I want to just be with Marvin. And he never talks about the future."

"Live with it. Marvin doesn't think in those terms, Lydia. And he isn't ever likely to."

"It's as though our paths are meant to be entwined. I want to wake up in his arms ... you know what I mean."

"No, I don't." Auriol sounded angry. "It sounds like something from *Woman's Own*. I've never felt like that. It's no good talking to *me* about it."

"Please listen. I'm trying to work out what to do. The Department has offered me a serious job. It's a big deal. I want that. But how am I going to combine that with a lover on a farm somewhere in the Pennines?"

"It's your decision, Lydia. Throw up the job. You can always do that sort of thing later in life. If you live that long. I'd lay down my life for Marvin Brewer." Auriol hesitated. "But I'm not accountable for him. How is he, by the way? Was he very sad about his father?"

"I don't know. He doesn't really talk about his family. The pigeons, yes, but not the people."

"He ran away from them. He went to London when he was a teenager. Like everyone else."

"Sometimes I don't know him at all. I think you are the only person who does."

"You don't have to know your lover, Lydia. It's better not, really."

They were sitting side by side in a small sandwich bar near Lydia's office, perched on high stools, their backs to a row of small tables that looked out through smeary windows on to Berkeley Square. Auriol raised an eyebrow at sardine sandwiches on thick white bread. But she didn't say a word.

"Sorry. I couldn't face the office canteen." Tears fell slowly down Lydia's cheeks. "I'm being pathetic. I ... I don't know ... I need to talk to someone. My university friends have finished their final exams and are scattered to the winds..."

"What did you do, mysterious Lydia, to be sent down from university? I can't imagine you not handing in your essays. And obviously you weren't found in bed with someone."

Lydia stirred her sludge-grey coffee.

"I bit someone."

Auriol laughed.

"It's a bad story. I can't face explaining it today." Lydia waved her hand at the soulless surroundings. "I behaved very badly. It involved my mother. Everything does."

"Family!" said Auriol. "Thank goodness you can escape them nowadays. That's the whole point. Imagine our mothers, stuck at home, waiting for a suitable man to take them away and install them in a different prison. Then stuck there for the rest of their lives."

"*You* may be able to escape your family, but I can't. Living under my aunt's surveillance. Like being on remand."

"Lydia, this is 1965. Things have changed. We can decide things for ourselves. You've got a job and a salary. There's a Labour government. There are women ministers. Go that route. Or run away to Marvin if you feel like it. Just tell them to go to hell."

Auriol had a splinter of steel inside her. Lydia wondered whether you were born like that and it grew inside you like a small tumour, or whether it could be implanted later.

"I know. I know. Emotional pressure. It's not as though you exactly see eye to eye with *your* family."

"Oh, that. That's been all over the papers. The 'Northumberland landowner's daughter rejects inheritance' business. Lydia, my coming-out ball cost what sixty pensioners live on for six months. You see why I had to set fire to the tables?" Her eyes blazed. "I love my father but I reject the way he has made his money. I suppose I'll make friends with him again when I'm older. When I've done what I want to do. But now I need the distance to breathe. That's what you need too. A distance from your family."

Lydia carried her distress at her grandmother's disapproval just behind her eyes, like an incipient headache.

"Forget *my* mother," Auriol went on. "A bitch. An insensitive controlling dragon. She loved my brothers and my pretty little sister. I don't care if I never see her again in my life."

Auriol stirred her coffee viciously, slopping some of it on to the white china saucer. "What horrid cups."

"Dead giveaway, Auriol. A proper socialist has to welcome thick chipped white teacups. And renounce delicate porcelain."

Auriol's laughter warmed Lydia. Auriol didn't laugh very often but when she did it was light and carefree.

"You're right. I reject all that completely. The only thing I miss is the dogs, and don't you dare tell anyone that."

"So you *are* human after all."

"Listen, Lydia, I must go. I've signed up for this MA at the LSE. I have to go and meet a famous professor."

"What's this about Cuba? Marvin worries that you will get mixed up in something dangerous."

Auriol raised an eyebrow.

"I'm not talking about it now. Let's meet soon. I've got used to you, although you're pathetic. For Christ's sake, just decide what you want and set about getting it. It's quite simple."

"What's the MA about anyway?"

"Philosophy. Philosophy of revolution."

"Sounds suitable for the 'Red Deb'. That's what they call you, apparently. The Red Deb. The brilliant young radical!"

Lydia smiled. Auriol walked away, eyes set on the far horizon.

* * *

"A personal call, Lydia. While you were out at lunch. A gentleman friend." Her colleague looked pained. Lydia's heart sank.

Fred was trying to contact her. He couldn't find her at the Matisse. She had held back from giving him her telephone number at her aunt's address. So he kept ringing her office. As luck would have it, Lydia was having lunch with Auriol when he finally got through.

"He said to tell you that he's lost all his money and needs you to get him out of a ... somewhere in Soho ... I've written it down ... an Italian place, a 'bordello' I think he said." She sniffed. "I told him that we don't encourage personal calls but just this once I'd take a message.

And then ... he ... er... told me to stuff a daffodil up my ... Oh dear... such a terrible word."

Lydia stifled her laughter, clapping her hand over her mouth. It was so typical of Fred – his instinct to shock when he most urgently needed support. She wondered whether he had said 'fuck', an expressive sort of word that she liked the sound of but would certainly be offensive to her colleague. Or the 'c' word, which she still couldn't bring herself to say out loud.

Oh dear. It was not a laughing matter and whatever he'd said, the people in the room would not let her forget it. She would be made to pay in various ways over the coming days and weeks, by the usual salacious innuendo.

She would like to say: "But you have to forgive him. He's only recently out of prison. It's his way of getting attention. Like a neglected child." But she couldn't do that.

She felt guilty about neglecting him herself.

The lonely street-facing windows of her office let in a meagre, unwashed light. You wouldn't know it was supposed to be summer. There were four of them in the gloom. They sat at their carefully arranged desks, almost head to head, but separated by a yawning gap.

Lydia apologised quietly, picked up her bag and left the building.

Fred was expansive when she arrived at the Havaga in Dean Street. "An unfortunate misunderstanding, beautiful one. Don't worry. All sorted out now. Seemed quite urgent for a moment or two. Now you are here, let me buy you a delicious cocktail."

She hugged him.

"Darling, you're perfect. So pale and ethereal. That curtain of hair. Those sad violet eyes. Really, Lydia, you're wasted on the civil service. You could make a fortune working for a funeral director. You're the only girl I know who looks as though she is going to cry unless she's actually laughing."

"But Fred dearest, I'm upset. You must have said something terrible to my colleague. She was very distressed."

"I only told her I wanted to put a daffodil up her arse."

"Don't you understand? Most people, almost everyone I know, would be horrified by that. It's not funny, really. That woman was seriously offended. Probably no one has ever said the word 'arse' in her hearing."

"But darling, what are you doing among these people? They'll stifle your beautiful spirit." Just the sort of thing Marvin might have said.

Lydia didn't much like Miss Fletcher but she could imagine her shocked features peering over the pile of files, skinny hands flapping to keep the obscenities off her face like flies.

"She loved it really. That sort of repressed woman gets a thrill from being shocked. It'll have made her day."

"Since when were you an expert on women?"

"Hush, darling one. I'm delighted to report to you that I have now made love to a woman. And you know what? She said I fucked like Lucifer."

If this had been anyone else, Lydia would have been shocked. She looked at him now. Hair creeping down on to his shoulders, embroidered velvet jacket flaunting his obviously handmade shirt. He must be doing quite well.

"How are things with you, Fred? It's ages since I've seen you."

"I keep a watch on you through Dave Perry. But look, that's why I want to talk to you. I've been down in the West Country but I'm planning to come to London for the summer. When the rich leave their London houses empty."

He liked saying outrageous things like that.

"Can I stay in your flat for a few days till I've sorted something else out?"

Oh dear, thought Lydia, that's a terrible idea. Aunt Patience would be horrified.

"Oh, I'm not sure about that. My Aunt Patience wouldn't like it at all."

"She'd love me, darling. That sort of woman always does."

"Seriously, Fred, she wouldn't hear of it."

"Don't tell her then. Look, Lydia, I need your help. I don't ask often, do I? Between you and me, I need to go to ground for a few days. Keep the head below the parapet. She wouldn't even know I was there."

Fred needed help. Fred was part of her life too. One of the jigsaw pieces that didn't fit together.

"OK, Fred. But only for a few days. On condition that Aunt Patience doesn't catch sight of you."

# Chapter 15

Lydia leapt off the train at the small Lake District station of Oxenholme and into Marvin's arms. They hugged each other for a long time. She could feel his heart hammering against her breastbone. After a while he stepped back and looked her up and down, freeing her hair from its coil on the back of her neck and letting it fall across her cheek. Then he fastened some of the buttons on the front of her dress, one by one, right up to the top, up to the collar, his fingers warm against her skin.

"Beautiful. More interesting with the buttons done up. Unsuitable though. There's no real summer up here."

This was another Marvin. He'd settled into this farm but his eyes were on the far hills. The brown-eyed look swept briefly over her and moved back to the horizon, as though his range had changed, as though he'd never been a London bohemian. High up on a ridge behind the house he pointed out landmarks, lingering over his flock of blackface sheep, and scanning the horizon for grouse and hares. They strode on, even further, whistling to Bruce, the border collie with the mad different-coloured eyes and the moods that alternated between defiance and grovelling submission. The rain let up, and the hills were rinsed in pure pale colours, yellow and sage green and indigo, stacked one behind another, the still wet surfaces of the rocks shining like quartz. The lingering gold of the sunset poured into the long, light evening. Lydia knew this scenery, a mere hour's drive from her mother on the Solway Firth. She shivered.

Marvin wrapped her in his coat.

"Look at you, you're freezing. Keep stuff here. I may never leave, Lydia. So you'll just have to keep coming."

His attention was fully taken up – as it had been with sports cars. She had expected the death of his father to spark something in him, inspire him to make some demands of the present, to build a home, to focus on the two of them together. At least on something more than asking her to keep her coat on a hook at High Fell Farm. She looked around in dismay. Marvin could turn his hand to anything, plumbing, brickwork, carpentry. She'd imagined him installing central heating, doing up the farmhouse, designing furniture, head bent over the carpenter's bench. Foolishly, she'd expected a sliver of settled middle-class behaviour in her nomad lover.

"I don't know … I thought you might have plans for your new home."

"It's a house, not a home, Lydia. A building is just a shelter."

"Like Kensington Park Road? Somewhere to eat and sleep and smoke grass?"

"It's the outside I've come for, the sheep and the hills. This room, this kitchen, it's all I need."

The kitchen was at the back of the farmhouse, leading out into the cobbled yard. At the front of the house, elegant high-ceilinged rooms were tall and empty, silent behind their faded curtains. The kitchen must have been here first, the original heart of a small farmhouse, with its huge fireplace. The stone floor seemed to have grown out of the earth, pushed up from the Lakeland hillside by some long-ago geological eruption and formed of great uneven rectangular slabs. Worn smooth, as though people had danced on them over the years, and hairline-cracked where someone had dropped a cauldron of soup or an old-fashioned flat iron, and near the fireplace there was one with a bite out of it, a triangular hole that collected dust and breadcrumbs, and ants in the summer. The same silver grey as the granite outside, the floor was both cold and comforting to the skin, hard and yet softly eroded by so many boots and slippers.

The back boiler puffed and roared in the old bread-oven chimney. Marvin tended it, lovingly, oblivious to time and the rest of the world, as though it were a substitute for something, a human baby even, feeding it with coke through the cast iron lid, riddling the clinkers of used-up coal into a tray beneath.

The walls had faded to raspberry red in the summer evening light, and the lime in the plaster leeched out in sprays of white pimples around the back door. The ceiling, once white, was stained yellow from the boiler and the smokers who sat round the table. Through the small square window the hillside rose steeply outside, alarmingly close, threatening to encroach on the house if you turned your back for too long. Leaning out of the window, Lydia picked white campion and scarlet poppies straight from the hill and put them in a mug on the kitchen table. Piles of *Farmers Weekly* and paperwork covered the faded cover of Marvin's father's sofa, the only piece of furniture he'd brought with him from anywhere. Lydia thought twice about disturbing them before clearing a space to sit down. In a mere few weeks, Marvin had created his own authentic world.

"I've got to learn to read better," Marvin said quietly. "To understand regulations and so on. There's a woman in the village, Mary-Anne, who'd have thought it, she's an expert in something called 'word blindness'. She thinks that's my problem."

He'd made new friends. The Kensington Park Road flat was being sold. He was neglecting the Bayswater garage. It had all happened so fast. It was as though her life and his were rivers, flowing along fast, in parallel, and you couldn't tell whether one was going to join the other or come up against an obstacle and veer away into another valley.

He seemed to know what she was thinking.

"Things change, Lydia. I've given all that up. The only person I miss is Auriol."

"Do you love Auriol more than me?"

"Why do you always want to pin everything down? The past is the past. It's you I love now. But I'm worried about Auriol. There's something restless about her. She's in Cuba now. I wouldn't like her to get mixed up in anything violent. There's so much chatter these days. It's difficult to tell what is really happening. There can't be any more wars, world wars, I mean, but people are turning against their own. She's angry, Auriol. Addicted to conflict and protest."

His Mini Cooper was still in perfect condition, but he took it out only rarely. Nowadays he preferred the old Land Rover that he had "improved" using disused pieces from local garages. This seemed to symbolise something deeper in him, pulling in his horns in some way. He drove it to livestock auctions, he explained, with Mary-Anne along for the ride to help with the paperwork.

Surely this Mary-Anne was no threat? Lydia tossed her head. It was she who had given Marvin the fountain pen, coaxed him to write, convinced him that his problems with reading had no bearing on what people thought of him. But she was left out of this. She wasn't here. She could only come at weekends. She felt a part of him sliding away from her and she wanted him back.

She got up and went over to him where he sat, half in the shadow of an old standard lamp, long denim legs thrust out in front of him. She sat astride him, hands on his shoulders, looking into his eyes, trying to recapture him. She moved her crotch softly against his. His eyes darkened. Turning his face away from her, he groaned. She dragged him away from his stove and his sheep, his *Farmers Weekly* and his dog and his new friends, and into the box bed he had built for himself in the adjoining room, the room that used to be the pantry. There, with the curtains drawn around the bed, she made love to the person she thought she knew.

"Don't go back to London," he said. "Stay a while. Come here and live with me, Lydia Renfrew…"

He spoke hoarsely, as though the words were dirty and disreputable and had to be dragged out of him.

\* \* \*

It was late on Sunday night when Lydia let herself into the flat at the end of Aunt Patience's garden. Part of her was still in Marvin's farmhouse under the starry Pennines' sky, in the clear air among the crouching hills, and the other part leaping ahead of her, towards the approaching deadline for the report on the comprehensive schools.

The blue tits had pecked open the top of the milk bottle on the doorstep that she'd forgotten to cancel. The purple and white stocks in the mug on the windowsill had died of thirst. The half-eaten tin of baked beans was still in the fridge. Nothing was out of place. No sign of Fred. Yet that tiny cold knot of fear refused to go away.

She fell on to the bed and slept.

She woke with a start. The door into the garden burst open. Uncle Edmund strode into her bed-sitting room, white-faced and thin-lipped. "Get up, Lydia. Come and explain yourself."

In her teenage years, when she had spent so much time with her cousins, Lydia had learnt to fear her uncle – the look in his eyes as much as his sudden rages. She would pay later, she thought. Now, wrapped in her old student dressing gown, she ran across the lawn between her flat and the house to confront an enraged Aunt Patience. Lydia ran her fingers through her tangled hair and tied her dressing-gown cord more tightly around her. Aunt Patience was smartly dressed and fully made up.

"Two oil paintings, a carriage clock, a set of silver candlesticks, and the pretty jade horse and my pearls," Aunt Patience hissed through clenched teeth.

"A rushed job," said the older of the two policemen. "You got off lightly, madam. Could have cleaned the place out."

"It's no consolation to me that it could have been worse." Aunt Patience glared at Lydia. "It is only because of my good housekeeping that my jewellery and the family silver were at the bank when we went away. It's dreadful, d'you understand? It's the things I love best. Is this how you repay our generosity, Lydia Renfrew? Your rackety life. Your low-life friends living under our roof..."

"He was only staying there till he found somewhere else. He's a friend. He wouldn't steal from my family."

"It seems that that is exactly what he did, Miss Renfrew. And now you have to tell us all you know about him," said one of the policemen.

Lydia was shaking. Protecting Fred felt more important than the loss of a few expensive objects belonging to someone who could easily afford to replace them. But a relation versus a friend? She clung to the idea that she was a law-abiding, responsible, serious person, even as she smoked illegal drugs and consorted with doubtful characters. Yet how could she condemn Fred to almost certain imprisonment? She hunched her shoulders, wrapping her arms round herself.

"I understand how you feel," said the older, more sympathetic of the two policemen. "We may not have to use your evidence. Chances are he'll have been up to more of this somewhere else."

Lydia watched the laborious handwritten account crawl across the pages of his notebook, building the case against Fred, beloved, outrageous, self-sabotaging Fred, who needed her support more than anyone except perhaps her own mother. It was unbearable to betray him. Once, late at night, he had allowed her a glimpse of the terror behind the bluster, the unembellished horror of the prison cell, but that was enough. Why hadn't she spent more time with him, these last few months, watched over him, found out what his circumstances were, helped to sort things out?

"Just an address. That's all we need. So that we can contact him, know what I mean. Ask him a few questions."

Lydia froze. She could just about admit her suspicions, but she couldn't lead them to him.

"A signature here. Then it's all done and dusted. Just an address."

"I don't know his address."

"Now, miss. I have to insist."

"It's true. He's not someone with a fixed address. He has been out of London somewhere. We met in a bar in Soho. I can give you *that* address."

There was a pause.

"Well, then we'll start with a telephone number."

"I don't have…"

"You told us that you phoned him on several occasions."

She played for time. Fred might not be there, at the flat of some relation who wasn't smart enough for his chosen lifestyle, his last-resort contact point, the place he preferred not to stay except in emergencies. But she didn't know what would happen if she refused. Was it a crime to withhold evidence? Could she lose her job? Would her university incident be on their files somewhere too? Could they dismantle the fragile structure of her life?

She formed a sort of idea that she would warn Fred before they could get to him. He might have a boy lover with him – might that not be a criminal activity too? She would have to admit her terrible betrayal to him, that she had told the police he'd been staying in the studio while she was with Marvin, but it would give him time to disappear. It was all she could think of.

"It's in the office. I will have to find it and let you have it."

"I'll come along with you now," said the younger, fiercer one. "No time to waste. Catch up with the bastard."

"Please. I'm not even dressed. Imagine what it would look like for me, being accompanied to the office in my pyjamas by a police-man." She thought of Michael Suffolk's comments on her private life. She imagined the expressions on the faces of her office roommates, the pleasure they would get from her disgrace.

The older policeman wrote something down in his notebook and tore it off.

"Ring this number as soon as you get into your office. If I haven't heard from you by ten o'clock, I'll be right round there myself. We know where you work."

\* \* \*

Lydia searched for a working phone box. The first one she found was filled with cards from prostitutes offering their services. There was a little pile of vomit on the floor in the corner. The heavy door swung shut, imprisoning her. Something went wrong and she lost two shillings worth of sixpences. She dialled again, carefully. Minutes ticked by before Fred came on the line. He protested. No one called him before midday. He received her news in silence and put down the receiver.

She got on a number 19 bus and went up to the top deck. She stared out of the window. At the next stop an old woman stumbled as she tried to step on to the platform. It was too high for her and she dropped one of her bags. Gleaming oranges rolled into the gutter and the old woman gestured desperately to the bus conductor, who was heaving her on. She attempted to get down again to retrieve the lost oranges, but he had pressed the button and the bus accelerated forward with a jerk. A passer-by picked one up and held it out to her, but it was too late.

Lydia cried all the way to her destination.

# Chapter 16

Eveline's fingers reached out for the squat black telephone by her bedside. She withdrew them reluctantly. It was too early to ring him.

She had awoken from a nightmare. A lovely walk on a familiar Perthshire moorland. Rolling hills. Still sere from the winter cold. But spring had arrived. Her favourite season. Pale green leaves creeping along the lichen-crusted branches of the ancient oaks. Eyebright and birds-foot trefoil at her feet. But something wasn't right. Something evil was creeping up behind her. She spun round to face it but there was nothing to explain the sense of threat, not a cloud on the horizon, but a tall stone cairn on the ridge that had never been there before.

It was half past five. When she woke early, she told herself to get on with life and not to think too much. If, with her arthritic fingers, she could still switch on the funny little device that Edmund had given her for her birthday and make herself a cup of early morning tea, then life was still under control. But it didn't feel like that today. Her fingers shook and the tea tasted bitter.

She patted her hair, leant back against the pillows and stroked the lace edging on the linen pillowcase. The leaves on the maple tree seemed to be crowding against the window, that uniform green of high summer that suffocated the early morning light, dusty, heavy, without differentiation. She longed to turn back the clock, go back to spring, the promise of new beginnings and possibilities. Even autumn was better, when you could check off the disasters that wouldn't happen again this year.

A weigela rampaged in a single pot on the balcony. She'd never liked weigela and couldn't imagine why she'd allowed Mrs Clutton to plant it and nurture it there. Flaunting its fleshy, glossy leaves and insipid pink flowers.

Still in her negligee, Eveline sat down at her elm-wood dressing table and ran stiff fingers over her silver and ivory hairbrushes, the familiar objects that had anchored her life. They had been with her since she was eighteen. Engraved on the back of each one, on the little hand mirror, the matching clothes brushes and even on the side of the big-toothed ivory comb, were her initials, ES, Eveline Sutton, her maiden name. They had travelled with her through her life, more constant than any friend.

The bristles were the colour of red squirrels. She couldn't remember what bristles were made of. It couldn't be red squirrels. Or was it pigs?

It was the eighteen-year-old Eveline Sutton who looked back at her from the hand mirror, red-hair, creamy skin, the slightly tilted nose, very blue eyes. She didn't think she had ever been vain. Just responsible for maintaining her reputation as a beauty. On a good day, she was resigned to the effects of age. She didn't mind wrinkles. They gave you a certain dignity. Her eyes were still 'the blue of northern seas', as the old General was always telling her.

It was the greyness of her skin that disturbed her, a sort of harbinger of something. A warning. She wasn't against grey as a colour – she liked it, in fact – along with other gentle colours that became her so well and piled up in her chest of drawers. Rose pink, lovat green and harebell blue. But as a skin colour it looked decidedly unhealthy. She must call Dr Field. And her 'man of affairs'. She sighed.

Her hair was a *good* colour – a strong silver-grey, very becoming. Not a word much heard these days, 'becoming', but describing it exactly. With the ivory hairbrush she now brushed her hair a hundred times, just as she had done since it was first given to her. A few strands came out, stuck in the bristles like a spider. When she pulled them out they wouldn't drop into the wastepaper basket beside her. They stuck to her fingers. She shook them fiercely away.

She examined her face again, and put on a little more powder. She looked at her nails and the pale, well-kept cuticles.

Then she let herself pick up the receiver and dial the familiar Frobisher number.

"It's urgent, Arthur. Forgive me for ringing you at this hour. For breaking our rules. No. It's not the theatre outing. It's about Lydia. It's urgent. It seems most dreadfully urgent. Can you come and see me?"

She nodded her head into the mirror at his response. She mentally patted her hair.

"You're sure about that? You're sure I'm not interrupting your writing?"

\* \* \*

The sun poured in through the drawing-room window, as it seemed to have done day after day this month. Eveline found it more than usually difficult to get to her feet, her knees creaking, her arthritis bothering her although it was summer; staring out of the window for inspiration, patting her hair and fumbling with the brooch at her neck for resolution. Arthur relaxed into an armchair, apparently delighted to be summoned away from his typewriter. Mrs Clutton brought in the Kenyan coffee that she prepared especially for this visitor. There were little cinnamon buns on an oval silver plate. Mrs Clutton knew he was partial to cinnamon buns.

Eveline waited impatiently until Mrs Clutton left the room.

"It's Lydia," she said. "Something really frightful has happened. There's been a burglary. A friend of Marvin's, someone who has actually been in prison, imagine her consorting with such people. She let him stay in the flat – Aunt Patience's flat at the bottom of the garden. He broke into Edmund's house and stole paintings and silver."

Eveline paused for breath.

"Lydia was away, staying in a farmhouse with this Marvin. All alone with him. No one else. Imagine that. I don't know which is worse." She put down her coffee cup with a little clatter. "She picks her friends from the sewers of society. She's no longer..." She couldn't bring herself to say the word 'virgin'. She sank back in her chair. "He was caught, I'm glad to say, but it seems he was hiding out in a house that belonged to this Marvin. And there were people taking drugs all over the place when the police broke in. Oh dear. Oh dear."

"But surely Lydia can't be blamed for all of that."

"Well. I don't know about that. But it's gone far enough, as far as I'm concerned. Lydia must be made to break off her association with this Marvin person."

Eveline poured more coffee from the silver pot with an unsteady hand, spilling a little into the blue-and-white saucer.

"Look how she repays Patience's generosity. Someone who's already been in prison, imagine, and Lydia's still in touch with him. Patience is desperate to secure Henry Sturridge and terrified that his family will hear about it." She sighed. "Arthur is such a nice name. So much more sympathetic than 'Henry'." Would she ever have said that a few months ago?

"I thought of changing it," he told her. "It doesn't sound right for a modern playwright. People say that it sounds like a ploughboy."

"Indeed." Eveline smiled for the first time that morning. "What were you thinking of instead?"

"A surname for a Christian name, like they have in America. Marlow. Or Mitchell. Or Monteith. Monteith Shortcross. It sounds much more distinguished, don't you think? People would sit up and take notice. Then I fancied something Russian, like Leon or Ivan. My father was a communist sympathiser. But the sons in his family have always been called Arthur."

"You must promise to tell me about your father, Arthur dear, when I'm not so terribly agitated. Patience has every right to turn Lydia out of that flat. But how will I watch over my Lydia now? She's earning money. She will just settle in with someone else, someone unsuitable, in some dangerous part of London. Worse still, she might throw it all up and go and live in sin with Marvin. Go off the rails like her mother.

"For Patience," she sighed, "it's all a matter of finding the right sort of young man. That's how Patience thinks. You haven't met Patience, have you? She is as sleek and immaculate as a swan, impressive and magnificent at a distance, but ruffled and hissy if confronted. She terrifies Lydia's mother, poor, misguided Flora. She scuttles away like a moorhen into the reeds. But I don't think Lydia is after a husband. I wish she was. She wants something else. But I don't know what it is. I'm not even sure she does. There are all these opportunities nowadays and she's out there searching through them. That job at the Department is so dreary but at this very moment even to me it seems like the least disastrous bit of her life. Socially, she's stumbled into something extremely unsuitable. And we must do something about it. Patience is right about that. The question is…"

"Eveline, tell me more about Flora. I've got a clear picture in my mind of most of your family. She's the missing piece in the jigsaw, if I can put it like that … one of the missing pieces, anyway."

Arthur hardly ever interrupted her.

She stared at him. She pursed and un-pursed her lips. Her hand fluttered to her hair, patting, patting the curls. Her sea-blue eyes were troubled. Minutes seemed to pass. The bits of her life that she wished to dismiss were threatening to line themselves up in front of her. Her thoughts bore heavily upon her. She hadn't let herself spend much time thinking about Edmund, who was so dear to her as a small boy. She had longed to protect him from his father's bluffness. "Leave my son to me, Eveline. He has to answer to his father." She had wanted to put a protecting arm around the small, pale child who came home from his bleak prep school with bruised knees and a wary, watchful smile, to insulate him from the hearty cruelty of his father: "Why aren't you in the rugby team?", "How is it that you have sunk three places in form order?", "Spare the rod and spoil the child", and, worst of all, "Leave my son to me, Eveline." She had steeled herself to watch Edmund's open nature seal over, excrete a sort of sheen of invulnerability like a scab, define him for ever as a secretive, strung-out young man who spent the last years of the war in Sicily and came back silent.

Her generation expected their traumatised menfolk to be grateful for surviving the war. To get on with their lives. So she'd handed Edmund over to Patience Muirfield and held back from interfering. She had to make do with what was left over – his assiduous stilted concern, his sudden explosive rages. She preferred not to dwell on the past but today the memory of the child Edmund made her heart ache. All the things she had done because she thought it her duty. A word the young didn't recognise.

With Flora it had been so different. She had been too much involved. Tried to channel her in her own image. Failed to let her learn to deal with the world. And the moment her back was turned, look what happened. Things unravelled. Eveline was preoccupied with reports from Sicily, she went out daily to comfort friends for their losses, and her seventeen-year-old daughter slipped out of her grasp. Somewhere in the West Country she met that fellow Rio Renfrew.

Then he went back to the war, some special job, he said, so he couldn't tell them where he was. Then Flora was pregnant and he married her in a hurry, and then he went away again, and as she held the month-old baby in her arms, the telegram came. Of course there were a lot of those, but Flora took it harder than most. Then there was the running after unsuitable men – none of them her own social class. So what was he – Mr Rio Renfrew – some sort of Irish country boy who got his claws into Flora? Who broke her spirit in some way? So that she ran after those terrible men? One after another, until the Rumanian violin player who lived in a caravan, the time when Lydia had nearly drowned trying to follow her. Then she and Uncle Edmund had taken a stand and she had driven Lydia away in the middle of the night and sent her off to boarding school and made her spend her holidays with the Ashfields in Suffolk. For a while, she had even discouraged her from writing to her mother.

She groaned out loud.

"Gracious me. No. I can't really talk about Flora. Certainly not today. There's too much on my mind already." She was silent, thoughtful. "So you *are* taking up my challenge to write a play about us."

Arthur relaxed when he smiled. He looked less northern and bleak. She wondered how *she* looked when she smiled. She supposed that she did smile sometimes, but she couldn't remember when she last felt like it.

"I'm writing from dawn till dusk, Eveline! Stuff is pouring out!" He wanted to encourage her, and it was nearly true.

"But today I'm talking about real life, Mr Playwright, and sadly you can't control that with your pen."

# Chapter 17

Lydia had been summoned to see Eveline. Urgently. Inevitably. But when she arrived, Mrs Clutton asked her to wait in the hall. This made Lydia even more apprehensive. Her grandmother had never done that before. If she was on the telephone when Lydia arrived, she beckoned her into the drawing room with an imperious finger or a raised eyebrow, or even a wink, as she listened to someone interesting or tedious.

Eveline had always liked the telephone. Flora ignored it, insisting that she couldn't be expected to hear it when she was out on the farm dealing with the pigs. Eveline made one of her stern and stately visits to the Post Office in Carlisle to demand the installation of a telephone with a customised loud bell tone. Flora had still ignored it. But in London it signalled Eveline's authority. She used it like a sort of lasso – to draw errant family members back within range.

Today, Lydia walked up and down the hall in agitation. There were huge oil paintings of stags either side of a narrow window, displaying their antlers against a background of lichen-covered rocks somewhere in Scotland. She used to admire these when she first came to visit in the school holidays, but today they depressed her. A glass-fronted bookcase took up a good deal of the wall opposite the firmly closed drawing-room door. Over time, Lydia had thoroughly investigated the contents. There were encyclopaedias, fishing manuals, a row of Everyman books and, on the top shelf, Eveline's precious collection of Georgian poetry. Lydia ran her eye over it fondly and noticed a few new paperbacks tucked in at the end of the row of cloth-bound hardbacks. She opened the glass door and pulled them out. They were modern plays – several Pinters – imagine Eveline reading those – John Osborne, *A Patriot for Me* – amazing – a programme for *The Pope's Wedding* by the outrageous Edward Bond – she can't have been to that – and *Thirteen Years* by Arthur Shortcross, the playwright who worked at Martel and Tillotson with the Poet. Well I never, she thought.

She hadn't noticed Eveline's approach.

"Put those back in the bookcase immediately, Lydia, and come into the drawing room."

"Let me just look at my favourite drawings. Please. It's been ages since I looked at them properly."

Lydia had been fascinated by the plant paintings as a child, their ugly shapes and sinister tendrils. She knew Eveline didn't like them but they had been done by her favourite uncle and her father had treasured them. They were from his last collection, commissioned for the Royal Geographical Society. Or maybe Kew. Eveline had hung them at the far end of the hall, out of the way, leading to Mrs Clutton's territory.

"Why do you always like the wrong things, Lydia? I despair of you. Come along."

"Who wouldn't be fascinated by them? The Bat Plant. The Bleeding Tooth Fungus. The White Egret Flower. Look. The Mandrake. What do you know about the mandrake root, Grandmama?"

Eveline gave Lydia a little push in the direction of the drawing room.

"But look what it says. *'Legend has it that the Mandrake springs from the blood and semen of a hanged man and when pulled from the ground it lets out a monstrous scream and kills all within earshot.'* Is that your uncle's handwriting? How brilliant and strange."

Lydia wanted to beg Eveline to give them to her in her will. But this was scarcely the moment. Today she was likely to be disinherited of anything that Eveline might have been planning to leave her. Lydia had neither interest nor expectations in anything significant, but she'd be desolate without a few objects that reminded her of her grandmother.

"Stop this, Lydia. You know why I want to see you."

She followed her grandmother into the drawing room like the peni-tent she half was. She tried to hug her, but Eveline pushed her away.

"Sit down. You must realise that this can't go on."

"I'm so sorry. Please understand. It's not as awful as it sounds. I knew that Fred had stolen stuff before. That he'd been in prison. But it never crossed my mind that he'd do it to me. To anyone connected with me, I mean. He needed a roof over his head. He's my friend, Grandmama."

"He's been in prison and he's your friend, Lydia. Isn't that bad enough? Why must you choose to spend your time with ex-convicts?"

"He needed my help."

Lydia could see it from Eveline's point of view, but she thought that some people had too many beautiful and valuable possessions and others too few. She wondered whether morality wasn't becoming a bit blurred these days, along with class distinctions and sexual taboos. Or was it just among the people she knew? She thought of Dave Perry and Finn Caradoc and their disregard for the consequences of their actions. And Marvin. Marvin working on getaway cars for the Kray brothers. For dangerous criminals who took them to expensive bars and night-clubs. With Marvin, it was the souping-up that he loved. He'd do that for anybody. And the bench-racing with the owners of powerful cars, whoever they were. She sighed.

"This is extremely serious, Lydia. Aunt Patience tells me that you've been ... er ... spending nights with that mechanic. The son of a pigeon fancier. There were illegal drugs in his flat. Oh, Lydia. I have tried so hard to look after you. And look at you now. Careless of your reputa-tion. Consorting with criminals. How did it come to this? Whatever shall become of you?"

"Grandmama, I'm doing all right. The Department of Education is encouraging me to take the entrance exam to the higher grade. Do you know what that means? A job for life if I want it. I'm a steady, responsible person. I'm earning money. I can look after myself now."

"That's exactly what I'm afraid of. You on your own. Don't you understand? Your judgement is all over the place. You're making all the wrong choices. It would be so terrible if you threw yourself away. If you had a baby without being married…"

Eveline was trying to be fierce, but she looked so frail and miserable. Lydia knew she was thinking about Flora, worrying that Lydia would ruin her life too. There must be a way of comforting her, of convincing her that she knew what she was doing. She felt hollow and uncertain inside. In fact, the whole contraception business had turned out to be simple. Dave Perry's doctor friend – who owed him some favour, drug-linked no doubt – hadn't turned a hair. He hadn't been pink and sleazy. He was young and bespectacled and brisk. It felt like the most straightforward thing that had happened to Lydia since she came to London. It was she who'd had the problem. She hadn't wanted it to be simple. She thought there ought to be obstacles to promiscuity. There ought to be edges to things.

And there was something fearful about being turned out of Aunt Patience's flat. She might find herself out at night, prowling the dark London streets like her mother had along the Solway Firth. She thought that for Eveline's sake she must appear strong and determined. She would have liked to sit at her knee and beg her to tell her all that she had learnt in life about love and sensuality, about the conflict between convention and trusting your own judgement. But Eveline didn't know that. Neither understood what was in the heart of the other that day.

"I have to make my own choices, Grandmama. And I don't want to get married just yet." The words sounded harsh in the elegant room.

"That's what's so terrible," Eveline wailed, her usual steady voice deserting her. "A granddaughter of mine living in sin with someone with no family background!"

"That stuff doesn't matter any more. Marvin's a good person. And I love him." What mattered was whether a farm in the Lake District was too far from her serious job.

Eveline rarely lost control of her posture. Now she slumped back in her chair. Lydia couldn't bear to see that. But her grandmother shrugged off her caresses.

"Love? What does love mean, Lydia? It's the stuff of poems and plays. Being settled is what matters. I want to see you properly settled. Don't you understand that you're breaking my heart?"

Lydia stood up, straightened her shoulders, tossed back her hair.

"Don't break *my* heart, Grandmama. Don't make me choose between you and him. Stop all this. Am I really so different from you? If you'd grown up in today's world I think you would understand, but you're not quite brave enough to accept it."

She shouldn't have said that. Some deep-rooted anger had stirred inside her. At the same time, ingrained attitudes and managed memories were wrapping themselves around Eveline like the coils of a python, stiffening her back and hardening her expression.

Eveline stood up too. She knew how to look stern and forbidding.

"I've heard enough. Give up that Mr Marvin Brewer. Or you're no longer welcome here. Do you hear me, Lydia Renfrew? If you can't do that for me, this is the last time we will meet."

Lydia nearly crumbled. Fighting tears, she tossed her head again, turned on her heel and walked out of the flat.

# Chapter 18

"Oh dear. I do feel rather out of sorts. Yes. But I'm going to the theatre. I don't want to miss it."

Eveline felt shell-shocked by her ultimatum to Lydia but she knew that in a crisis you must not think too much. You must not flinch from your duty. You must galvanise yourself to fight for what you believe in.

It must be the weather. "Riot weather", her admirer, the General, called it.

"Not a good idea to be out and about tonight, my dear Eveline. There will be a thunderstorm. You can always feel it in the air. Takes people differently."

The heat wave seemed to be on the verge of breaking. It fitted Eveline's sense of crisis.

Arthur was clever to get tickets. Mr Lashmar at the Prowse Ticket Agency had shaken his head. "I'd do anything for you, Mrs Ashfield. But Pinter. *And* the Royal Shakespeare Company. Everyone wants to see *The Homecoming*."

Arthur had used his connections. She could see that it pleased him to be able to get them for her. He seemed almost jaunty as he took her arm to guide her up to the dress circle. He smiled often these days; he seemed to have lost his haunted look. She decided it must be the writing.

"How's it going, if I may be so bold as to ask?"

"Inspired by my conversations with you, Eveline. I think of you as my muse."

She was delighted. Her eyelashes fluttered, she sprang up the stairs like a racehorse on a grassy track. She was young and dizzy again. She settled herself in the seat, arranged her purse on her knee and waited impatiently for the curtain to rise.

The words of unseen playwrights unlocking people's secrets, she thought. So neatly. So lyrically. Theatre as a substitute for the grim untidiness of real life. Their theatre outings were spaced out – strictly once a month – but they inspired her to question some of her long-held beliefs. And his too, possibly. Her frankness with him was partly because he was not of her circle.

Sitting there, close beside him, a sideways glance, Eveline realised that she was not quite treating him as an equal. Not as an employee, of course, more like an intellectual footman. And he was so much more than that. She had done a lot of realising lately because of young Arthur Shortcross.

"It's odd," she said, "we agreed that I can ask to walk out any time … if there's something horrid going on … or, you know, something explicit that I don't like, but I don't need to do that nowadays. When I'm seeing these plays with you, Arthur. I never have to leave, do I."

It was almost as though she was especially interested in the elements that used to outrage her, hungry for them.

But suddenly, in the middle of the second act, she tapped Arthur on the shoulder.

She had been utterly absorbed in this play. It wasn't that. Her chest ached. She found it difficult to breathe. It was this hot weather, not the words, she told herself. She felt suddenly that she was going to collapse. Now. Here. In the dress circle of the Aldwych Theatre. That would be so shaming. She whispered an apology. She had to get out into the fresh air.

In the foyer she held a tiny handkerchief soaked in sal volatile to her nose.

In the street it was hotter still. The air was like a heavy weight pressing on her body.

"I'm taking you straight to hospital." Arthur drew her arm firmly through his as though she were his aunt, and flagged down a taxi with unaccustomed authority.

"No, Arthur. It's not an emergency. But I'd like to get home and take my pills."

"Of course. Mrs Clutton will take care of you."

"No." She was adamant and fevered. "No. I don't want Mrs Clutton. Stay with me, Arthur." She used his name tenderly. In her head she often still referred to him as "the Playwright". She wondered if, long after she was dead, he would change his name to Ivan. She thought it would suit him.

Mrs Clutton helped her into bed and gave her the pills. Then she summoned Arthur into her bedroom.

"Would you mind terribly, Arthur, holding my hand? Just this once. I think I'm dying. I feel it tonight. I feel it approaching. To tell you the truth, I'm a little frightened after all."

She was silent for a while, her white hand limp in his. She hadn't fallen asleep. She kept her eyes open and they felt unnaturally dry and bright. She let her fingers tighten round his, like bird claws on a slender twig.

"You can't imagine what it's like. Your joints are stiff. In the morning they creak, like an old tree. You could be uprooted by the wind because you can't bend. You can't reach your feet to put on your stockings. You can't cut your own toenails. The humiliation of asking someone to do intimate things for you.

"When I get out of the bath I have to hold up my huge bosoms so I can dry myself properly underneath..."

She shouldn't talk to him like that.

"I can't hear without a hearing aid, eat an apple properly, or see without one of the pairs of spectacles that hang round my neck where my emeralds ought to be. I'm frightened of not being able to cope with what is going on around me. Being old is so terrible, Arthur. So messy and ugly. It's better to go out like a light, don't you think? Young even. All those young men who died on the battlefield. Forever beautiful."

Oh. Goodness. She didn't know exactly how Arthur's parents had died. His mother, she thought it was his mother, died of a stroke on the way home from work, probably she 'went out like a light'. Oh dear, she wanted so very much not to hurt him. She wanted to get over her own distress and preoccupations, to have time to get to know about Arthur.

"What's the worst thing that ever happened to you, Arthur dear?"

He didn't speak for a few moments.

"My father was dying. They did some tests at the local hospital. At first they said it wasn't lung cancer. But he was coughing. Coughing through the thin walls. Groaning. In the night. Unbearable. I didn't know how to help him. He was a very private person. Shy about physical things. Very modest. I was embarrassed about helping him."

She could see it so clearly.

"One evening we were washing up in the kitchen. He could still do that. He was standing there with the pan scrubber in his hand, staring out of the window into the back yard and the chimneys, and he said, 'I wonder what it would be like to go for one of those strange new cures I've read about, where they make you eat nothing but spinach. In South America somewhere, isn't it? Could it do any good, do you think?' You don't know what it was like, Eveline, to have our limited horizons. It didn't occur to me that it would be possible for people like us to go to such places. That conversation still haunts me."

Eveline squeezed his fingers gingerly. How could she comfort him? When it was all too late.

"I'm sure you were a wonderful son to him."

A clock ticked on the wall. There was an occasional rumble of distant thunder. Mating cats shrieked outside in the square. A car accelerated away from a parking place.

"The young things think I don't understand what's going on. But I understand all too well. That's the tragedy. I can see and foresee. I wanted a big family occasion, before I died. I wanted to preside over a grand wedding, hundreds of people, flowers and stained-glass windows and an organ playing. Watch Griselda and Lydia marry men I admired, clasp new grandsons-in-law to the bosom of the family."

She paused, tears running down her cheeks, pooling on her skin and dripping on to the bedclothes.

"And Lydia, my precious, cherished Lydia, the one that makes my heart ache because of all she has been through, all that I couldn't save her from when she was a child, Lydia who could shine so brightly if she didn't deliberately hide her light. I thought I had set her free from her past. But now I don't know. I can't separate her from the man whose life is tinkering with the insides of engines. Oh. No. He won't marry her. And it would be worse if he did. What sort of life would that be? She is throwing away her best years on the son of a pigeon fancier and some musty old documents in a government department. She should be out in the light. Dancing in cornfields. Surrounded by flowers."

Arthur patted her arm.

"Don't upset yourself, Eveline. Nothing is set in stone these days. Lydia can still do anything with her life, she can make it and remake it. You'll see." He hesitated. "Does she remind you of yourself, the young you? Imprisoned by convention? Is that what's upsetting you?"

She couldn't speak. She closed her eyes again. Her breath came shallow and panicky.

"No... Not me... She reminds me too much of her mother."

"These days we can escape our parents' fate. Look at me. The chances I've had. The futures your granddaughters can have. Shall I tell you what I'm writing about? Would it divert you?"

Eveline levered herself up a little so she could see him better. Her head felt heavy and she leant back on the pillow.

"You have to help me, Arthur. I've given her an ultimatum – that Marvin Brewer or me. She'll stick to him and I'll be too proud to back down. What can I do before it is too late?"

She fell back against the pillows, utterly spent.

# Chapter 19

He, Arthur Shortcross, a playwright from Burnley, found himself late at night in Eveline Ashfield's bedroom, sitting beside her and patting her hand. On piles of pillows, swathed in pale apricot nightwear, layers of silk and lace, surrounded by oceans of abundant white linen, she sank back. Her face grey. Too much cloth, he thought, for a night like this.

"Will you let me open the window, Eveline?"

It was one of those airless nights, when a thunderstorm was closing in on London, waiting in the wings to break the heat wave. He usually got away at this time of year, to Burnley for a few days to see his mother's younger sister, but he had been too busy this summer, tapping away at the neglected keys of the Olivetti.

Eveline had offered him a bridge between lonely desperation and human warmth. When she first saw him, in the half dark, outside the Aldwych Theatre, she had been frightened of him. He had no difficulty imagining what she saw – a haunted, wild-looking vagrant – and if it hadn't been for the familiar theatre and the street lights she would have turned away. And now they were – what? Companions? Collaborators in a strange enterprise? Friends?

But wait. She was saying something. A soliloquy in the best theatrical tradition. Centre stage. Speaking from her heart, all reserves dismantled, withholding nothing. Tears running down her cheeks, rivulets flowing over her papery skin. She talked so eloquently about what it felt like to be old, she whose young body must have been ravishing. She should have written something herself.

He saw her with her defences down, a vulnerable creature inside the perfected imperious shell. We all put up these facades. Could he have broken through his own mother's protective shell? Was it inevitable to take for granted your parents as they showed themselves to you?

He sat watching Eveline, mute and sad, thinking about the shadows that death cast backwards over his past, and forwards into the future. The deaths of his mother and father were in the room. His mother had been too young, her death too sudden; cut down after a routine day's work. Had she foreknowledge of it, any time for reflection, any adding up of the pluses and minuses? He didn't think she was like that, but what did he really know about his parents?

Fans had told him that their own parents spoke exactly like the beleaguered hero of *Thirteen Years*. He could write dialogue for people like his father. But real life hadn't been like that. The black-and-white photograph of his parents at a nephew's wedding, him with his arm round her shoulders, her looking shy in an elaborate hat. What did he really know of their innermost thoughts? Of their feelings for each other?

It was strange to him that while both his parents died young, along with so many of that generation, the men who went to war, the downtrodden who succumbed to the pressures of scraping a living for their families in the years of austerity, his own grandmother, like Eveline, had lived to her seventies. You would never have thought that they might have this in common, his grandmother's landscape so pinched in comparison. She had died without doubting her own upright and repressive standards. In that, perhaps, she was more at peace on her deathbed than Eveline would be.

As Eveline spoke to him, he was swept by a sudden wave of envy. He yearned to be one of her desired grandsons-in-law, the bridegroom whom she would see married in pomp in a large London church. To be welcomed by the matriarch of a privileged family, proudly paraded before her closed little world.

It lasted only a moment.

He knew he brought something important to her that no one else could. She relished the lens on life he had provided for her in their conversations. But would she ever fully embrace the working-class lad from Burnley, however talented, on a level with her family and friends? He thought about endings – the last scenes in plays, the unexpected twists in plots, how often the last act was a disappointment. How the great playwrights succeeded, Shakespeare satisfied, Edward Bond surprised. Why shouldn't he change the ending?

Eveline groaned and closed her eyes, her body still like stone, barely breathing and shockingly pale.

She was going to die. He panicked. How could you tell when someone was about to die? She must not die. He must do something. Call in Mrs Clutton. The doctor.

Suddenly, Arthur knew he must take that large old bundle in his arms, through the mountain of coverings, hold her, breathe life into her, be a male body to hold hers at the last. He would defy death, comfort her in the way he had not had a chance to do with his mother, the way he had not known how to do with his father. Tell Eveline that she had done well, that all her family loved her. That he loved her too. Fill the silence of his mother's death.

If it had been a play he would have thought twice about it, stood back and imagined it on stage. Dismissed it as crass. But this was real life. He climbed on to the high bed, slithering across the slippery coverlets, his shoe catching in a piece of lace and ripping a hole in it. He clambered over her, awkwardly, to the other side so that he had room to hold her without falling off. He pressed his arm gently under her shoulders and pulled her towards him.

"Don't die, Eveline. Don't die. I don't want you to die."

Eveline let out a long sigh and her grey head fell on to his shoulder.

That was how Mrs Clutton found them.

# Chapter 20

Entering the room, facing the whole of Eveline Ashfield's family for the first time, Arthur's deep-rooted uncertainty broke through the thin crust of swagger. No one acknowledged his arrival. Not one of them stood up and held out a hand, to welcome him or even to accost him as an intruder. It was as though a spell had been cast over them. They appeared to accept this stranger, Eveline's young playwright friend, officially entrusted with the task of sorting her father's papers, the last person to see her alive. It would have been disconcerting if one of them had pointed at him and protested that he had no place among them. But it would have been satisfyingly dramatic.

An arrogant, incurious lot, he thought, preoccupied with dynastic concerns, too self-absorbed to examine an interesting stranger, preferring their nails or their shoes or even the ceiling. Just look at them. A closed clan, fenced in by privilege. He, the outsider.

He slid into an empty chair. He thought he detected a movement of Edmund's heavy eyelids, a lazy lizard flicker, barely registering him. Arthur couldn't help feeling uneasy. He balanced his elbows on the slithery wooden arms of the chair, trying to hitch his trousers up over his knees without drawing attention to himself. He ran his fingers over his high-buttoned jacket, smoothing the dark wool. His clothes defined him, a hangover from his free-spending days in the King's Road. They protected him from the old-established Ashfields.

The desire for a cigarette was overwhelming. There were ashtrays set into the arms of each chair; the others untouched, even Lydia's.

He knew she smoked. He drew a packet of Russian cigarettes from his pocket, flicked it open with his thumb and fingernail, extracting the delicate cylinder with the little gold tip, stroking it lovingly. His battered Zippo coughed several times before it ignited. He bent his head over the flame, sucking hungrily, calmer already. He filled his lungs with the draught of anaesthetic, the cigarette as much part of him as an eleventh finger. He looked up to see if any of them had noticed. Lydia's hair fell over her face and her hands were clasped tightly on her knee. Almost imperceptibly, she rocked backwards and forwards, as though in pain.

First he inspected Edmund, Eveline's son, now head of the family, a large, upholstered sort of person, red-faced but active-looking, limbs trained for country pursuits, arms to carry guns or handle dogs on leashes, legs to carry him over privately owned hillsides. Representative of that class. But wait. Was he, with his domed head, flickering eyelids and fidgety hands, slightly more complicated than that? He mustn't jump to conclusions. The success of his assignment depended on observation.

A motorbike screeched in the street below. Briefly, the outside world intruded. It seemed to stir up the fairy-tale silence, bringing Edmund to life. He straightened in his chair and picked up the newspaper from the table in front of him. Then he looked at Arthur.

Without intending to, Arthur lowered his gaze respectfully to Edmund's shoes. Huge black-leather brogues, shiny and imperious. They had to be handmade. Surely you couldn't buy oversized items like that at Dolcis or Freeman, Hardy and Willis in the High Street. Suddenly, he remembered that Sunday afternoon in Burnley, years ago, when he and his friends were out and about looking for something to do, to make fun of or destroy, jostling each other on and off the pavement. Round the corner they had come upon his own father, sitting on the bench in Englefield Road, his day of rest from the factory, dressed in his good church clothes, a respectable and dignified figure. In the unexpected sunlight he had taken off his socks and shoes, and stretched out his feet, long and narrow, side by side on a copy of the *Sunday Mirror*, like a display of yellowish, slightly smelly fillets of haddock. Arthur's heart clawed at him. Eveline's death stirred up the memory of his own parents. He had strayed so far without escaping.

The chairs were ranged haphazardly around the room, a big echoing room, high ceiling, moulded dado rail, a large expanse of sage green carpet, and a pair of tall doorways from which you expected some violent spectacle to emerge, like in a Roman arena. Through the left-hand door the old lawyer appeared, a poor substitute for a lion or a manacled Christian. Arthur Shortcross wanted something more sensational than that.

He had pictured them sitting around a dark old-fashioned table, mahogany at least, suitable for the rented London offices of a country solicitor. This is how he would have written the stage directions: a shaded green-glass lamp, a pile of legal tomes, one of them studiedly open, a portrait of the Queen on the wall between lugubrious dead judges. That sort of thing.

"Good afternoon," said the lawyer. "You all know each other, I think. And why we are here."

This wasn't quite true. The family had been told the cover story for the commission Eveline had given him but none of them had ever cast eyes on him. But there was not so much as a murmur or a raised eyebrow. Silent and expectant, they seemed to dismiss him as inconsequential. They were grieving, of course.

The lawyer chose to remain standing in front of them. He was buttoned tightly into a pin-striped suit, overdressed by today's standards, a throwback to the pre-sixties' days when men still came to work in London on Saturday mornings in bowler hats. It looked as if it had been dusted down for the occasion, taken out of mothballs. The trousers were too tight across his stomach and too wide in the leg, and the stripes too far apart. He was not a tall man and they made him look

smaller and rounder than he was. Arthur noted these details carefully
– he had a good eye for clothes. Besides, it relaxed him to catalogue
such things. But don't waste your energy, he told himself. It is certain
that the lawyer has only a walk-on part to play in this drama. Two
of the people in this room would turn out to be the main characters, he thought. An additional one or two others could be admitted as
supporting cast. Don't jump to conclusions.

"As you all know, the late Eveline Ashfield wished her will to be
read out to her family in public. So here we are. I'll not take up any
more of your time. With your permission..."

Thinking dramatically, Arthur had encouraged Eveline to make
the reading of her will a formal occasion. Surrounded by her lifetime
collection of precious stones, the suggestion had amused her and
appealed to her imperious tendencies. They'd even discussed it. It must
be appropriately theatrical, he insisted. Perhaps he could make it the
new first scene in his play, though he would experiment with the chro-
nology later. He could almost see it on the page. The play with the
happy ending that she had begged him to write, that was already partly
written. "Oh Arthur. Beyond price. I would give anything for that.
Anything, Arthur, anything." But now his familiar doubts returned to
him, burning along his entrails like a fuse. He could fulfil Eveline's
instructions, yes, but could he meet her expectations?

"... either side of the River Earn ... acres of forest and moorland in
Perthshire, to her grandsons, Mathew and Marcus Ashfield."

Not grand estates, apparently, but a good few acres.

There they were, Edmund's twins, Lydia's young cousins, blond,
curly-haired, amiable young animals, still apparently malleable, fresh
from some smart fee-paying school and preparing to go to a good
university. Arthur couldn't remember which, though Eveline had
surely mentioned it. She didn't object to a university education for
boys. St Andrews or Durham, probably. Or one of the new universities
that resembled the old prestigious ones – York or Warwick. Not one

of the polytechnics that he himself might have gone to if things had been different.

Those moorland properties were valuable. In any other context Arthur would have been scornful. Landed estates seemed anachronistic to him, a sort of rural throwback to when the people who lived on them ruled the country. The days of petty feudalism must surely be numbered, estate duty must rise, or there was no point in the new Labour government.

Eveline had not got round to concentrating on the twins as real people, she told him, but she had set them up nicely, and they sat there together, the other side of the room, tweed shoulder to tweed shoulder, corduroy knee to corduroy knee, trying to hide their excitement. Eveline had told him that she wasn't interested in anyone under eighteen. Arthur had maintained that was a mistake, that he himself had written his first play by the time he was eighteen, that nowadays youth was a quality in itself.

"Then they're late developers," she said briskly. "They never say anything in the least interesting."

"That's only because they're twins. All their interesting ideas, they try them out with each other. They don't need anyone else."

"Is that so? How do you know? Would you like to have had a twin?" She was perceptive, even late at night. "A brother?"

"Anyone at all." He'd swallowed a sort of sob. Turned it into a cough. Eveline had stiffened in her armchair. She didn't like to be confronted with raw feelings, except on stage. Yet she could draw imprisoned emotion out of him like a fork extracting a snail from its shell.

The twins' blond curls would darken, he thought, and their shiny innocence tarnish. That was what interested him, was important to his assignment – which way would they go, backwards into the arms of the establishment or out into the changing world? Would they draw away from each other as their experiences of life and love ate into those comfortable foundations? Or were they too insulated from harm and disappointment, well enough set up – with looks, education, financial ease – to be imprinted by the world around them, unlike the rest of us? Arthur had licence to predict.

The lawyer described the main part of Eveline's estate, the grand Chelsea flat and her stocks and shares, divided between her two children, Edmund and Flora – Flora, the only family member not present in the room. Perhaps she had been unable to face the disapproval and stately presence of her brother and sister-in-law. It meant that Lydia was all alone with no one there to comfort her. His heart contracted. He wondered how she'd heard about Eveline's death – who told her, and whether they did it gently. The death of his parents had been shared by word of mouth along the row of houses in Burnley, doorstep to doorstep, window to window, the details stretching like a row of tattered flags the length of the street, the predictable lung cancer and then the unexpected stroke. He didn't want to think about that.

Griselda had her family and her fiancé to support her. Her fiancé, a stockbroker, wasn't he? It was all the same to Arthur, an utterly alien world. But there he was, already adopted by the family, invited to the reading of Eveline's will, sitting among them, a smug and proprietary expression on his face. Medium height, crinkly hair, wandering eyes. Arthur could see it all. Character notes.

It would be one of those long, sexually frustrating engagements in which Griselda was keeping herself pure for Henry Sturridge while he ranged about the town. Griselda, stuck the wrong side of the sexually loosened-up world, still brainwashed into believing that you had to be a virgin on your wedding night. Arthur shuddered. The little team. Patience, the mother who hoarded her daughter's virginity. The family doctor entrusted with telling her about "marital relations" and advising her to put her fingers into her vagina and stretch it a little so that the deflowering on her wedding night would be less painful.

In Arthur's eyes Griselda was a throwback, a perfect specimen of her class and background. Fine blonde hair, expensively cut, wide open blue-green eyes and breasts to adorn the bowsprit of a ship, well-constructed and accentuated by a pointed brassiere and pale blue cashmere. Smooth, honey-coloured stockings stretching over solid, hockey-girl legs. Not exactly to his taste, not slender or spindly enough, not mysterious or vulnerable. Oh dear. He was describing Lydia.

It was Griselda's skin that was enticing, nourished by air softer and more favourable than the chimneys of Burnley. Only in the last few months had his interest in women revived. While the lawyer was droning on, Arthur allowed himself to think what it would be like to run his hands over those soft pinkish contours, to press his fingers into her flesh, to penetrate that sense of privilege. He knew that she would not part those immaculate legs for someone like him unless he was rough with her, psychologically. He was good with words. Maybe she'd like that. Others like her had lined up for it when he was famous. But if he succeeded in getting inside her, invading her as it were, what then would he find? For all that silky impressionable skin, there would be nothing for him there. Emptiness – the thing that filled him with dread.

Arthur shifted in his chair, uncomfortably aroused by these musings. He reached down to the table beside him, moved his coffee cup and picked up the packet of Sobranie. There were already three cigarette ends in the ashtray. They must be his. He hadn't realised how nervous he was. Why was no one else smoking?

He was only half listening now. He knew what to expect and he was mainly interested in watching the reactions of the family. They felt it was almost over, shifting about in their seats, preparing to get to their feet.

"And finally," said the lawyer, "Mrs Ashfield left to her beloved granddaughter, Lydia Renfrew..."

There was absolute silence in the room. There had perhaps been an expectation that as well as allocating her valuable jewellery to Griselda, Eveline would express her disappointment in Lydia in a public way, somehow punish her younger granddaughter for rebelling against her background. Leave her something conditional on good behaviour, an admonition from beyond the grave to be read out in front of them all, or a possession that was precious to Eveline but valueless in their eyes, like her Georgian poetry collection, or her drawer full of pearl-buttoned opera gloves.

Everyone was looking at Lydia.

At last, Arthur let his eye alight on Lydia. Oh, Lydia. He had chosen to sit at a point in the room from which it was difficult to see her without leaning forward and turning in her direction. But he did this now, fiddling with yet another unlit cigarette in his long, thin fingers. She had dressed carefully for the occasion, in a way that Eveline's family would interpret as socially rebellious. A short grey shift falling straight from a priestly collar to somewhere above her black-stockinged knees. He recognised it at once. Biba. Sold out in weeks. His lingering eye spotted a little farmyard mud on her patent leather shoes. Her long, unbrushed black hair fell like tangled pondweed across her face and she was looking at her hands.

Oh, Lydia. Arthur Shortcross felt his heart dance. Then a savage little twist of something inside that left him breathless and his internal organs out of place. He shut his eyes and held himself quite still.

"And finally," the lawyer repeated, "Eveline Ashfield has left to her beloved granddaughter, Lydia Renfrew, The Brasserie on Hornbeam Road."

There was a sharp intake of breath. Edmund snapped to attention, hooded eyes suddenly opened wide. The expression on his face said it all. "What's that? A piece of property I didn't know about." His wife, Patience, clapped her hand to her mouth. Griselda shot a glance at her mother. A flicker of ancestral greed crossed the fleshy face of Griselda's fiancé. Only the twins seemed oblivious, preoccupied with their own delightful legacy.

"Excuse me," Lydia said softly, "I didn't quite understand what you said."

Arthur had no defences against the emotion it caused him to hear Lydia's voice. Eveline, who had invited him to witness this day, had insisted that the reading of a will should contain at least one outrageous surprise. But he hadn't taken it very seriously. He was as surprised as everyone else. His reaction was even fiercer. Eveline had introduced a whole new element of unpredictability to her commission to him.

# Chapter 21

The key Lydia held in her hand was huge, like the key to a castle dungeon. Heavy with significance. Heavy like her heart. Eveline must have used this key. Perhaps her fingerprints were still on it? Lydia held it to her nose, imagining that she could smell a faint hint of Cabochard by Grès, brought in from Paris especially for Eveline. It brought tears to her eyes once again.

She was grateful for Mathew's company, relieved that it was *this* twin who'd begged to come with her when she made her first visit to The Brasserie on Hornbeam Road. Mathew was the only one of the family she felt close to at the moment, the only one who understood how much Eveline's disapproval and death had affected her, and how she had to roll up her grief, along with this strange and momentous gift of a brasserie, into a carpet bag of emotions and fasten it securely. Unwrapping her emotions had to be put off till another day.

Together they parted the velvet curtains and found themselves in a high-ceilinged room, filled with reflected light. There were dust motes and yesterday's cigarette smoke in the air and a sort of raffish glamour. On the long wall opposite the bar, tall mirrors extended from handrail to ceiling, making the room feel larger than it was. Six of them in a row, old glass with discoloured patches, huge rectangular panels edged with gilt wood, relics of a more extravagant era.

"The mirrors. The cast iron tables. And even a little gallery. Oh, Lydia," said Cousin Mathew. "What a wonderful place. How did we know nothing of this?"

Lydia had to sit down.

"Dinner menu 7.30–10.30 p.m.," she read out. "Prawn cocktail, melon and parma ham, avocado and lumpfish roe, radis au beurre."

The corner of the menu was slightly stained with red wine. "The Brasserie on Hornbeam Road" was printed in gold letters at the top.

"Boring menu," said Mathew.

"Give it a chance. Sole meunière, coq au vin, steak diane. At least it's not chicken kiev and beef stroganoff like everywhere else. At least it's trying. Radis au beurre is authentically French. But no oysters. No carbonnade de boeuf. Not quite like a real Parisian brasserie."

"I've never been to Paris."

"What? Never been to Paris! Where have you been all your lives?"

"You know Father. It's cold country houses with echoing corridors for us. A birthday visit to Menton with Eveline. Hotel food and a tiny crème de menthe on the beach at ten at night."

"So deprived. And there was I thinking you were spoilt brats."

"You know what our lives are like, Lydia. All those holidays on the Suffolk coast. Mostly fresh air."

Lydia knew a lot about Mathew, including the ways in which his teenage years had not been easy despite his privileges.

"I bet Griselda jet-sets off to Paris with Henry Sturridge."

"Actually, it's more Monte Carlo with them. You're miles the most exotic person in our family, Cousin Lydia."

"How could that be, Mathew? All my summer holidays were in Scotland with the Poet."

"But you went off to St Tropez with the pigeon fancier. Sorry, Lydia. That's what our parents call him. And you're a member of that French Club."

"I do like French food. Do you think that's why Eveline left this to me?"

She had once bravely taken Eveline to lunch at the French Club. She felt the tears returning as she remembered Eveline's slightly haunted look, her fear of contamination from Lydia's dangerous social milieu, perching on a little pine chair with none of the comforting velvet upholstery she was accustomed to, bewildered by the limited menu, and appealing to Lydia for advice. Her eyes finally lighting up at the prospect of mousse au chocolat.

At least they had shared that, a love of chocolate mousse.

And here it was again on the menu in front of them. Had Eveline put it there? Was it a message from beyond the grave? A sign that she'd forgiven her?

Lydia's grief. This shock inheritance. The thread of chocolate mousse. She felt like laughing and crying at the same time. She linked arms with Mathew as they walked round the room.

"Loads of atmosphere. Would you bring a girlfriend here? Someone you were falling in love with?"

"Your questions, Lydia." He blushed.

She wasn't sure who Mathew would love. Or whether anything would go smoothly for him. Unlike his twin. It wasn't difficult to see that a career in the City would not suit him, and she feared that Uncle Edmund would try to crush his artistic son into the mould as he, in his generation, felt compelled to repress himself.

"Nice little tables," he agreed. "Intimate."

"You could have secret conversations every evening."

"It's not open at lunchtime, is it?"

"No. Maybe the staff work somewhere else at lunchtime. I don't have the details yet. Only that it seems to have fallen on hard times."

"Where is everybody?"

"It's shut on a Sunday, silly. Less comment and more action from you. You promised to work for the whole day long without a word of complaint. The brass table lamps need cleaning. I mean all the brass you can see. The little towel-rail things on the sides of the benches, and the door handles."

"I could come to love this place," said Mathew, sitting down and lighting a cigarette.

"Don't just sit there admiring it, Mathew."

Dishcloth in hand, absent-mindedly wiping down the bar counter, Lydia smiled at him. "There's work to be done. Come along with me. You and I are going to inspect the kitchen and the rubbish arrangements. If you've any inspiration left after that you can clean your beloved mirrors. Do you even know how to do that?"

Mathew picked up a discarded copy of the *Daily Mirror*, pulled out the centre pages and screwed them into a ball. He started shining the nearest mirror in graceful circular movements.

"Well done. I can see you're not just an idle layabout."

"Life at The Grange isn't quite what you think, Cousin Lydia. Mother is hard to please. Father is easy to annoy. That's why we're so pleased about Eveline's forests. We can escape. Think of it. The freedom. There won't be much to shoot, or anything like that, but what does that matter? A little hut in the woods. Somewhere to hide."

"Hey. Give me that paper. I love the Cassandra column."

"Isn't the *Daily Mirror* a red rag?"

"You don't have a clue, do you? It's Labour, yes, but it's serious. It criticises the government. Very thoughtfully. And that's the best political commentary around. I see that I'll have to educate you."

Lydia looked him up and down, his jeans and dark blue shirt. "You look much better in jeans. I can't think why you wear those terrible tweeds."

"Mother insisted. Respect for Gran Eveline. She was a stickler for appearances."

"I'm afraid she disapproved of everything I wore once I came to London."

"And of Marvin?"

"Marvin. Yes. It's so sad about that. They could have been such friends."

Lydia turned away, looking out of the tiny back window into the yard.

Marvin picking up Eveline's glove in the King's Road, as though it were an injured pigeon. His stroking fingers. His instinctive sensuality. The lost opportunity to show Eveline that she could love and appreciate him. Imagining Marvin helping Eveline across the road. Marvin looking into her searchlight blue eyes as he explained the inside of an Aston Martin engine. How sad that there was no way of rewriting life.

"But she loved you, Lydia. We all knew you were her favourite."

"I made her unhappy. Don't make me cry again, Mathew. Please."

"Were you surprised, when you heard she'd left you all this? You looked as though you were going to pass out."

"I thought she was disinheriting me. That she might weaken and leave me a small amount of cash, with big conditions. But that's all. I had absolutely no idea that she owned anything like this. I don't think anyone did. Even your father. I didn't know that The Brasserie existed. Let alone the flat upstairs."

"You must have known something. She must have prepared you."

Lydia had listened to the reading of Eveline's will with a sinking heart, resigned to humiliation, not that she really wanted anything except the row of botanical paintings from the hall. She knew that no one else would give them a home. Where were they now, she wondered?

Every aspect of this brasserie reminded Lydia that Eveline was really dead, and that her death left the sort of gap that could never be filled by new friendships. And cheated her of all the things she wanted to know about her grandmother. All the things she hadn't got round to asking. And those that she was too shy to ask.

Parents built sandbanks around their children to protect them from the tidal streams of fate, to hold the outside world at bay, to soften its blows. Eveline had taken on the role her mother had left empty, when all that her own mother offered was a macabre dance of passion along the dangerous tidal flats of the Solway Firth. You needed to have forethought if you were to erect a ring of defences for yourself. Some people did it by instinct. You could see that Aunt Patience had built unbreachable ramparts around herself, and put up for Cousin Griselda a fine palisade made out of jewellery and tissue-wrapped dresses. Eveline had tried so hard to do it for Lydia. And now she was bereft.

"I had no idea. I promise you. It's the last thing I'd expect of Eveline – a run-down brasserie in a rough area and a secret flat."

"So what are you going to do about them?"

"I have a job, Mathew. And Marvin is three hundred miles away. But it's exciting. I'm meeting the manager tomorrow and then I'll have to decide what to do."

"Do you think she wanted to distract you? So you wouldn't be too sad? Father said she changed her will just before she died. I'll come and run it with you if you like. I'm meant to be doing some work for a friend of Father's in the City. Not my sort of thing at all. I'd much rather do this."

"And turn it into a drug den? There's enough of that around here already."

"Live music. What about that? Up in the gallery."

"And who would come? This is a Caribbean area. They're way ahead of your tastes." Who would come? Dave Perry and his friends? "I have to think about it."

"Look at that row of bottles behind the bar. And there's French wine in a cupboard at the back. Do you think she used to come here – Gran Eveline, I mean – to meet a lover?"

Lydia laughed.

"She didn't use the word 'lover', Mathew. They were 'admirers' or 'gentleman friends'."

"Gentleman friend, then. I wouldn't be surprised. She was beautiful, wasn't she?"

"An admirer could be someone who never even touched her, except to press a bunch of flowers into her hands. She had one of those, an admirer I mean, I met him on the doorstep. A small retired general."

"Maybe she had a dashing former playboy with slicked-back hair and co-respondent shoes? A secret lover who bought the flat with some of his ill-gotten gains? So that they could have dinner together and retire upstairs to bed. You never know about people, do you? What secrets they have."

Lydia studied Mathew carefully. Eveline thought that the twins had nothing to say for themselves. How wrong she was. About this twin anyway.

"The flat belonged to our great-grandfather," Lydia explained. "Lionel Maybury Sutton. He bought it for his mistress. An actress or a dancer. She was much younger than him, Eveline's age I believe. She outlived him and she had a life tenancy, or whatever it's called. She only died recently. According to the lawyer the flat is still full of her frocks and hats and things. You can imagine it, can't you? All silks and frills and feathers. And Eveline's mysterious playwright friend, with the hooded eyes, the one who was there at the reading of the will, he's going through Lionel's papers. There are stacks of those too, apparently. There's so much I didn't know about Eveline."

Lydia started to cry.

Mathew passed her his handkerchief and they went back to the cramped kitchen, the pile of clean copper-bottomed pans, the row of gas rings and an ancient plate-warming cupboard with blackened doors.

"It's all quite overwhelming."

Mathew took her hand, walked her gently back into the dining room and sat her down at the nearest table.

"I'm making you a cup of coffee, Cousin Lydia. Look, it's a Gaggia. A fancy Italian coffee machine."

Marvin would approve of that.

"Or would you prefer brandy? You look as though you need something like that. There seems to be plenty of it here."

Then he was up a stepladder dusting the glass chandelier, leaving her staring into her coffee.

"We should paint the edges of the mirrors some other colour," said Mathew. "Gold is a bit passé, don't you think? Racing green? Or Oxford blue."

Sports car colours. If only Marvin were here. To share the excitement. To make suggestions. To fix intricate and delicate things. His long fingers and the golden hairs on his wrist. Why wasn't he here? If only he would leave the farm for more than a few hours. Are you out on the hill now, Marvin? Sunday is a weekday on a farm. I know that. I wish all those sheep could just disappear.

"Look at the carpet, Lydia. Concentrate. We'll have to get rid of that. There are flagstones underneath it. I've had a look."

"Maybe just leave it bare."

"It's autumn already. How are we going to bring in the diners if they freeze to death when they're inside? The boiler has all sorts of terrifying warnings on it. We'll have to find you some help. Really, cousin darling, you are the most impractical person I know. What was Eveline even thinking of, leaving you a loss-making restaurant? What can possibly have possessed her?"

\* \* \*

Marvin's Kensington Park Road basement was only a few streets away. So recently leaning against his shoulder, the look in his eye as he first passed her a spliff, testing her, loving her. Oh, Marvin, why aren't you here?

She got through to him finally on the brasserie pay phone.

"Where were you? I've tried so many times."

"I'm a farmer. I was out on the hill. You sound sad, darling honey, I wish I could hold you."

"I wish you were here."

"You know I can't leave the stock."

"Can't Jack look after them for a couple of days?"

"Not again, just now. Last week was exceptional because of your grandmother. I can't keep doing that. It's the lamb auctions next week. You should see them. You come up here."

"I can't. I took time off work for the funeral. And tomorrow too, to meet the staff and see the brasserie in action. But it's so exciting, Marvin. I want you to see it. You'd love it. A wonderful room full of gilt mirrors and cast iron tables and rows of bottles of alcohol – like a real French brasserie. I wish you could see it. You'd have all sorts of ideas…"

She thought of Marvin's farmhouse. The beautiful stone floors. How cold it would be in Marvin's kitchen in the winter, but there'd be the stove and the blazing fire, and the curtains round the box bed in the back room.

"What's the weather like up there?"

"Wet and windy. As you'd expect. There's lots of red berries on the holly bushes and the rowan trees. More than I've ever seen. Means a hard winter. I have to think about that – timing the lambing. Risky if there's a lot of snow. Or very frosty."

Neither spoke for a moment, each in their separate worlds.

"How's Auriol?"

"I don't know where she is. I think she must be off on one of her protest trips. It's very kind of her to let me live in her flat, but she never tells me anything."

"I hope it's not something dangerous."

There was another pause in the conversation.

"Are you all right, Lydia? I miss you. Forget everything else and come up to me."

How could she do that?

\* \* \*

On Monday, Lydia left work early and walked from Holland Park Tube station. She wanted to pace how far the residents of the smart end of

Ladbroke Grove would have to go to reach a brasserie in Hornbeam Road. They might perhaps press on north along Portobello Road and stop off for a drink at the Duke of Wellington, the pub she had been to with Marvin on cold days. Even drift on a little further north, keeping to the Portobello Road, looking for Victorian china and long cotton nightdresses. But they would almost certainly turn back to familiar territory before they reached Hornbeam Road.

An unforgiving rain was falling. The sky was low and grey, rehearsing for autumn, and the pavement slick with wind-blown maple leaves. The tall buildings of Ladbroke Grove gave nothing away, sullen and inward-looking.

The brasserie was a couple of blocks beyond Ladbroke Grove Tube station. Hornbeam Road led off the Golborne Road. There weren't many restaurants. One Italian sandwich bar, with a few tables if you wanted to sit down to pasta or chicken in breadcrumbs, cheerful and friendly, small and crowded and neon-lit.

Lydia stood in front of the brasserie for several minutes, wondering what to expect. Just as she was fitting the huge iron key into the keyhole, the door opened and a cool-looking young black man appeared. In a slight American accent, he asked her who she was looking for.

"I'm Lydia Renfrew. The new owner of the brasserie. Who are you?"

"I'm Joel. I'm a friend of Trevor's. I'm delighted to meet you. I must explain – I don't actually work here. I'm with a contemporary dance group. I'm just off to a rehearsal."

He was soft spoken and immaculately dressed. Tight jeans and a dark reefer jacket, with little raised seams, clearly tailor-made, and a glimpse of pale shirt with exaggerated cuffs spilling out over his hands. He looked Lydia up and down, raising an eyebrow.

"Come on in."

A tall figure came out from the kitchen, wearing a striped apron and carrying a tray of cutlery. Reasonably presentable from the front but his shirt tails hung out over his trousers at the back as though he had dressed in a hurry. He had a tic in his left eye, like a tiny camera shutter, and grey streaks in his brown hair. He looked gentle and battered.

He sat down beside Lydia, stared at his hands, and started talking.

"There's nowhere like this in London. That's why I came to work here. A brasserie. I came for the name. No one bothers me here. I just cook what I want. Real French food. There's Parkes, Parkes in Beauchamp Place where the cool people go. But it's all froth and glamour. Not proper French food. Lots of people go there, of course, and truth to tell" – he looked up at Lydia – "we don't get enough diners here. But it's wonderful, isn't it?"

"Oh, Trevor, I love French food too," said Lydia. "Have you ever been to the French Club? There's real French food there."

She listened, spellbound, as Trevor sketched his dreams for the future of the brasserie on the tabletop, with a fork.

* * *

"Mondays are nice," said Trevor. "Not too many people. More manageable."

A few hours later almost everyone had left and Lydia was taking stock of Monday evening at her new brasserie. In her opinion, it had been a fair degree of chaos. The service was not quick enough and a group of four men in suits complained that they were in a hurry. The starters worked fairly well. But the problems started with the main courses. Trevor prepared each dish from scratch and the production line was slow. There was no sole today because it was Monday. So why was it on the menu? A couple of people considered the steaks too rare. No one ordered radis au beurre. Lydia was disappointed by her clientele. Why come to a brasserie if you didn't want French food?

"Too many items on the menu," said Trevor. "We know that we need to cut it down. But the Ferret says it has to be classy."

Lydia laughed.

"Is that what you call him? My grandmother's 'man of affairs'? I'm meeting him soon."

Martha, the waitress, took orders without writing anything down but remembered them, word perfect, and added up the bills faultlessly. She had a pinched pale face as though she suffered from malnutrition, but she smiled at the diners with her green Irish eyes, whatever they said to her. She should be running the country, thought Lydia, sorting out the balance of payments problems, the International Monetary Fund eating out of her hand.

As well as Trevor and Martha, there was Didier, apparently a trained barman. Didier had failed to turn up. Evidently, this often happened on a Monday. He got 'tanked up' at the weekend and had 'a bit of flu' on Mondays. Lydia had no choice but to stand in for him. She hovered behind the bar herself, taking it all in, delivering glasses of white wine or Cinzano and occasionally a bottle of something red. Only about a third of the tables were filled at any one time and suddenly the place was nearly empty. A small grey-haired woman was getting up from a table near the door, bending down to pick up her handbag and umbrella.

"You're new, my dear, aren't you? You didn't know which was my table."

Lydia was ashamed that she had not even noticed her. She didn't know how to say that she was the new owner.

"Well, dear, I always have the corner table to the left of the door. Here. That is *my* table. I hope you stay longer than some of the others. There was a rumour that the brasserie was closing down. I do hope that's not true. I love it. The service can be a bit unpredictable. But it's the only place around here that a woman on her own can eat interesting food without people looking at her and wondering whether she's been jilted or is trying to pick up somebody. And I do so like eating out. I come here every Monday. Just me and my book. Mondays are special, you know. Trevor calls them 'Mainstay Mondays'."

Lydia wanted to sit her down and ask her advice about the menu, whether she would ever order boudin noir or tête de veau or any other authentically French dish if they appeared on the menu. What did she like about the brasserie? What should change? Did she live nearby? What interested her in life?

There was a fracas at the far end of the room and the old lady had gone.

"You bastard! You absolute creep!"

At the alcove table in the far corner – the one Trevor referred to as the "foreplay table", and was apparently always in demand – a girl scraped back her chair and kicked it to the floor, a girl who looked like a model, an ash-blonde Jean Shrimpton, tall with a short chequered skirt and very long legs. She was the sort of person who drew attention to herself, effortlessly, exactly the sort of customer Lydia needed to sashay about in a successful brasserie.

Leaving her companion still at the table, with his back to the room, she started walking towards the door. Then she thought better of it, turned back and slapped him hard across the face, and was running out into the street.

Ha, thought Lydia. This was the true test of the restaurant owner. It wasn't all cutlery and garlic, this business. There was a lot to learn about handling clientele. Should she go over to him and pour him another cup of coffee, as though nothing had happened? But Martha was already there. "Your usual, sir?" He nodded, a sleek, dark-haired nod, and swirled the brandy around in the glass – as though nothing had happened.

"Nothing out of the ordinary," said Trevor. "We call him the Philanderer."

# Chapter 22

"One moment, Miss Renfrew, can I have a word?"

Lydia was on the point of leaving the office. She had to meet Eveline's 'man of affairs' at the brasserie before they opened for dinner. Luckily, she was wearing her sensible skirt for the Ferret. One day women would wear trousers to the office, she thought, as she followed Michael Suffolk's pin-striped back view down the corridor.

He was smiling. She wasn't sure whether that was better or worse than his thin-lipped pen-tapping pained bewilderment when she failed to meet his expectations.

"You've done very well, Miss Renfrew. This is an excellent piece of work. State of knowledge, I call it, about non-selective education. The high-ups are very pleased with it. You still have to learn, of course, to use civil service language – here, look, you talk about 'exciting results'. You can't say that. D'you see what I mean? You must find detached ways of saying it – 'better than expected', 'ground-breaking'. But generally I would say that you have the makings of a good civil servant."

Lydia didn't know what to say.

"I can teach you about that. We can go over it together, line by line, and I'll show you what I mean. Friday afternoon, shall we say?"

"I was, er ... wondering whether I could take Friday off?"

"Is that strictly necessary? You've had a number of days' leave lately, Miss Renfrew."

"My grandmother's funeral ... a number of things ..."

"Look. There's something else. We are transferring you out of the research department. You will be joining the new Comprehensive Schools team. Very busy team. As you know, Circular 10/65 requires every local education authority in the country to turn their grammar and secondary modern schools into comprehensive schools. All-ability schools. Taking in their technical schools too, if they have them."

Lydia nodded. Of course she knew this.

"There's very little money for specially designed new buildings, so in some areas they are faced with the difficult task of joining up their existing schools to make comprehensive units. The team in Room 301 are studying proposals from all over the country to check that they are genuinely comprehensive and that no child will have a worse education than before."

Ha. This was really exciting. She would escape her disapproving colleagues and be part of the implementation of a dramatic new policy. 'Dramatic' was almost certainly not civil service language.

"As expected," he continued, "Labour local authorities up and down the country are rushing to submit their plans as quickly as possible. And Conservative authorities are dragging their feet, and some are refusing to do it altogether. The team looks at the proposals and makes recommendations about whether the Secretary of State can approve them. Your recommendations will come to me first of all, of course, then to the deputy secretary, then to the Minister of State, who will make the final recommendation to Mr Crosland. He wants progress. You know, show success. But your team has to make sure that local authorities aren't joining up their old grammar schools into academic units, and pairing off secondary moderns into clandestine sink schools in poorer areas. You see what I mean?"

"That's wonderful. I'm really pleased. Thank you, Mr Suffolk."

"You start next Monday. With the proposals submitted by Liverpool. Big local education authority, lots of schools, but very pro-government. So it should be straightforward for you. And now I'd like to take you along the corridor and introduce you to the team in Room 301."

"Oh goodness. Would it be possible to do that tomorrow morning? I'm so sorry. I'm hoping to leave a little early this evening."

Mr Suffolk limited himself to raising an eyebrow.

\* \* \*

"Just look at these figures, Miss Renfrew."

Eveline's 'man of affairs' had brought a pile of papers with him. His face was thin and his eyes small and restive but it wasn't only that which made Trevor refer to him as "the Ferret". He seemed to be hunting all the time, sniffing at piles of bills, nosing through accounts, and running a pointed claw down the list of entries till he pounced on an error.

Years later, Lydia would think how unfair it had been to react so negatively to him. He was only there to help her. He repeated that several times. He had nothing against Mrs Ashfield's "rash" inheritance. "Unusual", he meant to say, leaving this rather uncertain business to an inexperienced twenty-year-old girl. Women didn't usually own restaurants. For good reasons. Tough businesses. Full of chancers. You needed to know your way around. Did she have expert help, a knowledgeable man whom she could turn to? A man who knew something about the business?

A rough area too. Maybe she hadn't appreciated that. Probably more used to her grandmother's Chelsea setting? Not so salubrious here. She might need to take that into consideration.

And now for the figures. Men's business. The brasserie had been losing money for some time.

Lydia bristled. Of course a woman, a girl, could run a restaurant. All you had to do was to think it through. Attention to detail. It was no more difficult than writing a government report. So far she'd been toying with the idea of the brasserie. She had played with the menu, intending to take no real responsibility, no significant decisions. Watching and listening and picturing its future success.

Now the Ferret was going to leave her with sheets of figures showing their expenditure and what they paid the staff, Trevor and Martha, and the erratic Didier, alongside the profits from a series of weekday meals of sometimes no more than twenty customers at a time. How could that be made to work?

"How about the bar takings? They are creeping up."

"Clever girl," said the Ferret, infuriatingly patronising. "You're on to something there. If you could boost bar takings, that would indeed help. But then again, you'd have to pay staff if you decide to open at lunchtime. Swings and roundabouts."

She could hire Martha full time, Lydia mused. Martha would welcome that. She could stop doing her other job, the one she wouldn't talk about, which tired and depressed her, and caused bruises to appear on her arms. She and Trevor and Martha could run an interesting lunch destination with a dish of the day, like a Parisian brasserie. How about that? But how could she combine it with her job in the Department of Education?

"Reducing the menu would be wise," continued the Ferret. "Very wise indeed. Using fewer expensive ingredients. That sole meunière was always dicey."

Lydia had had enough of the monthly loss figures now. She flipped through other sheets of paper.

"What's this then?"

"Potential income from the flat upstairs. The lady tenant having died very recently, Mrs Ashfield was planning to rent it out to subsidise the brasserie. She had an instinct for finance. Oh yes. A fine woman."

He pointed up to the ceiling.

"Mr Shortcross – that's quite a mouthful, isn't it! – is making an inventory. Everything left by the tenant when she died." The Ferret gave her something between a wink and a leer. "I wouldn't be surprised if he was checking for... something, you know, scandalous – between you and me, I don't think Mrs Ashfield wanted to face up to what she might find in her father's little love nest. There's lots of stuff up there. Some of it may be quite valuable. Mr Shortcross's orders are to 'disperse or destroy', Mrs Ashfield said, and pocket anything that interests him.

"We can't do anything with it yet, till Shortcross has finished his work. But then, grasp the nettle. Paint it up. It's a nice piece of property. With a bit of work, it could be made into a smart little two-bedroom flat. Rented out. Or even sold."

"I've been wondering about that. He has his own key, I believe, that Mr Shortcross? How long will he be there, do you think?"

"Your grandmother gave him a year. Same as she gave you, Miss Renfrew. That's the reality. What is it now? Nearly October. If the brasserie isn't making a profit by December next, December 1966 that is, we rent or sell the whole thing, brasserie and flat. The area is coming up in the world. Artists and intellectuals. You know the sort of people. Slowly they're creeping north along Ladbroke Grove."

Lydia thought she would like to give Trevor and Joel somewhere nicer to live than the room beyond the kitchen and the stained enamel bathtub on the first-floor landing. But she assumed that the Ferret shouldn't know about Joel. Nor that Mathew put up an army surplus camp bed each night beside the jukebox.

"Actually, it'd be quite convenient for *me* to live above the shop," she said suddenly. "Is there anything to prevent that?" She couldn't live on Auriol's sofa for ever. It would mean she could spend more time at the brasserie.

"Well. It can't go on making a loss indefinitely, Miss Renfrew. That's all I'll say now. When the year is up, the brasserie or the flat has to bring in enough to cover the costs of the other. The flat is the natural money-spinner. Or you could let the brasserie and turn your back on it and live on the small income."

"I'm certainly not turning my back on it."

"Surely you're not thinking of running this place yourself?"

Lydia didn't answer.

"I doubt very much whether you could make a success of it."

He stood up and dusted down his trousers, as though he might have sat in a bit of overlooked dust or chip fat.

"In the meantime, I'll be around once a week with the accounts. Please be sure to study the legal documents before then."

Where were the legal papers? Lydia sat there thinking about it all for some time. She'd been the owner of a restaurant for nearly two weeks and still hadn't seen any documents.

Perhaps they'd been sent to her c/o Marvin Brewer, High Fell Farm, Shap, Nr Carlisle. Was that her home? Was that who she was? Care of Marvin Brewer. She kept trying to telephone him from the call box behind the bar. There was never any reply. She listened to the ringing tone and imagined it echoing through the unused front hall of the main house. He'd be on the hill with the sheep or out in the yard. And after dark he would be sitting in his low-ceilinged smoke-filled kitchen, out of earshot of the telephone. Her heart lurched. Longing mixed with guilt and uncertainty, those familiar ingredients.

# Chapter 23

"I wish you were here," said Marvin, when she finally got through to him. "The pigeons are arriving."

"What pigeons? When? Why didn't you tell me?"

"I did tell you, darling, when I came to see you. It seems like a long time ago, doesn't it?"

"It's been very busy here, Marvin. All sorts of new people are coming. Sometimes it's really busy. New customers. It's so exciting. Word seems to have got out that there's something going on. Some days this week we've been nearly full."

"Listen, Lydia, Friday. The pigeons are coming on Friday. Please be here. And stay a while this time."

His voice was crackly on the long-distance line, choked or something.

"Friday? Oh, Marvin, I can't. Griselda is bringing some friend from the *Tatler* to check out the brasserie on Friday evening. I *can't* not be here then. You must see that. Publicity. Is it all right if I come first thing Saturday? I might just catch the night train."

"You'll miss the moment. Putting them into their lofts. The moment when I become a pigeon breeder. The lamb auctions didn't matter that much, whatever Auriol may have said. But this will be a very special moment."

Lydia sat down with a glass of house wine, elbows on the table. She lit a cigarette and studied the coils of smoke as they drifted towards the high ceiling. Her high ceiling. In her tall, gold-framed mirrors, she watched Martha clearing coffee cups and emptying ashtrays. She was tired. There was still a lot to do tonight. She envied Mathew his handy camp bed. She had to steel herself for Auriol's sofa. Auriol was in Cuba, researching revolutionary politics for her MA. There'd be no one to talk to.

The idea of returning to university to retake her third year and get her degree seemed unreal in the days that followed Eveline's death. Lydia was juggling with the pieces of her life enough, without moving back to Oxford. How could she spend long weekends with her lover at the farm and make something of the brasserie and write up a proper summary of her recommendations on the Liverpool schools?

\* \* \*

Griselda's *Tatler* friend brought three people with him, apparently journalists too, and they sat down at the round table in the middle of the room, talking loudly.

"Two bottles of Entre-Deux-Mers. At once, waitress, if you please."

"Expenses. Mark my words," said Martha sourly. "Starting off with loads of alcohol. They can't be real food critics."

Lydia thought she should wait on them herself.

"One main dish of the day. What sort of deal is that?" said one of them.

"You should really try the dish of the day – the Bouillabaisse. The chef makes it very well," said Lydia.

"What's Bouillabaisse when it's at home?" asked another.

"It's a Mediterranean fish soup." She spoke quietly. "I'm sure you'll like it."

"Very French, yes, but I don't fancy fish today. Don't know about the rest of you."

This was the *Tatler* journalist himself. She'd counted on him being adventurous.

"Then have the coq au vin. You can't go wrong with that."

"Can't go wrong with a cock and some vin," said the slob on the right, already holding up a nearly empty bottle of Entre-Deux-Mers. "More of the 'between the two breasts' please, waitress."

They didn't complain about the main course and one of them actually praised the fish soup. They seemed to enjoy the crème brûlée. The slob beckoned her over again.

"Another crème brûlée for me, waitress. And one for this gentleman too."

Lydia took a deep breath. "I'm afraid we've run out of crème brûlée. Sorry about that. But I'm so pleased you enjoyed it."

"Run out of crème brûlée? At nine-fifteen on a Friday evening? What sort of set-up is this?"

"It's a compliment to chef, as I see it. There's been a run on it," she said briskly. "I can get you some tarte tatin. Or some coffee?"

She knew what was coming.

"I'll have a tart myself. I like a nice fruity little tart. As long as it's not the sparrowy one over there," he said, nodding at Martha.

Lydia turned away in disgust.

"What do you mean, treating a customer so casually? I can make trouble for you." The slob leered at her.

"I am very sorry. There is no more crème brûlée. That's no reason to make personal remarks about the staff."

The slurred-voiced journalist put a restraining hand on his friend's arm, but to no avail.

"You're very rude, miss. I demand to see the manager."

"I *am* the manager." That wasn't quite true. Trevor was the manager. But she wasn't having Trevor subjected to insult.

"The manager? A dolly bird like you can't be the manager of a restaurant. Get me someone in authority."

"I'm the proprietor as well. And, as the proprietor, I am asking the head waiter to bring you your bill at once."

As they stalked out, Lydia turned away towards the bar. "No idea how to run a restaurant," muttered the slob as he passed her. "Nice ass, though." And he slapped her on the bottom.

* * *

"Christ Almighty," said Mathew, once they'd left.

"Pity," said Trevor. "I did my best with the food."

"You did too well," said Lydia. "I don't think they were here for the food. I got the impression that they were deciding whether to write it up as something social, an 'in' place to come to. The setting, not the food. What d'you think they'll do?"

"What can they do?" asked Mathew. "They're just a bunch of drunken journalists."

"Journalists are the most powerful people in the country nowadays," said Trevor gloomily. "They go back to their Fleet Street offices, light their fat cigars and bring down governments. Look what happened to Harold Macmillan. They'll kill us stone dead. No one will ever come again."

"Difficult to imagine that lot could write anything after all the wine they drank." This was Martha.

"We're off their beaten track anyway. I can't see many journalists coming this far from Fleet Street." Lydia sat down and rolled a cigarette.

"That's why people like the Philanderer are regulars," said Martha. "Safe from journalists."

"Make that a marketing feature," said Lydia. "Far from prying eyes. 'Lunch with your lover in safety in Hornbeam Road.' Shame it's not 'Hornbeam Lane' actually. Sounds much cosier and more discreet."

"It's not enough," said Mathew. "Drastic action is needed. We have to bring in a new type of customer. A group called Pink Floyd is playing at the art school up the road, Lydia. Next week. Crowds will swarm to see them. Smart young Londoners trying to be hip. Showing they know that things have moved on since The Beatles. Signalling to their friends that they are part of something new. They won't appreciate the music, of course, most of them anyway. They won't be locals from Talbot Road. They'll be public school boys, young professionals, well set-up in life types. Let's offer them a free drink afterwards. People we are trying to attract won't know the area. They probably won't have heard of Ladbroke Grove, let alone Hornbeam Road. They'll come from Chelsea or South Kensington or wherever. They'll be imagining the place is full of black locals prowling around with knives."

Lydia bristled. "That's prejudice, Mathew. You shouldn't say that sort of thing. They're living their ordinary lives, like us."

"Are we living ordinary lives, Lydia?" Mathew laughed. "It's not what I think. It's what other people think. They won't dare go into the local pubs. They'll be delighted to come here."

Mathew was sitting beside her at the table nearest the window. A little street light slanted in through the dim panes, and a chill draught lifted the velvet door curtain. Autumn seemed to be arriving early this year.

"I know exactly what they'll be like," said Lydia. "And I don't want them. I want naturally cool people like Joel. Artists and writers."

"We need the publicity, Lydia. People who can afford a night out."

Lydia leant her elbows on the bar, carried away by the image of a throng of cool and interesting people she wanted to attract to the brasserie, a mixture of the sort she'd met with Marvin, bohemian, fashion leaders on the hunt for sensation, one or two from the art world, like the Poet. But they had to be enticed in and they hadn't turned up yet.

"We could entice them in with a drink and tempt them to stay to eat."

They had to start somewhere.

* * *

Michael Suffolk popped out of his office and blocked her way to the tea trolley. Wearing her new patent leather boots, she was taller than him. She felt it gave her an advantage. She followed him into his office.

"How are you getting on with the Liverpool plans? The Secretary of State is especially interested, you know."

Sitting at her desk in Room 301, Lydia pored over a huge map of Liverpool, trying to make sense of the proposals.

"I'm getting on fine. It's fascinating, but there are so many schools. I'm working my way through the different areas."

"It seems to me that you've been sitting on those plans for some time," said Michael Suffolk. "You've taken a few days off lately too, I believe. No recurrence of the tonsillitis, I hope."

"There are parts of the plan I'm unhappy about, Mr Suffolk. It looks as though some children will have to move long distances between buildings during the day."

"Aren't you ready to recommend that we approve them? Big Labour authority, Liverpool. The Secretary of State is anxious to approve the proposals as soon as possible."

"I know it's Labour, but there's definitely a problem in one or two areas of the city."

"Liverpool is a leading advocate of comprehensive schools. You aren't suggesting the Secretary of State should turn them down?" Mr Suffolk looked horrified.

"I think it's a rushed job. In a few areas it looks as though children will not get as good an education as they do now. That's the test, isn't it? I'm in touch with the local inspector to check. But at the moment I couldn't recommend the Liverpool scheme without some amendments."

"Tell that to the Secretary of State at the meeting next week. He won't be very pleased, I can tell you."

"I'm only implementing his circular." She thought she sounded a bit aggressive. "Look, I'll try and get the inspector on the phone. It takes so long to get written reports."

"I'll expect something from you early next week, then."

She'd have to get the sleeper train back from Carlisle on Sunday night – the inside of two days with Marvin.

* * *

The train scrambled north towards what Lydia thought of as Marvin's country. After Lancaster, the Lakeland hills rose on both sides of the track, pushed up from under the Pennine crust. On the left, there were square white houses, rows of them, in the bowls between the hills, sheltered from the west wind driving in from Morecambe Bay. Grey-tiled rooves, easily maintained but ugly. Piles of aggregate for building more of them. Flooded fields patrolled by seagulls. Naked grey trees hugging a river as it flowed alongside the railway embankment, white horses where it tumbled over the rocks, sparkling in a glint of sunlight. Patches of newly planted forestry fir clung to dark crags ribbed with early snow. Sheep waited patiently for tractors to bring feed to supplement the dying grass. Farmyards with corrugated iron sheds and battered-looking barns, and drystone walls scribbling messages over the hillsides for mile upon mile.

Wind-battered white wooden fencing signalled the approach of the station. A small station for a mainline train. Two long, narrow platforms. Oxenholme. Marvin. At last. It seemed like years, but it was a mere three hectic weeks since she had last seen him, since he'd come down to comfort her when Eveline died. Neither of them could talk about Lydia's failure to be there when it mattered to him – for the arrival of the pigeons. His disappointment unspoken. He didn't complain. He didn't need to. It hung in the air, crueller to him, it seemed, than casual infidelity.

Hand in hand they inspected the row of pigeon lofts and the breeding nests, sheltered from the prevailing wind, like a precious art installation.

"I've named the pigeons after Greek gods and goddesses," said Marvin, "in honour of Auriol. Auriol was here when they arrived … straight back from Cuba."

Lydia said nothing.

"Soon. Soon," Marvin whispered softly to Persephone and Hestia. "These are both red hens."

Lydia didn't know about red hens. She'd never heard of Hestia.

"Goddess of Home and Family. That one there, the speckled hen, is Eos, goddess of the Dawn. Her loft catches the first light."

He opened the door of a cage, murmuring softly to Hestia. His love object. He held her backwards against his heart as though she were a tiny baby, stroking her dark grey head with one finger. "Look at her, Lydia. So precious. So beautiful. So wise."

Jealous of his tenderness, she was brusque.

"So, when are they going to mate?"

"I told you that we don't say 'mate'. That's too crude for pigeons. You 'pair' them mid-February. The same day every year. February 14th. My father called it 'the Pigeons' Wedding Day'. I had no idea that Valentine's Day had any other meaning till I left home. The hens lay their first eggs about ten days after being paired. At five-thirty in the afternoon."

"You're laughing at me, Marvin."

"I'm not, Lydia. That is exactly what happens. Always. With all pigeons. They lay two eggs, one ten days after pairing and the second of them always arrives two days later. At around two in the afternoon."

"How incredible."

"You will be here, won't you, for their Valentine's Day?"

Marvin looked at her. He touched her cheek with his cold fingers.

"Then they 'sit tight'. The cock bird sits on the nest with the hen for the whole incubation period, the cock during the day and the hen at night. Did you know that? Are you listening to me? You see how wonderful pigeons are. How much in advance of humans."

"They actually share sitting on the nests?"

"Yep. Birds are the only creatures that do that, as far as I know. What's more, the cock and the hen pigeon both produce milk and they share the feeding too. You see why you have to be here. You will come, won't you, Lydia?"

"For the pairing? Or the births?"

"For both. Of course."

Are these your babies, she thought? A nomad substitute for a human child? But he wasn't a nomad any more. He had settled. In fact, he hardly moved off the farm. Did he want children with her? Was that why he pressed her to stay? Why couldn't she ask him these questions? Did she really have to wait for him to make his intentions clear? Was she still brainwashed by Aunt Patience?

But if he did, would she say yes?

Valentine's Day might be an important date for an up-and-coming brasserie. Mathew might already be planning something special. And eighteen days afterwards? The beginning of March. She couldn't work out what day of the week that would be without a calendar. It was a long way ahead. A lot could happen before then.

# Chapter 24

'FREE DRINK AT THE BRASSERIE ON HORNBEAM ROAD'. The publicity handouts littered the pavement, glued flat by the recent rain. He stopped to read the words at his feet. My God. Was this Lydia's idea? Reckless girl. He had no idea she was planning something like this.

Arthur had been watching her from a distance. On his visits to the Hornbeam Road flat to sort Eveline's father's possessions, he avoided her. He didn't trust himself not to give away his emotion. For so long his heart had been empty. Now there was grief for Eveline and a sort of fascination with the brasserie and little flat above it. And his feelings of love for Lydia. A commotion that felt like an illness. Not since Joyce at grammar school had he felt this sort of tumult. The posh girls who had adopted him while he was famous flattered him, left their mark on him, yes, especially when they moved on, but no more than scratch marks that quickly fade. Skin deep.

A cellar. Dark and enclosed. A lot of brick, a few spiny arches, and a faint smell of incense. Mixed with marijuana. Half-dead flies woken by the clamour, buzzing at grimy windows, trying to get out. Crowds jostling to get in, pulsating with excitement. Scrubbed young West Enders, straying from their normal pleasure grounds, dressed-down posh, Irish cotton shirts over archaic trousers, protective arms round girlfriends with added hairpieces and subtracted skirts.

He was always interested in the look of the women. A few stood out, a fashion statement all of their own, a beret or two, a floor-length velvet coat, but mostly it was a rent-a-crowd selection of young Londoners whose sense of entitlement was beginning to spread its tentacles into new kinds of rock music and new areas.

He reminded himself he was not writing this down. This was real life. He hunted for Lydia in the half dark and the strobe lighting and the expectant bodies, and caught sight of her leaning against the far wall of the cellar, half-closed eyes, letting the sound flow through her. He watched the spotlit colours washing over her slender body. He wondered how much she knew about music. Would she understand what Pink Floyd were doing? Or was she simply soaking it up? Inviting demented waves of sound to rise and break over her?

He had been to a Pink Floyd event before and so he expected to be battered by psychedelic lights and quadraphonic sound. But this exceeded all expectation. Rhythm and blues lifted to new heights. The beat ricocheting off the walls. Mind-searing reinvented colours. It was physically thrilling, like he imagined stag hunting might be for some people, or jumping from a parachute. More a sensation than a concert.

Lydia and Mathew slipped away early, to be ready for possible customers, he supposed. He would like to have stayed. But he left too, following discreetly at a distance, waiting quietly in the shadows outside until the brasserie started to fill up with people. He didn't want to speak to Lydia just then. He wanted to watch.

He saw at once that the free drink idea was a mistake.

And certainly a misjudgement to offer whisky sour. He could see what they were trying to do. Send a message that the brasserie was sophisticated. But it is too complicated a drink to prepare when you have no idea of numbers. Few of the crowd that tumbled through the brasserie door seemed to have any idea what a whisky sour was. He guessed that many of them had not even been to the concert. They had picked up the free drink leaflets off the pavement and wandered in out of thirst and curiosity.

Many demanded free beer, which complicated matters for the struggling team. They seemed to get drunk very quickly, the beer drinkers hammering on the bar, the whisky sour drinkers helping themselves out of the bowl. It was easy to be beguiled by whisky sours. And impossible to keep track of who had already had their free drink. People were shouting and gesticulating, arms waving, the confident shouldering the others out of the way.

The enticing 'starter' items on Trevor's menu were ignored. A few chastened-looking people seated themselves at tables as far away as possible from the bar. They had hung up their overcoats and stowed their handbags safely by their feet, settling in for a quiet three-course meal and solemnly consulting the menu.

Trevor came out of the kitchen to find out why there were so few orders. He stood in the doorway, wearing his apron, trying to catch the eye of one of them behind the bar, Lydia, Martha or even Didier, who had deigned to come in especially for the event. But all three were occupied by the shouting swarms. You could see it dawning on Trevor that the mob was not the discerning French food lovers they had imagined, and that an extra hand was needed behind the bar. He was not stupid, Trevor, just a little directionless sometimes.

A red-faced, red-haired man took issue with an intruder from a smarter part of London, dressed in the sort of blazer and cavalry twill trousers that only an innocent abroad would wear in this part of London. The words "Get out of my face, you posh git" reached Arthur. Cavalry Twill stood his ground, tossing back his cowlick of blond hair and swaying slightly. He wasn't going to be bested by a low-life son of a bitch. Words floating slurred and unretractable above the throng.

If Martha had been serving those two, she would have known how to defuse the situation, but Lydia was out of her depth. The red-haired man drew his right arm slowly across the bar, sweeping a row of whisky glasses on to the floor in a thrilling Wild-West gesture. He paused for a moment, then brought his beer tankard down in slow motion on to the counter, in a shower of tinkling glass. Holding the base by its handle, he shoved the jagged section into the face of his tormentor.

There was a horrified hush. The crowd fell back from the bar, a circle opening up around the protagonists, the posh young man on his knees on the glass-spattered floor, hands to his face, blood streaming between his fingers.

Arthur himself had plenty of experience of brawls, Burnley style, in his days with the Park Street gang. He knew that speed was essential, and you needed a confidence that Lydia did not possess, even if Marvin had introduced her to all sorts of undesirables. It was her safety he cared about, more than the reputation of the brasserie. He reached the bar in two strides.

Two men in raincoats had already grabbed hold of the red-haired man, who, perhaps stunned by his own action, chucked the jagged glass on to the bar, without Arthur's intervention. "It's all yours," he said. "He had it coming to him."

The three of them slipped out. People seethed about. A few of the younger crowd followed them, sheering off along the pavement away from trouble or the police. This wasn't what they'd signed up for. Men made protective gestures to their horrified girlfriends. Others fell back, as though the main event was over, sinking down at the tables, clutching their own drinks and pulling out packets of cigarettes.

One of the people who had hoped to order dinner came forward. He was a young doctor and offered to look at the injured bloke's face. There was a lot of blood and a couple of deep cuts, one on his forehead and another on his right cheek, but his eyes were undamaged. Thankfully for him, not to mention Lydia and the brasserie. Trevor found a first aid kit, miraculously in its place above the jukebox. The doctor cleaned the cuts with neat vodka, "excellent emergency antiseptic" he said, and in a surprisingly short time the victim was sitting down at one of the tables, face covered in plasters, with yet another whisky sour.

"Should be OK now. No glass in the cuts that I can see. But you should get a stitch put in that cheek. If you don't want a scar." He turned to the bartenders. "I wonder if we could order our dinner now?"

"Do you want us to call the police?" Lydia asked Cavalry Twill, patting his shoulder.

"Are you mad?" said Trevor. "They'll close the place down, if you do that."

"I'm OK now. My car's outside and I don't want to leave it here overnight."

His friend would go with him. No one asked if either was fit to drive.

Now the brasserie became curiously peaceful. Who'd have expected that? What it is to be an observer of human behaviour. Surely everyone had had enough and would go home, grateful that they had experienced nothing worse. It can make people feel a bit shaky, that sort of thing, a fight in a bar, a streak of violence escaping like gas into a roomful of people. It excited Arthur, but then he'd grown up in Burnley. You relied on a fight or two to get through the grey winter months.

Some of them did drift away, slightly shell-shocked, but a hard core stayed.

They settled in, forming an improvised circle among the tables and chairs, a group of them, music aficionados some of them, people who lived locally, at ease in the area, long-haired, polo-necked, donkey-jacketed, several of them wearing shades, despite the dim lights, equipment for their roll-ups resting on their knees like tiny animals. Trevor moved around quietly, occasionally fetching a dish from the kitchen. Didier was nowhere to be seen. Lydia and Martha leant on the bar, elbows parallel, heads tipped close together. Someone put something on the jukebox. Not Pink Floyd. Ray Charles.

There was just enough whisky sour left for Arthur to have his first one – his free one, really. He leant against the far end of the bar and watched them.

Into this unpredictable scene entered Joel, ballet performance over for the evening, standing stock still inside the doorway, slightly surprised, used to picking his way through sleeping tables at this time of night, out through the back to where he shared Trevor's hidden bedroom. Of course, no one was supposed to know about that. Arthur was not sure what the official version was, what the Ferret knew about the set-up. In theory, Joel lived somewhere else. He was a well-paid member of some exciting contemporary dance group, not the sort of thing ballet audiences were used to, but thrilling. Not *Swan Lake* obviously, but so much the better for that, as far as he was concerned, not being much of a classical ballet fan himself.

Joel literally glittered. He could have just walked off the stage, something about the way he held himself and the traces of stage make-up in the light of the table lamps. He moved into the centre of the semicircle, slowly, through the now unmistakable haze of marijuana, picking his way among shards of whisky glass still littering the floor, appearing to soak up the dramas of the evening without being told the stories. Suddenly, he started to dance.

What he performed might have been stage pieces, bits of them, or something entirely improvised for the music and the setting, but it was magic, part erotic, part dream sequence, the intimate decadence of the casbah mixed with the jungle. Arthur was spellbound. One moment he made you think of a python, the next a leopard, and then he turned into something aerial, a woodland sprite, pure and light, dancing on that old stone floor, the shards of broken glass glittering like rogue diamonds. There, in the half dark of the brasserie, it was simply breath-taking. If that was what the London contemporary dancers did, well, no wonder they were attracting new audiences. Arthur wondered what Eveline would have made of this performance. The thought made him smile.

Others joined in. Then Lydia too. Arthur truly did not want to watch Lydia dancing in that exotic setting, far away in her head, revolving slowly and sinuously, entirely at ease. He hadn't known that she loved to dance. As one of the dancers put his hand on her hip, only lightly, to swing her away and back again, touching that thin jut of hip bone, Arthur turned away as though blinded and walked out into the night.

* * *

There was Lydia next morning, pale, dressed in that purple shift, cascades of beautiful hair, tumbling Brigitte Bardot style out of an inadequate hair clip as she swept up the remains of the broken glass from the floor by the bar. She jumped when he opened the door. Shouldn't she be at the Department of Education on a Friday morning? She was anticipating a visit from the police, she said. He sighed. She wasn't his, to take in his arms.

How did the best playwrights convey love? He searched for words that weren't corny, ways of describing the physical sensation in a way that wasn't embarrassing. There was anger and betrayal in his plays. But not much love. Yet here he was, overwhelmed by love for Lydia, and unable to express it in words. He laughed out loud. He felt something lift inside him. Sometimes you had to choose life over artifice, even if it meant you couldn't control it.

"Lydia, we've hardly met. I've seen you in the distance several times…"

"Oh, Arthur, yes. I was just thinking about you. You came to my rescue last night." He felt she was really looking at him, inspecting her grandmother's strange playwright. "And the reading of my grandmother's will. The smell of your cigarettes, Sobranie Russian, weren't they? I don't suppose I could have one now, could I? They'll always remind me of Eveline.

"Coffee and Sobranie for breakfast." She seemed quite talkative. "Perfect. Especially after last night. I had to struggle not to cry at the reading of Eveline's will, Arthur. It was all so overwhelming. And when the solicitor announced that she'd left me The Brasserie, you knocked over your coffee cup. The perfect reaction in that horrible hushed room."

He was conscious that Lydia was examining him. What was she seeing, he wondered? His waistcoat buttoned up to a Nehru collar, the long pale-grey cuffs of his most interesting shirt, put on specially for her? His closed-in, intense expression? What he used to think of, when he was successful, as his mysterious, burning-eyed look? He thought of his face as unremarkable. He knew that his eyes were disturbing. One was lighter grey than the other, as though he were hiding something, or feeling two different emotions at the same time, and there was a kink in the lid of the bluer eye – the result of a teenage fight.

"I keep seeing you here … sort of in the background. As though you were, I don't know, checking up on us." She laughed. "You have a key, don't you?"

"I didn't want to disturb you. Yes. I have a key to both floors of the building."

"So no secrets from you, then. How are you getting on with your research? Or should I say inventory? What have you found? I suppose everything belonged to that actress. Please don't throw away anything that might have belonged to my grandmother … I'd like to see that first … at least. I don't want to lose her. Mind you," she laughed, "Eveline still seems to have a pretty strong presence here."

"I miss her very much too," he said. "Would you like to come upstairs and have a look now? There are some photographs you might be able to identify."

They climbed the narrow flight of stairs to the flat. He had spent a number of days here, sorting and reading papers, listing contents and sometimes an hour or two writing a scene of Eveline's commission. But watching Lydia, it was as though he saw it for the first time.

A tiny box-like front hall opened directly into one large room, half dark, lace curtains covering the windows. Two lamps gave off a soft light through shades made of glass beads linked with filigree ironwork. They shook and jingled as you crossed the floor, as though they were missing dalliance and salon conversation. Limp curtains hung from cast iron rails. On the far wall was a huge four-poster bed, separated from the rest of the room by a silken screen. At its foot was a chaise longue in pink damask, and a spindly Georgian table. A series of little cupboards led off the opposite wall – a tiny kitchen, a basin and mirrors on three walls, a lavatory encased in a mahogany throne, and a walk-in wardrobe. Lydia was evidently enchanted.

"This flat would suit me fine, just as it is."

She ran her fingers over a leopard-skin jacket, a sable wrap, a floor-length velvet coat. She inspected the row of hat boxes on the shelf above them and the fox fur stole that hung from a brass hook on the wall, its moth-eaten tail in its mouth and its glass eyes glaring. Satins and chiffons fluttered and whispered from padded coat hangers.

"She must have died suddenly, or surely these beautiful things would be protected in bags?"

"All I know is that they want an inventory of everything. Then I recommend what to keep and what to sell or destroy."

"Look, Arthur, please don't throw the clothes away. I want you to think of me as a serious civil servant and a professional restaurant owner, and I'll probably have to face the police today, but please may I go through these clothes sometime? I have my eye on that fox fur. What a lot of secrets Eveline had."

Arthur went over to her.

"Is this upsetting for you?" he asked. "The actress was almost the same age as your grandmother. Her father's little girlfriend. Hard on Eveline, I would have thought."

"Did she ever talk to you about it?"

"Not really. I got the impression her father could do no wrong in her eyes. A lot of papers" – he pointed to tin trunks in the corner – "but mainly accounts and lists of purchases. He seems to have had a number of business interests."

"I think he made a lot of money somewhere. But possibly questionably. They bought the Suffolk house on the proceeds. The one that belongs to Uncle Edmund."

"I doubt if I will make head or tail of all that. I'm not very good at finances." He smiled at her. "The theatre stuff, that's quite straight-forward. There's an interesting correspondence with …" – he named a famous actor – "which I've sent to his family to have a look at. And the rest seems to be ephemeral. The main thing is to decide what Eveline would have done. I believe she wanted me to be ruthless about throwing stuff away."

"You won't throw those away, will you?" Lydia pointed to some pictures stacked against the wall.

"The strange botanical drawings?"

"They were in Eveline's front hall. Have you looked at them, Arthur? I used to stare at them, fascinated. In fact, they are the only things I hoped she'd leave me."

"They're intended for you. Look, there's a label. And the stags over there are for Marcus and Mathew Ashfield. I don't know why they are here."

He watched her kneel beside the pictures, turning them one after another to the light. "Look," she said. "Have you ever heard of these? The Bat Plant. The Bleeding Tooth Fungus. The White Egret Flower. The Mandrake is meant to shriek like a human when it's pulled out of the earth. Will you keep them safe for me, Arthur? I don't live anywhere at the moment. You know … Marvin … er … lives far away and I'm staying in a friend's flat since my aunt threw me out. I'm a sort of nomad."

"Put them up in the brasserie. They'd look wonderful."

"What a brilliant idea. Goodness, I must get back. I'm meant to be making it look presentable in case the police come to call."

"Will you have a quick look at these photographs? See if you can tell me who anybody is?"

The huge old-fashioned album lay on the table, thick green leather binding and page after page of dark grey paper scattered with small black-and-white photographs, here and there a date, and occasionally an illegible handwritten note. He hoped she might identify some of them.

An hour later he got up from the roll-top desk at the other end of the room and laid a hand gently on Lydia's shoulder.

"You're in another world," he laughed. "It's nearly eleven o'clock. You may be needed downstairs."

She looked up slowly, brushing away her tears with the sleeve of her purple shift.

"Lydia, what is it?"

"Photographs... photographs of my mother... lots of them ... optimistic ... laughing ... before ... before everything went wrong. It's so upsetting to see what she was like before."

# Chapter 25

The brasserie closed for a few days over Christmas. Christmas Day was a Saturday and Boxing Day a Sunday, and the civil service were given Monday and Tuesday off in lieu and one added 'privilege' day. Lydia went up to High Fell Farm without a sense that she should be somewhere else. Looking forward to walking on the hillside, sitting in the kitchen in front of the fireplace, spending time with Marvin.

They had Christmas dinner at the Ramsay Arms in Shap village.

"With all these chickens in the yard, Marvin, couldn't we grab one of them and cook it in the stove?"

"I wouldn't trust a sparrow to cook in that stove."

"Why don't we get a new cooker? There's money enough, isn't there?"

"Spoken like a true restaurant owner. I like that stove. It suits me. When you come and live with me, then we'll see. Anyway, you'll like the pub. It pulls out all the stops at Christmas. And I want you to meet my friends."

Marvin introduced Lydia to Rob and Jack and old Fergus, their wives, and the occasional teenage hanger-on. All of them seemed to know Marvin well, and joked with him. Lydia drank what was put in her hand, not knowing what it was, and began to feel dizzy. She was worried about forgetting people's names. She met Mary-Anne, the dyslexia expert, small and inward-looking, with curly brown hair and intelligent eyes. Lydia didn't know what to say to her. She didn't think it was appropriate to thank her for helping Marvin with his reading, as though she were a parent, or to ask her whether she was married and had a family. They stood together in front of the huge fireplace, eyeing each other warily.

The Ramsay Arms was dark and smoky, not unlike the kitchen at High Fell Farm, but there was a long refectory table, scrubbed till it shone silver-grey in the candlelight, places laid with red paper napkins and large beer tankards, and plain white plates. In the middle of the table crouched an enormous goose, crisp and glistening, and a row of Cumberland sausages stacked around it like kindling at the foot of a bonfire. And a tray of roasted potatoes and a pyramid of green cabbage and Brussels sprouts, turnips and carrots.

Lydia wanted to sink her teeth into the goose, lie down on the pile of vegetables and never think again.

Marvin tapped her on the shoulder.

"Come and sit down, darling."

Jack was next to her and there, on the other side, between her and Marvin, was Dave Perry.

"What on earth are you doing here?"

"Nice you're so pleased to see me," he said. "Surprise visit. Checking up on my favourite lovebirds."

Dave waited for her to say something.

"Didn't Marvin mention it? I've come to stay for a few days. Don't usually take in Christmas. Planning to be with this bird I know, Belinda. Nice place in the Borders. But her father caught us in bed together, smoking a substance he didn't approve of, and he chucked me out on the long gravel drive. Dragsville. But gave me a chance to descend on you both for a day or two." He looked at her closely. "Brasserie shut then, is it? No conflict of interest?"

Lydia had been looking forward to five days alone with Marvin on the farm. Relaxing with him, getting to know him again, talking about when and how she would give up the civil service and the brasserie and be free to come and live with him. The last thing she needed was a sneering hanger-on.

\* \* \*

She and Marvin spent Boxing Day out on the Lakeland hills, hare coursing. She forgot about Dave.

As they walked back to the farm, the sun was still holding its own behind wisps of ashy cloud, surviving a little longer each day. They crested the last ridge and looked down. Pale light glittered on the unused front windows of the farmhouse, silver and ghostly. They leant against the wall, just looking.

Marvin was uncharacteristically short of breath.

"Not like you to struggle up a hill. Are you OK?"

Marvin took hold of her shoulders, crushing her against the rough-hewn stones, kissing her urgently, growling at her in a strange passion. Gone was his usual slow sensuality. Some creature crouched inside him, someone she'd never encountered before, savage and demanding. Desire and longing blotted out surprise.

Later, she padded along the icy passage between the bathroom and their bedroom, wrapped only in a towel, her naked feet leaving high-arched prints on the slabs of stone. Stone was everywhere. The floors. The hills. The drystone walls. And in her heart, something ached like a stone.

"At least keep a dressing gown here, for Christ's sake, Lydia." Dave spoke aggressively. "Better still, come and live with him. I thought you were meant to be intelligent. What sort of girlfriend are you?"

"What's it to do with you, Dave Perry?"

"Haven't you worked it out? He needs you to look after him. Time is short."

"Whatever d'you mean?"

They heard Marvin come in from the back yard, the collie snuffling and whining, the bang of the cupboard door, the scrape of the dog food bowl on the floor.

Then the telephone rang.

"Oh. Oh. OK," they heard him say. "Yes. Just a minute."

"For you, Lydia. Your cousin Griselda."

"Griselda!"

Lydia's heart missed a beat. Something must have happened to her mother. It must be bad news. She was hard-wired for worrying news, especially at Christmas. Christmas put a special strain on fragile psyches.

"Greetings, Lydia," said Griselda. "Guess what? I'm at Penrith. Just a few miles away. And I'd like to come and stay the night. And dinner. If that's OK with you."

Griselda and Henry Sturridge – "my fiancé and I", as she kept saying – were touring, for her to be inspected by his grand relations strewn both sides of the Border, an old-fashioned custom that she had been very much enjoying.

"We were about to leave Tarrow Castle in Northumberland to go to those polo-playing cousins of his in Cheshire. Henry got this telegram from his father and made me drive him straight to Carlisle to get the London train. Looking very grim and forbidding." She laughed. "So I guess it's business, even over Christmas. Ha ha. So here I am, all alone in my little car" – meaning her showy red Triumph Spitfire – "practically passing your front gate."

"We don't really have a front gate," said Lydia crossly. "You just drive into the farmyard. I hope you won't be disappointed."

"You don't sound all that enthusiastic. I thought you'd be delighted to see me."

The thought of Dave Perry and Griselda Ashfield together in the farm kitchen was fairly disturbing.

"It's just that I'm freezing. I'm dressed only in a towel. Of course I'm pleased to see you. What time will you be arriving?"

\* \* \*

Griselda and Dave hit it off immediately. Lydia might have guessed, she thought afterwards. Dave either knew, or wanted to know, most of Henry Sturridge's smart friends and relations. Griselda was unusually relaxed, much easier without the fiancé, with whom she always behaved like a plump geisha girl servicing a client.

She looked good too, Lydia thought, a bit dishevelled, blonde hair escaping from its stiff hairspray, elegant trouser suit roughed up from hours in the car, and a little slip of chiffon peeking out from under her jacket. She seemed genuinely interested in sheep, too, dropping names of breeds as well as local landowners.

"Oh, of course I know Belinda Brunswick. Not an original thought in her head. Wildly photogenic, of course. Those photographs of her in October *Tatler*. I'd die for that."

This was exactly what Dave wanted to hear.

"Fancies herself a lot," he said. "You can divide all dolly birds between the spoilt and the doormats. And she's definitely spoilt."

"Which do you prefer?" Griselda was perky. She found it easy to talk to Dave Perry.

"Nothing to choose between them. There's a third category. And that's the worst. Spoilt and needy at the same time. The spoilt abused."

"And what am I?" asked Griselda, openly flirting.

Raising his eyebrow, Dave looked her slowly up and down. "Bit soon to say. I need to know you better. Tell you what. Give me a lift down to London with you tomorrow and I'll give you my verdict."

"And men?" asked Lydia. "How many categories of men are there?"

"Only one," said Dave at once. "Excepting homosexuals, that is. Most men are only interested in having a good time and latching on to something – women, money, drink, drugs, clothes. Even politics.

Being part of something. They are all the same. Including me. Sheep. To a man. No. That's not quite right. There's just a few precious exceptions. A very few individuals who are oblivious to all that, who go their own way, following some inner compass. They think for themselves, immune to society's pressures."

He looked round the table. He had his audience.

"Like Marvin," he said.

Then Dave Perry taught Griselda to play *Love, oh Love, Oh Careless Love* on the guitar in the candlelight.

# Chapter 26

Lydia was consumed by the brasserie all over again, her eye ranging around the room, checking for anything out of place, anything that should be done to improve it.

She put Bob Dylan on the jukebox. *Like a Rolling Stone.*

"Time seems to work differently in Notting Hill," she said out loud.

"Talking of time, Lydia, we must open at lunchtime," said Mathew.

Mathew told Lydia that once a week. Since the fight, all sorts of new people were coming in the evenings. There had been new faces again today, too, but most of the tables were empty now. It was nearly eleven. The sleek-haired Philanderer was there too, breaking his tradition of Fridays, whispering something to Martha. There was an understanding that Martha waited on him, that she was discreet. He always tipped her generously and that was important too. Martha's day job was causing problems again.

The Philanderer had booked his usual corner table, the one Trevor and Martha referred to as the 'foreplay table', but he always did it through his secretary, never in his own name. This time he was here with someone new, a chalk-faced, black-haired, black-mascaraed girl, vaguely familiar to Lydia. The only relief from black was a large purple brooch fastened to her dress, drawing attention to her billowing moon-white breasts. That and a pair of purple suede shoes with very high heels.

Lydia decided that the Philanderer must like living dangerously. The blonde who had slapped him seemed tame in comparison. What would this one do to him when he proved faithless?

"I don't mind how many different girls he brings," said Mathew briskly. "I'm delighted with them all. The Ferret says we've pushed the customers up to four hundred per week. He's quite impressed, though he won't admit it. But it isn't enough. We're still losing money. As I keep saying, we have to open in the daytime."

Lydia laughed. It delighted her that Mathew was behaving like a manager. He was all of eighteen. She couldn't do without him – lunchtime opening would be impossible.

"I think we have to extend the licence to serve alcohol at lunchtime. That might be difficult, according to the Ferret. After the Pink Floyd business. Apparently they have to make further investigations before they are inclined to extend a licence 'to an inexperienced young female restaurant owner in a shady part of Notting Hill'. That's what the Ferret told me."

"I bet he enjoyed telling you that. We'll have to invite the inspectors soon, Lydia. Do you want me to have a good look at the kitchen with Trevor today?"

"What are you trying to tell me? Surely we don't have cockroaches!"

"Possibly mice, though …You should spend more time here."

"What about the Department of Education? They're already suspicious. I keep taking odd bits of time off. I'm lucky to have someone like you, Mathew. I ought to be paying you."

The restaurant door opened, the blue curtain was flung back, and a swirl of red maple leaves flew in out of the night. Auriol Wedderburn appeared on the threshold. She stood still, looking round the room. Lydia was reminded of her role as a gatekeeper in Marvin's Kensington Park Road basement, fierce-eyed, dressed in black as usual, commanding everyone's attention.

The Philanderer's girlfriend looked up and visibly blenched. The Philanderer glanced over his shoulder, whispered something to Martha and slipped out in the direction of the Gents. His girlfriend got up slowly, picked up her handbag and walked over to the door, swinging it menacingly. There was a fixed smile on her face.

"Why Auriol," she drawled. "Long time no see. I heard you were in Cuba."

"So this is where you have dinner, Maria? Do you know the proprietor, my friend Lydia Renfrew?"

Each of the three of them smiled stiffly. After a brief exchange, the actress – her name was familiar from the newspapers – swept out through the door with a little wave of her hand.

"Super to see you, Auriol. Super. Let's meet soon."

Lydia tried to hug Auriol. She stiffened.

"For goodness sake, let's sit down," she said.

"What can I offer you? We should be closing but there's some very good onion soup…"

"I don't want food, Lydia. Just a cup of coffee. I'm in a hurry. Can we sit over there in the corner, where they were?"

Lydia laughed.

"We call that the 'foreplay table'."

"Oh yes. So who was Maria indulging in foreplay with?"

Lydia realised she had given too much away. Martha was always reminding her that a restaurant owner had to be discreet. The Philanderer would be bound to know Auriol's father.

"Oh, I really don't know who he is. He always pays in cash. We call him 'the sleek-haired Philanderer'."

"London seems to be full of philanderers these days. Do they come here together a lot, those two?"

"I've never seen her before. Except in the papers. He comes fairly frequently, but with different people."

"I can see that this is all very fascinating. If you have time for long, lascivious meals."

"The diligent student. How was Cuba?"

"I've been in the north with Marvin. This is all very well, Lydia, but what about Marvin?"

Lydia was silent, refocusing her thoughts.

"He misses you but he won't say so. He wants you to be involved in the important things that happen on a farm. You've missed the livestock sales. Daughter of a pig farmer, I thought you knew about that sort of thing. And now the pigeons. Don't you realise how much they matter to him?"

Auriol stubbed out her cigarette, lit another and strode out of the brasserie.

* * *

Hundreds of final year students packed into Kensington Town Hall for the qualifying exam for graduate entry to the civil service. Rows of serious-looking men – almost all men, quite intimidating – bent over their papers, like an education institution in a communist country. Was she really one of them? Three hours of precis, an essay and comprehension. Half of Lydia's mind was on the brasserie – its second Monday lunchtime opening.

"I'd like to make you full time, Martha."

"But can we afford to do that?"

"Who are those two?"

"Never laid eyes on them before," said Martha. "Wrapped up in their conversation. Sulky about being asked to order."

Lydia watched from behind the bar. "Sulky, are they? I'll do their table. I'm quite intrigued by them. They look like the sort of people we need to attract."

"What? Posh intellectuals?"

Lydia blushed. "*Local* posh intellectuals."

The two of them had taken over a table for four and covered the surface with typescript and newspaper cuttings. The ashtray was full and a bottle of Algerian red already half finished. They had concentrated enough to order that.

"Here is a menu. Would you like to order some food?"

They looked up. The tall blond one smiled, and the curly-haired one with spectacles went on reading a typescript and tapping the end of his pencil on the table.

"The dish of the day for two, please," said the blond one.

"But you don't know what it is," she laughed.

"I'm a 'dish of the day' man on principle. And Piers here does what I tell him."

"Anything else?"

"You mean, does he do anything else that I tell him to? No. Not very often. Another bottle of Algerian red and some water, please. Are you the owner?"

"That's right."

"I've heard about you. And the brasserie. It's nice here. It's got character."

Piers tapped his pencil again.

"OK. OK. We're meant to be having a meeting."

Arthur Shortcross came in. He greeted them and sat down at one of the spare chairs beside them.

At first he had seemed to Lydia to be aloof and retiring, but since her visit to the flat he ate at the brasserie now. Like everyone else, he opened up when Martha waited on him. Lydia had even heard him laugh. It was a nice laugh, light and musical. Lydia kept meaning to ask Martha what she talked to him about. She wondered whether he was a bit in love with Martha.

"I like this weekday lunch opening, Lydia."

"Would you like me to lay you a place?"

Arthur looked up at her, as though by mistake, and his gaze shocked her. It seemed to pour over her, like some liquid, thicker than water, purer than oil.

She stepped back.

No, he explained. He couldn't stay now. He was just checking up on these two. But he'd be here tomorrow.

She delivered two pork chops à la normande. The pork came once a week on an overnight train from a neighbour of Marvin's. Lydia told them this. They just nodded. But later, when she offered them coffee, the one called Piers invited her to join them.

"I'm sorry I was rude to you earlier, but it's impossible to get Adam to decide anything unless I bully him. You're Lydia Renfrew, aren't you? We met somewhere."

Lydia had dreaded this moment. When one of the diners would be someone she'd met somewhere before, in the dimly lit basement at Kensington Park Road, or worse still at one of Cousin Griselda's cocktail parties. That's why Martha always served the Philanderer. Lydia was pretty sure it would only take a few minutes to find a connection between him and someone she knew.

But she couldn't place these two. They had public school accents but were dressed in polo-neck sweaters and donkey jackets, the uniform of left-wing intellectuals in Notting Hill.

"Didn't you work at the Department of Education?"

"I still do. I should be there today but I'm doing their terrifying qualifying exams – for the graduate entry thing."

"I saw you at a press meeting," he went on, "during the launch of the comprehensive school programme, wasn't it?"

"Oh. Are you involved with comprehensive schools too?"

"Not just them. Labour party policy. Need for change – that sort of thing. I edit an underground magazine. An outlet for left-wing ideas. It's called *The New Generation*."

"I'd be interested in that. Where can I buy it?"

"They refuse to stock it at W.H. Smith. It's subversive, apparently. We give it away on street corners. To be honest, it's not come out regularly yet. Adam here is very rich. I'm trying to persuade him to put more money into it."

"That's good. Is he going to obey you?"

Adam nodded. "I guess I'll have to."

"Shall I get him a brandy on the house in the interest of revolution?"
She came back with a couple of glasses of Calvados.

Piers wanted to talk to her. "This must be very different from
the DES."

"But interesting too. Choices. Always difficult, aren't they? All this
is difficult to combine with a serious job."

"I believe in the comprehensive schools. They could really
change things…"

Lydia put down the tray with the coffee cups and pulled up a chair.

"Yes. I do think that, Piers. More important than running a brasserie in the grand scheme of things. But I've only got a year to make this
work." She waved an arm round the room. "A challenge from beyond
the grave." Piers raised an eyebrow, but she rushed on. "Look. It's been
really interesting talking to you, but I must get back to work. This *is*
work too, you know. I hope you will both come again."

Piers looked at her intently, holding her eye for longer than
strictly necessary.

"Look here," said Adam, "before you go. This is the perfect place
for us to meet. Our editorial team – what we call our editorial team,
four of us – meet once a week. I know you don't normally open till
noon, but if you'd let us in at eleven o'clock, we'd have our meetings
here, coffee and so on, then stay for lunch? And bring the occasional
interesting visitor along? How about that?"

"I think we could do that. I'll have to check with Martha."

Lydia was delighted. The brasserie as a salon. This was exactly
to her taste.

# Chapter 27

"Darling honey, I don't want you to miss our first lambs. They're very special, the first ones."

Lydia came as soon as she could. She jumped on the train north once the inspector had finished going round the brasserie and the kitchen and the Ladies and Gents. She left Mathew and Trevor in charge of dinner. She'd taken another day off work. She felt torn in three directions. But she couldn't keep letting Marvin down. She must be there for the first lambs.

It was dusk when the train dropped her off at Oxenholme. There'd be no answer from the telephone at the farm. She knew that. Marvin would be out on the hill, watching over the ewes. She couldn't call him away, even briefly. So she hitched a dubious ride in a little white van. When she asked the driver to drop her at the Shap turning, he squinted at her, undecided. He braked, leant over towards the door handle as though to open it, but ground quickly back into gear instead. But she was half expecting this and she was out and stumbling away in the dark. She walked the last mile from the A6, her high-heeled boots clicking on the cold tarmac like an over-wound clock.

From a distance, she could see lights in the farmhouse kitchen.

She was back. She was home. Longing for Marvin burned inside her. Why did she keep leaving him? This is where she wanted to be. In the kitchen with him. Out on the hill looking for ewes in trouble, relaying news to him. Helping him. This was who she really was, wasn't it? A farmer. Daughter of a farmer. Not a civil servant. Or even a restaurateur.

The brasserie faded into the dark night.

She found Auriol Wedderburn sitting in the kitchen, installed like an empress in the high-back chair at the far end of the table, the one that Lydia liked to sit in. Of course Auriol had been there when the first lambs were born early that morning. It was Auriol, not Lydia, who had shared this important moment. And there she was now, she and Marvin at the kitchen table, both of them exhausted, smiling foolishly like new parents, elbows among the half-filled coffee cups and over-flowing ashtrays.

Auriol didn't have a job. Auriol was a privileged rich girl who could come and go as she wished.

Lydia burst into tears.

Marvin reached out a tired hand and laid it on hers. "Don't be sad, darling honey. The first ones are safe. They're usually the most difficult ones. And you're here now. That's what matters."

He went out again into the moonless night. He hadn't even taken off his coat.

"He wanted you to be here for the first one," said Auriol. "That magical moment. They're his babies, don't you see? The substitutes."

"Substitutes for what? Why won't he talk about having children? What is this all about?"

"You have to ask him."

"I did. He said, 'Now is not the moment for that.' For the explanation, whatever it is, or for us to have babies, I don't know."

"Was that ... before the brasserie? Exactly. Why would he talk about it now? Unless he thinks you are ready to come and live with him."

There was no time for conversation that night. There were nearly forty ewes. The first births were always spread out, Marvin explained, but then the pace sped up, lambs arriving more frequently, the ewes and newborn lambs moved under cover, as others out in the field were watched for signs of problems. Together she and Marvin fitted the skin of a dead lamb on to the back of a rejected twin, securing it carefully round its body, pushing its front legs into the dead lamb's leg skins like stockings, and persuading the grieving ewe to adopt it as her own. Together they injected and branded each new lamb and guided them into a pen where they could be watched over for their first twenty-four hours of life. Together they scoured the hillside in the wind and the rain for two ewes who wandered away in trouble. They tramped through mud and over wet rock until she could hardly stand. Marvin collapsed into the kitchen armchair, looking pale and haggard. There was nothing particularly odd about that.

Auriol stayed in the kitchen, bottle-feeding the weakened ones that wouldn't survive on the hill.

The next morning the rare Cumberland sun came out. Jack and the boys took over, swallowing hot coffee and thick toast, and going back to the field. Marvin was exuberant. Almost all the lambs had survived so far. Auriol relaxed. They sat round the kitchen table together rolling their own cigarettes, the silky little Rizla papers between their fingers and the scent of the Wills tobacco filling the room. No spliffs during lambing.

She and Marvin went to bed for a few hours. Marvin made love to her intently, as though there was nothing else in the world.

"I have to be here, darling honey. You know that. There is sage on the hills and mountain thyme too. The air smells so pure. Give up that job and come and live here. Live in the moment. None of us can afford to waste a single summer. Come here, darling, come closer."

"I can't yet. I can't yet."

Then he was fast asleep, head against her shoulder, hair longer now, skin rough from the cold on the hill. Sleepless, she watched him. She wept, quietly, wondering what would happen next, unable to talk about it. When she was here London seemed unreal, the brasserie absurd and frivolous, the civil service unthinkable. The real Lydia was up here and it was a cardboard cutout of her that operated in London. Marvin stirred and reached for her, and she made a decision.

\* \* \*

Lydia strode along the familiar lino-covered corridor, rather hoping her patent leather boots were puncturing little holes in it. She knocked on Michael Suffolk's office door more loudly than usual.

"Could I come in and see you for a moment, Mr Suffolk? It won't take long."

She walked confidently towards the chair opposite him. Defiantly, she had not brushed her hair. Michael Suffolk seemed hypnotised by her fishnet stockings. It took him a moment to get into his stride.

"Good morning, Miss Renfrew. Good to see you back. What can I do for you?"

"It's about my future…"

"My dear, the very subject. I was on the point of calling you in to see me. To discuss exactly that. I happen to know that you have passed the qualifying exam, though the results are not yet public. On to the interviews next. I'm sure you'll do well. Your experience working here will stand you in good stead."

"Mr Suffolk, I've come to tell you that I've had second thoughts about it…"

"Because of the security vetting? Only a temporary blip. The security people, they want to know a bit more about the people you spend time with in the evenings. Unusual to ask all these questions, I know, but my dear, these days, I'm sure you understand, we can't be too careful. Soviet blackmail is a real issue. Ah, here it is. They think you may have links with a known communist. They need more references, more details. But you know this already. They've already questioned you, haven't they?"

Lydia didn't know any card-carrying communists; none who adver- tised themselves as such, anyway. She racked her brains to think which of her friends might be regarded as a communist by the security people. She knew a number of people who called themselves radicals and she obviously didn't enquire about the political allegiances of the brasserie clientele before she gave them a table. The Poet was a natural anarchist, but he wasn't interested in politics. It must be Auriol. Perhaps they thought Auriol was a communist because she'd been to Cuba and protested against the war in Vietnam.

Lydia thought that the policeman in uniform who had interviewed her wouldn't be able to distinguish between someone like Auriol and a paid-up member of the Communist Party. But that wasn't important now.

"Excuse me, Mr Suffolk. But that isn't it at all. I'm trying to tell you that I've decided I don't want to get into the civil service after all."

"Hold on, Miss Renfrew. Don't go off the deep end because of a little setback. It's only a hiccup."

"But I'm going to leave the department. I'm giving in my notice. Now. To you."

"Now then. Sit down again, please, and talk this over. I really must advise you against any such hasty move. You do realise that we are talking about a job for life, don't you? And an index-linked pension? You are within a step of getting into the sought-after administrative grade and becoming a permanent member of the British civil service. You can't just walk away from all that."

"I assure you that I have thought it over very carefully and I believe I know what I am doing. I really am resigning. I'll obviously work out my notice period..."

"But the administrative grade ... Very few women..."

Lydia stood up.

"I know you've supported me all along. I'd like to thank you for all you have done for me."

With her hand on the handle of the door, she turned back to him.

"I've got nothing against the civil service. I think the work is really important and I might try to come back one day. I'm leaving because I am going to run a brasserie in Notting Hill."

Michael Suffolk was speechless. He stared at her as though she had turned into an alien or a dangerous animal.

"Don't forget you've signed the Official Secrets Act, Miss Renfrew," he spluttered. "You are committed to not telling members of the public the secrets of government…"

Lydia nearly laughed out loud. But it would be hurtful. He really believed that revealing her doubts about the Liverpool comprehensive schools proposals was a serious threat to the nation.

# Chapter 28

Arthur began writing feverishly at dawn, the Olivetti keys ringing in his ears, pages piling up on his desk. He didn't read what he had written. Stuff was pouring out again. Thanks to Eveline, he thought. He missed her. Sometimes he thought he heard the telephone ringing in the front hall of his lonely flat and when he picked up the receiver he imagined that firm yet uncertain voice saying: "Frobisher 3173? Are you writing, Arthur? Are you writing the play with a happy ending for Lydia?"

He thought about his commission. He didn't like the word 'ending'. He felt that Lydia was all beginnings, beginnings that she might eventually untangle. And then…

Mid-morning, he stopped, exhausted.

Today he walked out along the King's Road and past Eveline's flat in St Leonard's Terrace, glancing up at the window of the bedroom where she died. He sat down on the bench in the gardens opposite. There were nannies in uniforms chatting, children shouting and playing, and babies in huge dark-blue prams with monograms and coronets on their sides, big enough to hold a litter of goats, the eight little kids he had found curled up in an old discarded pram on the rubbish heap at the end of Purley Road when he was eleven. Eight little caramel-coloured goats, which he had carried home wrapped in his grey school sweater.

His mother had complained about their piles of "doings" under her washing line. "Dirty little creatures. If I get that stuff on my work shoes there'll be hell to pay. They're rubbish feeders, those goats. They belong on rubbish heaps. I'm telling you. You're not wasting good bread and milk on them."

"Please, Ma. They're so small. I've always wanted a pet."

"I won't hear another word, Arthur. You've got enough on your hands with that eleven-plus exam."

He begged her to let him keep them. He stroked their thin fur with the tips of his fingers, one after another, until it was dark.

When he came home from school the next day, they were gone.

"Don't waste your tears on the little blighters neither, d'you hear me. Your tea's ready."

Arthur felt sad, so he went straight to Hornbeam Road. He had taken to spending a good deal of time in the brasserie in the mornings, now that they opened at lunchtime. He liked the actress's flat but he persuaded himself that he needed a break from Lionel Sutton's papers, which were mainly financial, dull or incomprehensible to him; and that now he was working so fast on Eveline's commission, he needed to be there for research.

It was very comfortable in the brasserie. He sat at the corner table that the old lady with the book used at dinner on Mondays. He had come to recognise the clientele. He liked the round cast iron tables and the tall glamorous mirrors. He liked the staff – Trevor, whose dedication to the brasserie was unshaken but whose mood had turned gloomy when Joel left to go on a world tour with his dance group, and infallible Martha with her perfect recall of orders and her sly sideways look. Didier had more or less ceased to turn up but occasionally responded to emergencies, like a firefighter. Lydia's cousin Mathew was always around. He had evidently persuaded his father that he was better off learning about finance and marketing in a struggling brasserie than by sitting in a smug striped suit in the City. His brother, Marcus, was learning about insurance, as his father wanted.

Mathew was impressively steady for someone so young and had a natural instinct for publicity and marketing – he had introduced him to the advertising agency, Martel and Tillotson, and he now worked there a few days a week until he started at university in the autumn. He spent the rest of his time at the brasserie, but it wasn't enough. Now that they opened for lunch, they were rushed off their feet.

Lydia came in from the kitchen, stage right, and went to the pay phone by the jukebox. He coughed but she didn't notice that he was there. Martha was behind the bar, making his coffee. Lydia was oblivious to her too.

He could only hear her side of the conversation.

"You knew I couldn't come. I wanted to. But Marvin darling, it's a job. Like any other. To be done properly. I can't just take off when I want."

"I know. I know. I mind terribly too. I didn't forget the wedding day. It's so poignant. Of all the things I didn't want to miss. They insisted on seeing the manager. I didn't have a choice."

Arthur picked up a copy of the *Daily Mirror* and tried to read it.

"Don't say that, please. It makes it worse."

"That's not fair. *You* put the pigeons before me. And the lambs. You always have. You didn't even consult me before you bought the farm and disappeared up there for ever."

"You've never said anything about the future. You just do what interests you next. And expect me to fit in and follow."

"Oh, I do want to follow you. I miss you all the time. I'd never do that. There's no one. It's the brasserie. That's all."

She was sobbing now. "Please, Marvin, don't say that. I couldn't bear that. Please forgive me. Please."

Lydia leant her forehead on the jukebox as though to cool her head. Then she punched some buttons and *Unchained Melody* filled the room.

"O...h, my love,
My darling
I've hungered for your touch

A long, lonely time

T…ime goes by so slowly…"

Arthur felt he couldn't creep away. He put a hand on her shoulder instead.

Lydia looked up, suddenly conscious of his presence. Tears were streaming down her pale cheeks. His heart twisted inside him. He tried to pull himself together. He wasn't very good at eye colour. He mostly avoided mentioning it in his plays, occasionally assigning blue eyes to a character to portray something about her. But it was no good trying to distance himself. This was real life. Lydia's eyes were not blue. They were the most beautiful bruised violet colour he had ever seen.

"S…so, Lydia," he stammered. "I didn't realise you'd be here in the morning."

"I've stopped working at the Department. To concentrate on this."

The telephone rang.

Arthur walked rapidly out towards the kitchen, where there was a communicating door to the upstairs flat.

"Arthur." She was calling him back. "Don't go away. It's for you. It's the Poet. He seems to think you live here. I like that idea. I hope you are going through those papers really slowly."

She was laughing now.

# Chapter 29

Marvin met her at Oxenholme station, Bruce at his heels. He was standing on the platform, wrapped in his thick grey coat. He didn't throw his arms round her, hugging her, shutting out the rest of the world, as he usually did. He let her wrap herself around him.

"Marvin darling, you're shaking. What's wrong?"

"Not shaking, honey, shivering. A bit cold, that's all."

The wind blew along the platform, whipping around her ankles, sweeping in under her coat. It was dark and chill, but it wasn't cold enough for this. Marvin didn't feel the cold. Normally, he strode over the hill in his checked shirt, impervious to the elements.

The yellow station lights turned the healthiest of complexions a sickly grey, but that didn't explain what she saw. Marvin looked haggard.

"You're ill. You should be in bed. Why didn't you tell me?"

Marvin didn't get ill. That was another thing about him. He didn't seem to get the routine illnesses and physical weaknesses that afflicted other people, nor the psychological dramas that battered them. This was something she loved about him. He was like a tree, she thought. You would have to cut through one of his limbs and count the rings inside to account for the years. And like a tree, the only changes in him were due to the seasons – lambing in February, pigeon breeding now, and what next? Pigeon racing beginning in April and lasting through the summer, when the sheep were on the hill pastures. Then the autumn – the lamb sales once again and the renewal of the land.

The pigeons were sitting and Marvin's eyes lit up when he talked about them.

"Aphrodite is beautiful, as she should be. Look at her. Eos seems like a natural breeder. The others are all doing well. But Hera, there's something about her, a look in her eye. A huntress. We should have called her Diana. She's a blue. I'm starting with a mix of breeds. I won't specialise till I've worked out which is best suited to here."

Lydia loved the names, though she couldn't yet identify them accurately – red hen, mealy hen, blue hen, mosaic cock, chequer cock.

Marvin laughed and started coughing.

In the night it happened again. He was feverish, hot in her arms, then shivery. Then the coughing again.

"You've got flu, Marvin. You'll have to stay in bed. I'll take care of the pigeons."

He shook his head, but he lay in a pool of sweat.

She watched over him in his sleep. His hair kept growing longer, the near crew cut he had when they met outside the Scrubs a thing of the distant past. It was soft and silky now and there were even a few dark-grey strands. He reminded her of a monk, from one of those orders that produce their own food, or a sort of itinerant preacher. He went about his daily life as an ascetic, breaking out to laugh and smoke and make love.

At dawn she crept out from under the covers and looked through the window on to the sudden hillside. The sky above it was dark and threatening, reluctant to relinquish winter. But he would never give up this land. Their love had changed her, not only her, but him too, as though swapping bits of each other's natures. She had become a Londoner with a mission and Marvin had withdrawn to the countryside. She wondered if this was an unstable mix, like random elements in a test tube in a school chemistry lab.

She returned to Marvin and stroked his hair, murmuring to him.

"I can look after the birds. You just stay in bed and get well."

"There's the lambs too."

"I can feed them ... I can drive the hay up to the field."

"For how long though?" He spoke softly, as though he hadn't intended her to hear him. "What happens on Monday?"

Marvin seemed better on Sunday. She wanted him to see a doctor. She guessed that he wouldn't go unless she took him herself. But she really wanted to be at the brasserie on Monday, when the people producing the magazine were coming again. And the old lady had converted to lunchtime with her book. "During the winter, it's easier for me," she said. "I'll review the situation in the spring." Arthur would be there too – he always checked in on Monday. She'd rather miss 'Sexy Friday' than Monday, intriguing though it was. Friday lunchtime had quickly developed its own louche character – clandestine assignations and whispered conversations, a wine glass held in a lace-cuffed hand and at least a liqueur to round off the meal. It seemed to be filling a niche in London bohemian restaurant life for those whose working week ended at one and whose train to the Home Counties didn't depart till five o'clock.

She'd try to come back to Marvin in the middle of the week. She could take him to the doctor if he wasn't better by then. And the baby pigeons were due to hatch next weekend too.

She sighed. She took a deep breath.

"Give me a year, Marvin," she said in a low voice. "To make the brasserie work. To make a success of it. Because of Eveline. Give me a year. Then I will come and settle here with you."

She expected him to be pleased, but he turned away.

"And I'll be back on Thursday at the latest. In time for the pigeons. Take care of yourself. Do you hear me, Marvin, don't turn away, dearest. Do you promise me?"

Jack drove her to the station. He shook his head a lot but offered no opinion.

"I'll look in on him, lass. Same as I always does."

\* \* \*

Why had she gone back to London? Why hadn't she stayed with Marvin? Why had she let herself think he was better?

Marvin had pneumonia. She must get there. She must be with him. It was for her to look after him. The terrible journey, the agony of minutes ticking by. Time must be made to stop. For five or six hours, for the interval needed to get from Euston to Penrith. For some reason this train didn't stop at Oxenholme. Penrith was further from the farm. It would add unbearable extra minutes. But no. Maybe not. Penrith was more likely to have taxis. But on a Wednesday evening? After dark?

She fought against rising panic and helplessness. Everything seemed pitted against her. It was wet and cold, the sort of conditions that made trains slow down. And taxi drivers go home.

Was she being punished?

She couldn't breathe properly. She couldn't concentrate on anything, newspaper, book, food. She roamed the dirty corridor, hands on the window to steady herself, peering out into the suburban, neon-lit gloom.

The journey went on and on. Heart-stoppingly slow through miles of dark countryside, a sprinkling of lights, embankments closing in and falling away, jolting through rib-vaulted stations. Was that Crewe? Then speeding up through the next, so fast that she couldn't read the signage. She had to know where they'd got to.

Nearly empty. Where were the other passengers? Might they decide it wasn't viable and shunt her off into a siding for the night?

The train ground to a halt. In the dark, in the middle of nowhere. A signal failure near Preston. Biting her fingernails. Crazily jumbled ideas of getting down on to the track, running to the nearest road, hitching a lift, screaming that she had to get to him. The train lurching forward slowly, stopping again a few hundred yards further on. Beating her fists on the windowpane.

Lydia lunged a few steps one way down the corridor. Then back in the other direction. A mad dance. How could she have not understood how ill he was?

A woman passed her in the corridor, stopped and stood beside her, patting her arm.

"Can I do anything, dear? You look in a bit of a state."

"I've got to reach him. I should be there. He's got pneumonia."

"I see. Well, perhaps you can telephone at the next station."

"But look, we're not moving. We'll never get to the next station."

"Calm yourself, dear. There is nothing you can do but wait. And pray, if that's your sort of thing." She examined Lydia doubtfully. "I suppose you might ask the conductor to ring ahead to the next station. Lancaster, isn't it? Have a taxi waiting for you."

"I have to get to Shap. Can you do that? Get the conductor to ring someone for you?"

"Shap. That's a long way in a taxi. I'd stay on till Penrith if I were you."

Lydia stumbled along the corridor towards the front of the train. It lurched forward again, picking up speed as though trying to make up for lost time. It swayed violently along the tracks, crashing her into the windows and the compartment doors, people looking up from their books in slight disapproval. All clustered together in the front compartments. Would they get out more quickly? And take the only taxis?

Eventually she reached a sealed door, the section where the driver must be. There was no conductor.

She turned round and set off back again, the full length of the train, passing the sympathetic woman again, and one set of sour-faced glassed-in travellers after another, panting, heart hammering, something to do, until she arrived at the luggage compartment at the back of the train. There was the conductor, standing over a couple of large trunks, checking something on his list, just as someone had done with her trunk when she was sent away to boarding school.

Finally he looked up and took her in, a desperate, dishevelled, dark-eyed girl in a pink PVC raincoat.

"Look, miss, I'd like to help you. We're about to stop at Lancaster. You *could* get out and find a bus or a taxi, but the line's clear now. We should be in Penrith by" – he looked at his watch – "by, let me see, about quarter past six. Quicker to stay on."

She asked if he could make a call for her.

"Just arriving at Lancaster. Must deal with these trunks. After that I'll see what I can do…"

Another wait. Another bolt out of the station and plunge into the night. And five minutes later, the inevitable lurch to a stop. Why hadn't she got out at Lancaster? It would be quicker to walk.

By the time the conductor returned to her, she was huddled in the corner of the luggage compartment, head down, hugging her knees, hands over her ears.

At Penrith she begged him to telephone the farm. Jack picked up at once.

"He's refused to go to hospital. Because of the pigeons… Come straight here."

Jack was there, Rob too, and Mary-Anne.

Mary-Anne held out her arms to her. "It's too late. He's dead."

They were standing round Marvin's bed in a circle, as though reluctant to share him. It seemed to Lydia that he had only recently departed from his body, and his spirit was hanging around waiting for her, or that he had only just left the room and would be back in a few moments. Only just departed, but, like a bus disappearing round a corner, he couldn't turn round and come back.

He lay stiff on the box bed, his feet sticking out of the blankets, his long legs unmoving. He would be uncomfortable like that, she thought. She took off her raincoat and covered his toes. The PVC wouldn't tuck in properly. The lipstick pink signalled derangement.

She leant over and put her cheek against his.

Then she fainted away.

The next thing she knew she was sitting in the kitchen in the armchair by the fire with a cup of tea in her hand. She sipped it automatically, expecting a heavy dose of sugar. But it was laced with whisky, the restorative tea and whisky that she and Marvin drank together after a day hare coursing.

She must have let out a howl of grief, because they all rushed back into the kitchen and stood looking at her.

"There now," said Jack, "don't take it so hard. The end was quite peaceful. He wanted to die at the farm, he said. He's been happy here. Walked along that passage, not two hours ago, Lydia, don't know how he did it, stood there," he said, pointing to the archway, "gave me the shock of my life, I can tell you, so ill ... said he would just check on the pigeons ... I'm caring for them, I told him, just like he'd taught me, just like they were my own ... and he smiled ... that smile of his ... and collapsed on the floor. We put him to bed and soon afterwards he breathed his last ... I'm sorry, Lydia, lass. Leastwise he died here ... in his home ... close to his pigeons."

Marvin hadn't been thinking of her, hadn't talked about her in his last moments, hadn't held out against death to say goodbye to her. The pain was like a knife disembowelling her. She bent double.

It was Mary-Anne who broke the silence.

"He talked about you, Lydia ... he said that you'd come ... 'She'll be late maybe...but she always comes.' And something else. 'Tell her that I have been happier with her than I ever thought to be.' Something like that."

Lydia turned her head against the wing of the armchair and sobbed into the faded yellow cloth.

The dog, Bruce, refused to leave the bedside where Marvin's body lay, growling each time a stranger entered the room. Head between his front paws, on guard, he lay flat on the cold stone floor. He wouldn't go to his basket and he refused to eat.

Marvin was like a carved stone sculpture, rigid features, a medieval knight or a crusader in a church. Austere. Without his smile. His brown eyes closed. It wasn't exactly Marvin any more, Lydia could see that, but nor was it yet time for him to leave the farmhouse. He was still an inhabitant. The funeral people insisted that out of respect he should lie in a coffin. It could be an open coffin if she wanted, but he couldn't just lie on the bed.

A number of village families came to view his body the next day, the children too, for that was the custom there, taking a special interest in a dead person. Lydia noticed how well all these families knew him, how little she'd really known of his life here. Her cold little vow haunted her. To give the brasserie the year, then come and live here.

Auriol arrived just before midnight, with Dave Perry. Dave always seemed to know where his friends were and what they were doing. Without telegram or telephone or postcard. Lydia wasn't surprised that he turned up. What did surprise her was his grief. She saw another Dave, a new aspect of him, devastated by loss.

They ate bread and cheese on a little table they found in the scullery. It seemed disrespectful to eat round his body. Each of them got up every now and then to check on him.

"I wasn't ready for this, Lydia. I loved him. I knew he'd go, but not so soon. So little warning."

It came out bit by bit, the things Dave and Auriol knew about Marvin that they had kept hidden from her.

"A terrible inherited illness," said Auriol. "An immunity thing. Like Huntingdon's disease, but not that. Some name I'd never heard of. It killed his mother when she was young. He knew it would kill him too. He wouldn't have children, wouldn't risk passing it on. He'd been horrified by what happened to his mother, her decline and death, when he was only ten. So he promised himself he would never get involved with anyone and never have children. Then he broke his promise. He let himself love someone. You," she added bitterly. "You, who didn't know how to love him."

"Give her a break, Auriol," said Dave. "She loved him and look at her now. She's pathetically sad … Pneumonia got him first, Lydia. Or whatever it was. Sudden. No terrible decline. That's something to be thankful for."

Lydia watched Auriol rocking in her chair, contorted by grief, and perhaps a little jealousy.

"He coughed," said Lydia. "He coughed a lot last weekend. A flu sort of thing that wouldn't go away. He even cut down on the smoking. But I didn't know it was so serious. Was that the immune thing?" Icy jigsaw pieces slotted into place. "He insisted on checking on the lambs. Out on the hillside in the cold …"

"You won't press for an autopsy, will you, Lydia?" asked Auriol. "You don't want to know whether it was the other thing, underneath, weakening him, waiting to pounce. Better not to know really."

Lydia blew her nose and stuffed her damp handkerchief back up her sleeve. She could feel the wet against her skin. She poured herself another tumbler of whisky and passed the bottle over to Auriol. Dave drank very little alcohol. He concentrated on drugs.

"But why didn't he tell me all this?"

"He wanted to protect you. It was one of his gifts to you. Not to tell you. He wanted you to come and live with him because you wanted to, not because time was short. He looked after all of us, if you think about it, but he was especially protective of you." Auriol laughed, a strange hoarse sound that bounced off the flag-stoned kitchen.

"He shared everything with you, Auriol. He was closer to you…"

"But it was you he loved…"

"When he got to be thirty, he vowed never to get seriously involved with a woman again," said Dave. "He knew roughly when he was likely to die. Around forty – like his mother."

"I don't know what he really felt about me. He just had this mission to stop me being a civil servant."

"Well. He won that battle, even if he couldn't beat a London restaurant."

"No, Auriol, that's not right. He didn't think he'd failed. He knew he could get Lydia to come and live with him, but he didn't like to press her."

Lydia cried some more.

Each was exhausted by grief. They sat silent for a while, staring into the fire.

Around dawn they talked some more, in that weird, intoxicated way that comes over people after a death and before the reality has sunk in. A respite from the pain that can't be held at a constant level. They told stories about him, shared him. Laughed. They drank and smoked as though he were with them. A curiously happy time, with none of the usual barriers between them.

"He amazed himself. He didn't expect to build anything. But look what happened – the farm, the pigeons, the pretty girlfriend," mused Dave. "That nomad drove more stakes into the earth than he ever expected to. He expected to drift. Along with the rest of us."

"How old was he?" Lydia asked suddenly.

"He wouldn't celebrate his birthday. His mother died on his tenth birthday... after a thing like that ... birthdays upset him."

That was why he cried when she'd given him the fountain pen.

"Do either of you know how old he is ... is ... was?"

"What's it got to do with anything?" said Auriol. "Don't make such a fuss about it."

"For Christ's sake, Lydia," said Dave, "if it's that important to you, look at his passport."

There wasn't much in his desk. There were photos of pigeons and copies of *Homing World*. There were some letters tied in a bundle, which Lydia would look at later, much later, when Dave and Auriol had gone. It wasn't difficult to find his passport, but it was upsetting, reminding her of their only foreign trip together, when she'd fallen in love with Marvin and with the Côte d'Azure, to which she'd never now want to return.

He was only thirty-five when he died. Only figures, but freighted with so much history. She might never get over those numbers. Or the timing. She could have been here. The pigeons were due to produce their first eggs – eighteen days after Valentine's Day – at 5.30 p.m. on the day after the funeral. They would be back in time to check on their safe arrival, to watch over them, to stand in for Marvin.

The dog howled when Marvin's body was taken away, scrabbling at the front door. Lydia put on his lead and held it in her hand, dragging him gently with her wherever she went, from kitchen to cupboard, from larder to stove. She tried to eat. Her head sank on to the table. The dog settled down on her toes.

# Chapter 30

The play required a happy ending for Lydia, an ending that Eveline might have wanted. And now this tragic death. Arthur Shortcross didn't yet know how his half-finished script could make sense of this. He ached to comfort Lydia.

It was this, as well as Eveline's commission, that drew him all the way up to Marvin's funeral. No one else would record every little detail of it. He travelled with the Poet, not speaking much, but glad of his sweet-natured, ungainly companionship.

They arrived at the crematorium chapel early. Arthur slipped in and sat near the back in his dark-suited, unobtrusive way. He could see that Lydia was already there, head bent, alone in the front pew on the left, the cascade of her beautiful black hair over her shoulders. He longed to go up and sit down beside her, put his arm round her and promise to look after her for ever. He watched as the Poet ambled up the aisle, his limp more pronounced by anxiety and sadness, hugged Lydia and shuffled into the row behind her.

Arthur assumed that she chose to be on her own, couldn't face shaking hands at the door with each of the odd assembly of people who were drifting in. She wouldn't be praying in a Church of England sense, of that he was sure. Why was he so sure? He imagined that she would be wrestling with her sorrow, for being at the brasserie when Marvin was taken ill. Perhaps she had a hangover too. They'd drunk enough the night before, according to Jack, the farmer who handed out service sheets with tears in his eyes.

Lydia hadn't wanted Marvin to be cremated. Arthur heard later that she had argued for a grave on the hillside behind the farm, near his sheep and his pigeon lofts. Or at least in the churchyard at Shap. Somewhere for her to visit, perhaps. People always think like that when a loved one dies. But how often do they actually visit the grave afterwards? Sometimes it's just romantic, a piece of theatre really. They visualise themselves weeping as they kneel to place flowers on the heap of earth. Yet how seldom had he visited those graves in the churchyard at St Andrews?

But Marvin had cremated his father, and Lydia could scatter the ashes on the hillside, to leave Marvin with his sheep and pigeons. He could hear the tone of voice Auriol would have used. Auriol would be trying very hard to be tough. He was interested in what she thought she was doing with her life. Playing with revolution? Or was she serious about it? He was considering her for a bit part in his play. But not today.

Had Lydia ever been to a cremation? Eveline had been buried in a grave in a little village church in Suffolk. The funeral service was in Wilbraham Place, just off Sloane Square, in that big aloof church, convenient for her decrepit old friends, but she had chosen, at the last minute, to lie beside her second husband. People reverted in funny ways when they prepared for death.

Who was to say whether Marvin was preparing for his death? The secret was out now. Everyone knew that some fatal inherited illness had been hanging over him. So in one sense he had had all the time in the world to prepare. Yet apparently he left no instructions. He didn't seem to be the sort of person who cared much about preparations. Arthur had never met Marvin. He had to construct him from his imagination. The character notes he had made about him when he started writing about Eveline's family were inadequate – "Marvin Brewer, Lydia's boyfriend – compelling rather than conventionally good-looking. Late thirties? Specialist sports car mechanic turned sheep farmer. Pigeon fancier by background and inclination. A grown-up on the fringe of a fast, smart, rich, drug-taking, thrill-seeking social group." Factual. Banal. No insight. Now he wondered who and what Marvin really was.

Apparently, Auriol had insisted on the minimum of religion on Marvin's behalf. That was surely right. It turns out that very little of the Church of England funeral service is mandatory, though many people don't know that. Who better than a lapsed Catholic to sort that out?

Now the priest went up to Lydia.

Oh, Lydia! Poor girl! Now he could see her pale, strained face. The thoughts he had attributed to her were as ashes in the wind once he had glimpsed her face. The scene-setting, the dialogue he had been creating in his head, the revealing movements and gestures he was planning for them, all turned to dust. All pretence of the detached playwright was gone.

He could only watch. He wished the service would start. The priest introduced Lydia to someone in a tweed jacket. Lydia stepped out of the pew. It was then he saw that she'd brought the dog, Marvin's dog, right there into the chapel. Arthur was a little shocked by that, but no one else stirred. It might have warned him about her state of mind, but at the time it struck him as the sort of action a smart country person would feel entitled to, if they chose, but that people like him would never presume to take.

It turned out, of course, that there is no bar to bringing animals into chapels. He found that out later. Were there limits? Could you bring a sheep? He thought of Marvin's pigeons.

It was difficult to take his eyes off Lydia. Then Auriol arrived, like a diversion. She looked good in black. Arresting, without being conventionally attractive. Pale face, feathery curls down to her jawbone, what he would call dirty blonde, angry eyes, an aggressive way of walking. A freedom rider. She strode up to the front row, across from Lydia. Did she deliberately put distance between them?

Surely someone should sit beside Lydia. He imagined that she would feel most comfortable with Jack, another lonely sheep farmer –

not that that properly described Marvin. Jack was his closest friend in
Shap. But Jack and the others had insisted that they would shoulder
the coffin. So there was Lydia, a lonely, stiff little figure, the long black
hair tumbling over her stiff little shoulders.

The crematorium chapel was filling up. Mostly people he didn't
know, hadn't researched, but there were quite a few of them. A funeral
in these country places was inevitably a village occasion.

Women had put on their best anoraks and lace-up shoes, their
good tweed skirts and presentable beige tights. There were caps and
hats and scarves, and a sea of pinched, anxious faces. This wasn't the
funeral of someone 'whose time had come', who 'had lived a good
long life and was ready to meet his maker'. There was something tragic
and out of place, something they didn't know the meaning of, and the
young girlfriend left bereft.

There was a stir.

Edmund Ashfield, sombre, metropolitan, striped-suited, black
polished shoes. He walked steadily up the aisle and into Lydia's pew.
He seemed more substantial than the villagers – taller, broader, as
though nourished and inflated by London.

Lydia rose and turned to him and let him embrace her. Presumably
she was as surprised to see him as Arthur was. It turned out that
Mathew had sent him. Of course Mathew wanted to come himself
but had promised to look after the brasserie till Lydia returned. He'd
instructed his father to support Lydia in his place. Mathew had gained
a sort of natural authority in a mere six months at the brasserie. He was
barely recognisable as the schoolboy Arthur had seen at the reading of
Eveline's will.

The Ashfields rearranged the front row. Griselda went in first, in
a little black suit, very smart and expensive, Chanel at a guess, black
tweed with a lovely knobbly texture and a little white edging around
the collar and the cuffs. She slid along to the end of the pew, followed
by Aunt Patience, a ship under sail, then Marcus, the other twin, a

trifle smug-looking as usual. He'd put on a little weight. It was interesting that Arthur knew immediately that it was Marcus. The twins were easily identifiable to him nowadays. There was no Henry Sturridge, thank goodness. Arthur could see from Lydia's body that she was comforted by the bulk of her Uncle Edmund beside her. He had his arm round her. She swayed against his shoulder several times before the service started.

During the waiting, Arthur caught sight of her face a couple more times, although she never turned round to see who might be there in the chapel. Her lovely eyes were half shut, black eyelashes against white skin. She looked alarmingly stricken. Oh, Lydia.

She barely glanced at the coffin when it was brought in, leaning just a little closer to Uncle Edmund. It seemed very large, and perhaps it was larger than normal to accommodate Marvin's height. How poignant.

Six dark-coated farmers walked steadily up the aisle, shoulders tensed.

He noticed the flowers. Thankfully, no one had ordered those terrifying wreaths of lilies and chrysanthemums that reek of death and misery. There were bunches of daffodils and narcissus, and a lot of green moss. Not tidy but beautiful, and how could he put it? – quietly promising of spring and new beginnings.

The service started.

The door banged. Someone had come in late. He caught a glimpse of wild red hair and a tattered coat. Ha. So she had come after all.

Auriol read a poem, very moving, which Arthur had never heard before. He knew a lot of poetry and wondered whether she had written it herself.

Dave Perry played *Pick Me Up on Your Way Down* on his guitar, a little unsteadily, that louche figure offering his tribute to Marvin. Most of the people there were bewildered by the words.

Arthur had been lulled into a stupor by the service, the music and those beautiful words. The coffin was being put on a sort of trolley and launched towards the doors of the cremation chamber. Suddenly

Lydia was out of her pew, screaming, the dog following her, howling, like something out of a horror movie. Her long purple skirt streaming around her, the dog at her heels.

"No. No. You can't. Not yet. Not yet. He's not ready to go. I'm not ready…" Scrabbling at the coffin, trying to grab a handle, screaming, "Stop. Stop. You can't do that…"

Screaming. Barking. Confusion.

And there was Lydia, in a dead faint, on the cold tiled floor of a Cumberland crematorium.

It was time for him to choose between life and writing.

# Chapter 31

Flora's words drove into her skull like nails.

"Lydie, Lydie, go up to bed. Grief makes people tired."

"You have to eat something, Lydia, or you'll fade away."

"Get out there and look after the pigs, for Christ's sake, Lydia Renfrew. Physical labour is better than thinking."

The Tamworth pigs followed Lydia down to the shore. Her mother's pig-keeping was wild and strange. She kept them, all forty-two of them, in a grassy meadow. When people claimed that pigs were dirty, churned up mud wherever they went, she contradicted them fiercely. "Pigs like to be clean. They are only thought of as dirty because they are confined to small spaces and then it rains. Really, they are the most fastidious of creatures. I could keep mine in the kitchen."

People responded warily, more because of Flora Renfrew's reputation than her actual words.

Flora liked to tell a story she had read in the *National Geographic* magazine. High in the hills of Papua New Guinea, pigs were more important than children. They came and went in the mud-brick houses as freely as humans, running through the kitchens on their neat little trotters, and lying on mats in the sleeping quarters. Women put down their babies to suckle the piglets, if the sows were unable to.

At this point, her visitors would shuffle about a bit and remember urgent errands.

But just in case her own pigs were missing out on a bit of wallowing, Flora took them on a daily outing across the sedge and down to the muddy flats of the estuary at low tide.

Lydia's body ached and she was limping. Her mother's old mare had trodden on her toe when she was too dazed to concentrate. Pig farming was physical. The mixing buckets, the stampede to the troughs and the shoving and grunting. Keeping so many pigs in sight and under control was demanding. It required concentration. But grief intruded. She bent her head and rocked backwards and forwards till the wave of grief subsided.

They told her that she had tried to throw herself on to the coffin, and later, in her still deranged state, she had apparently grabbed hold of the clippers that Marvin used to shear the sheep and taken them to her own hair, leaving a shaggy bloody corona. They thought it was an act of unmanageable grief. But there was penitence in it too, for not under-standing, not picking up on the clues, for choosing the brasserie, for being late for the first lambs, and, most of all, for missing the 'marriage' of the pigeons on Valentine's Day. That felt overwhelmingly significant now. As though she'd missed a wedding day of her own. Cutting her hair mirrored the rawness festering somewhere deep inside, invisible to the outside world. She expected there to be long-lasting scars, but to have scars there had to be healing first.

Meanwhile, the pigs rootled merrily in the slime. She had to watch them. Here the sea came in fast, turning the mud into dangerous quicksands.

It was dusk when Lydia rounded them up and drove them back to the farm. Maybe she should have been a farmer after all. She hadn't managed anything else very well. Jack had begged her to keep the High Fell pigeons for Marvin's sake, to watch the chicks hatch. It came back to her now. She nearly agreed; but she didn't think she could bear to do it without Marvin. Some instinct must have told her that she would desert the pigeons at some stage, that she wasn't going to spend her life on a farm in Shap. So Auriol was taking the decisions. Putting the farm on the market with a clause that saved the pigeon lofts for Jack in his lifetime.

Now the childhood smell of pig food filled the kitchen. Her mother was boiling potato peelings, leftover vegetables, stale bread and more risky stuff, past its best, unbearable to throw away, like old cake. She chucked it all into a pan on the stove and then mashed it in an aluminium bucket on the floor. When she was satisfied with its consistency, she added meal from a sack under the sink.

Lydia should pull herself together and offer to help. Her eyes felt too heavy to keep open, her body too tired to get to her feet. She leant her elbows on the table.

A neighbour peering through the window of that low-ceilinged kitchen, rubbing the ghosts of winter storms from the panes of glass, watching this daily ritual, would be struck by the similarities and differences between mother and daughter.

Lydia was shadowy, darker, paler, narrow-shouldered and heavy-lidded. It used to upset strangers that it was the child who looked after her sturdier mother. Flora Renfrew didn't look fragile. She was not tall but she had wild red hair, freckled skin and the wiry physique of a farm girl. It was her state of mind that made her seem deranged and forlorn. She had huge grey-green eyes in which people claimed to see depths of tragedy and delusion. She was short-sighted and had lost so many pairs of glasses under the trampling of pig hooves that she'd stopped buying new ones. She no longer tried to decipher anything far away from her. She relied on other senses, so she said, to predict the tide, the weather and people's moods, and on the dogs to round up straying pigs and to warn her of danger. She rode horses with fearless abandon. She had almost been barred from driving after a couple of incidents, but made a pact with the policeman in Silloth in which her last remaining pair of glasses must be kept permanently in a pocket of the Land Rover. And he would receive a large ham at Christmas.

"Just eat that soup, Lydia Renfrew. I made it specially for you. And you know how I hate cooking."

"Did you know about the brasserie and the flat, Mother?"

"I had no idea. Nor did Edmund."

"Nothing at all? Do you think Eveline might ever have used the flat for assignations herself?"

"Certainly not. Her admirers visited her in St Leonard's Terrace. Entirely innocent and above board. Gallant courtships. No secret liaisons."

Lydia laughed.

"Everyone has secrets."

"We knew that Grandpa had an unsuitable sort of liaison. A little love nest. We did know that. Not from Eveline. From Nanny Ashfield, I think."

"Who was Nanny Ashfield?"

Flora laughed.

"Nannies were called after the families they worked for."

"Nameless people. But that's terrible."

"I don't think it was terrible for all of them."

"Come on. Like slavery."

"Things were different then. Many of them never married. Maybe they'd lost boyfriends in the Great War. Some of them became part of the family. Stayed on for ever. More loved than the parents by the children. Sometimes more loved by the parents than their blood relations. It was all right for many of them."

"It's not all right. Thwarted of a chance to do something out in the world. To show their talents."

"A nanny we knew saved the life of her charges by lying on top of them in the Blitz. She lost her own leg." Flora hesitated. "I thought Aunt Patience had nannies, when ... when you were sent to live with them?"

"Come to think of it, there were several. One really horrible one. She was called by her own surname, though. I suppose that's a kind of progress. Nanny Murray. From Dundee."

"Nanny Ashfield had a uniform. But then so did I. Tweed coats with velvet collars and little felt hats with elastic under the chin."

"And look at you now." Lydia smiled at her. "Never out of a boiler suit."

"I was always a disappointment to Eveline."

A tremor passed through Lydia, like a horse scenting danger. She needed a cigarette. She remembered where she'd left her roll-ups at High Fell Farm. In the hole in the stonework of the fireplace. By the armchair in the kitchen. Her heart ached with longing for the rustle of the Rizla papers between her fingers, the harsh scent of Wills tobacco and a gypsy kiss in the box bed with the curtains drawn.

She reached out for one of her mother's Player's Medium and struck the match harshly against the side of the box to distract from her emotion. She passed the packet back to her. How old had she been when her mother had first insisted on her smoking to keep her company in her evenings of despair? The first time was after the gypsies moved on and the horse-trader rode away with them. She must have been about eight.

"Nannies looked after me and Eveline prepared me for 'society'. Eveline set her heart on a grand marriage for me. She wasn't interested in my small successes, a school poetry prize, the show-jumping competitions, that sort of thing. She wanted me to snare someone with a title and a stately home."

Flora had never talked to her like this. Lydia thought of the eager, vulnerable child in those photographs. There, above the brasserie, caught in the leather-bound photograph album, her mother was a different person altogether. She wondered if she dared mention them.

"Why didn't Eveline see through all that? She was so intelligent."

"Being beautiful is a curse, Lydia, it restricts your life. Everything else gets smothered. She was put on a pedestal by flattery, fixed like a butterfly on a pin in a collector's tray. It was only when she got older that people began to treat her like a normal person. It took her a long time to stop being nothing but a beauty. Everything – except beauty of course – came to her too late."

Lydia stared at her. She wanted to put out her hands and take Flora's across the table. Flora had rarely touched her.

"No one expects a mad woman to understand what's going on around her. I like your playwright, by the way. He's very percep- tive. I suppose you have to be something like that to be a successful playwright."

"'My' playwright? Arthur? He's Eveline's playwright. What do you know about him?"

"He's been up to see me. Brought me some photographs to look at. He and the Poet came together. We had a long chat ... about Eveline."

"What?"

Lydia opened her eyes wide, as though there was something she was failing to see.

"It was his idea to bring you here."

She dimly remembered Arthur and the Poet putting her into Flora's Land Rover and giving her something to make her sleep. Flora, the mother who had never cared for her when she was a child, who never went further than the auction mart in Carlisle, had driven fifty miles to Marvin's funeral and brought her back here.

"I thought you hardly saw Eveline after..."

"No. That's not right. She only set foot on the farm in emergen- cies, my emergencies I should say, but she used to summon me to meet her in Carlisle. She caught the train from London, strode into the Station Hotel, and demanded a table by the window. I would see her, through the glass, in her silks and cashmeres, patting her hair, as I ran along the pavement in my muddy boots. She brought clothes for you – Griselda's cast-offs, I suppose, delicate things I would never have thought of getting you. She was always generous with money. Even in the worst times she tried to help ... Till she took you away from me."

Flora got up from the table. She put on the kettle. She busied herself measuring tea leaves, warming the teapot, arranging the cups and saucers and getting the milk bottle out of the fridge.

Lydia couldn't leave it any longer. She feared that she might even now tip her mother over the edge, but she had to ask the questions. She needed the missing pieces if she was ever to put her life back together again.

She went over to her and picked up her mother's limp arms. "Put your arms around me, Mother. Hug me. I need your help."

Flora stiffened. After a while she seemed to get the idea and put her arms slowly around Lydia's shoulders. Lydia wanted to cry. The skin on her mother's cheeks was rough and slightly mottled, the lines on her forehead deeper than she remembered. Flora was barely forty. She looked both younger and older. To Lydia, she was both beautiful and haunted.

They sat down at the table again. The clock on the mantelpiece struck eleven. Their tea had cooled. The wind howled off the estuary and whistled under the door. Cigarette smoke mingled with the smoking of the fire in the grate.

"Why? Why has it been so awful?" Lydia asked. "I need to know. You must explain. You must talk about my father."

"You can't change anything by talking about it."

"Still, it's time to do it. For my sake."

"You know the story, Lydia."

"I don't. Only bits and pieces. And the gossip. I want to hear it from you. Properly. All of it. Tonight."

"I fell in love too deeply with your father. That's all there is to tell."

Lydia knew that. The crinkly dark hair, the blue eyes, the Celtic colouring. The jaunty air, the intense locked-in smile. There was a single photograph of him, sellotaped to the wall in the scullery, curling up at the edges. Lydia had stared at it as she rubbed soap into horses' saddles as a child.

"I was younger than you, Lydie. I'd never met anyone like him. And I would never have met him if I hadn't gone to that party on that particular day. It was my fate. He didn't even know the people. Someone brought him along. That happened quite a lot in the war. People on leave went round in packs to feel secure."

Lydia knew all this. Flora had met him on a Saturday and run away with him the following Monday and never returned to her mother's roof.

"Eveline got hold of the farm to keep me from prying eyes. Here on the Solway Firth there was no danger of her pregnant daughter running into her fancy friends. In those days an illegitimate child..."

Lydia knew all this too. Aunt Patience's oft-repeated warning ringing in her ears.

Each time Flora told the story, Lydia found out a little more. There were clues if you listened carefully. But never enough to explain the cloud that had hung over her childhood.

"He came back to marry me. I was seven months pregnant."

Lydia couldn't look at her mother's face.

"He left again before D-Day. He wrote to me saying that things were moving, that it would all be over soon." Flora hesitated. "Then nothing. Then nothing. Then you. Then other people's menfolk drifting home."

Lydia lit herself another cigarette, drawing the smoke deeply into her lungs as though it were anaesthetic.

"The telegram – 'Missing, presumed dead'. A month after you were born. I couldn't bear to look at you. So pitiful and small. He'd never even met you. No connection between the two of you. You only made sense as part of being with him. It felt as though I could have him or you, but not both. And I wanted him. I felt that you weren't safe with me. So I handed you over to someone else."

"It's OK, Mother. Nowadays it's got a name. It's called a nervous breakdown."

"The people here didn't call it that."

"They're quite common in London. Fashionable nowadays."

"They said: 'Poor Flora. So young. Such a shock. She's having trouble getting over it. So cut off from her family. So sensitive. But it's no excuse. She shouldn't neglect that child.'"

"Most of the time you managed. The farm and everything..."

"Peace came to me from the animals, the coats of the horses, the snuffling and nudging, the upturned snouts of the pigs at the gate."

"Poor Mother. I understand all that. But the bit we've never talked about. The men."

Flora was silent. Lydia focused on the cigarette in her fingers. Eventually she stood up.

"Look. You owe me an explanation. Think what it was like for me. You running away after the rabbit man. The gypsy with the horses. The time you disappeared into the mist along the Firth after the waiter. I thought you would drown."

"It's too difficult to explain, Lydia." Flora lit another cigarette with the stub of the unfinished one, her hands shaking. "I'm sorry, of course. But I couldn't help it."

Lydia stood up and paced up and down the kitchen.

"You have to tell me. I need to understand. Is it an illness? Are you a nymphomaniac, like people say? I'm worrying that it's inheritable. That I might be like you. Is it in my blood or something? Am I going to sleep with the next man I like the look of? With Marvin barely cold in his grave?"

He wasn't in a grave, of course. The thought of him reduced to ashes was unbearable. She turned on her mother in her anguish.

"You owe it to me. Don't you see?"

"Oh, Lydia. Sit down, for Christ's sake. I can't stand all this pacing up and down."

Flora laid her hands palms upwards on the table.

"How can I make you understand? It wasn't every man I liked the look of. It wasn't that." She glanced at the ring on her left hand. She stared at her upturned right hand as though it was all written in her lifeline. She sighed. She pushed her hair back from her face and at last looked at Lydia. "One dark night…

"One dark winter night, months after I got the telegram … I was upstairs … I heard the outside door banging. No one locks their doors around here, you know that. You leave it on the latch for the lost stranger."

Flora covered her eyes with her hands.

"A wild black night, like this. A problem with the generator and only a lantern."

She twisted her hands together.

"I came downstairs. The flame light flickering, throwing shadows on the wall. I pulled aside the old curtain, you know the one, with the blue stripes on it…"

There was a long pause before she continued. "And there he was, Rio, my love, your father, Rio Renfrew … Rio, leaning against the stove, eyes fixed upon me. I thought he was a ghost. He was looking at me with a hard look, like a stranger. I whispered to him to tell me whether he was a ghost or not. He just kept leaning against the Rayburn. Like something out of Shakespeare. Then he spoke. 'You have to search for me, Flora, you have to find me. It's up to you to claim me. To bring us together again.' His expression never changed. I must have collapsed or fainted. When I came round, he had gone. Afterwards, after the shock, the breakdown or whatever they called it, people said that I had imagined it. I couldn't be sure whether he had really been there or a voice from beyond the grave."

At first, her mother used to run over the sand dunes in her nightie, calling out Rio's name. Lydia had been told about that, had come to accept it, it hadn't seemed so unnatural, just a dangerous habit on a starless night with an incoming tide. Over the last few days Lydia had felt like doing it herself, crying out for Marvin. As though after all she shared something else with her mother.

Flora continued more calmly now.

"So I searched for him. The first time I thought I saw him was among the gypsies at the Kendal Horse Fair. Then it was the rabbit man. Then..." – she hesitated, and almost smiled – "then the beautiful Rumanian... Something about each of them. The colour of his eyes or his smile. Do you understand? I thought he wanted me to find him and claim him."

Flora got up and poked the fire. It blazed furiously and she fed it a couple of logs.

"And Aidan?" Lydia sighed. "You seduced my own boyfriend." How could she have done that? She didn't need to ask the question out loud. She understood now. The dark curly hair and blue eyes. Even Aunt Patience had noticed it. "He could be your father as a young man. Strange, these attractions." Her own mother seducing the university boyfriend she had taken to Wester Ross that summer. The one who said, "If you won't go to bed with me, Lydia, I know someone who will."

"It's all over now. It will never happen again. It has played itself out, Lydia. Death. Death broke the spell. A real death. Your lover cold in a coffin, your lover who could not possibly be Rio. And you on the floor of the crematorium." She paused. "I am a mother now. Too late. Too late."

Lydia swayed in her chair, then got to her feet unsteadily. She listened to the chains that had constrained her as they rattled to the kitchen floor.

# Chapter 32

A jangling noise came from the front porch. Mother and daughter raised their heads and looked at each other. Up till then, both had kept their eyes lowered, unable to face the raw emotion on the other's face, the dark-haired one with purple rings under her eyes and the red-haired one with the windblown forehead and the bewildered lines each side of her mouth.

"What on earth is that?" asked Lydia.

There was another bellow from the hall.

"It's the telephone, Lydia. Don't you recognise it? Your grand-mother made the Post Office people install one with an extra loud ring. So I could hear it from the yard and actually answer it."

"*I*'ve never heard it before."

"I've hardly heard it myself. For a moment I didn't know what it was."

They listened in wonder to the third set of jangles, as though to a child prodigy playing a concert piece in a next-door room.

"It won't be for me, Lydie. No one rings me. Neighbours come and sit in the kitchen if they want to talk. And your grandmother sends me postcards."

"She's dead, Mother."

"I know she's dead. I'm still getting used to the idea."

"Ah well. It's stopped now. How nice and peaceful." They took up their glasses of whisky in unison. And smiled.

There was the slight slurping sound of their drinking, the tick of the mantelpiece clock and the intermittent howling of the wind in the estuary.

The telephone rang again.

"Lydia, someone's dead. It can only be death or disaster when it keeps on ringing like that. You answer it."

Lydia thought about ignoring it again. The world beyond this kitchen didn't seem real. Then she ran through to the front porch, dived under the pile of coats on the window seat and snatched it up.

"Lydia. Lydia, is that you? You sound so distant."

"I'm a long way away, Mathew."

"I can hear the wind clearer than you."

"There's a south-westerly."

"How are you, dearest cousin? I've rung you several times."

"And I haven't spoken to you?"

"Don't you remember? After the funeral? You sounded drugged, actually. But now it's about the brasserie."

"I thought it might be. Please can you keep it ticking over till ... till I come back." She had no idea what she meant by that. Weeks? Months? Was she ever going to go back?

"It's been a while, Lydia. You can't go into a decline. It'd be good for you to come back. And it's really urgent. A journalist wants to come and write up The Brasserie. The awful patronising one. But he's bringing a real restaurant review person with him."

"You and Martha can deal with him. Much better than I can."

"No, Lydia. That's not fair to us. You should be here. The brasserie is *your* business. Someone told him about Sexy Fridays and he's coming this week." He paused. "He's booked in and it is time for you to come back."

Lydia looked at the holes in the sleeves of her sweater, the blisters on her hands. She swept her hand over her shorn hair and sighed.

"Oh, Mathew, I don't think I can..."

"You must, Lydia. The style, the mood ... it all depends on you. It's like a piece of theatre. You have to do it."

"I'm not a performance artist. And my hair. I … seem to have … chopped most of it off with the sheep shears. You can't imagine what I look like, Mathew. I can't be seen for a while."

"My God, Lydia. Are you OK?"

"No. Of course not."

There was a long silence the other end.

"Listen to me. You've still got to come. Gran Eveline trusted in your spirit. This is a big chance for us. Get a hairpiece. Everyone wears them nowadays."

Lydia laughed. It came out like a croak. She'd forgotten how to laugh.

"In Carlisle? Have you ever been to Carlisle?"

She felt the naked bit at the back of her neck and shivered.

"Can't you put him off?"

"He'll go somewhere else and forget all about us. Just come back. I'll get you a beautiful wig. I'm telling you. I'm not putting this off."

Lydia took a deep breath.

"How much time do we have? What day is it today? No. Of course not. Pigs don't distinguish between weekdays and weekends. Don't be silly. I'm still just about capable of reading a train timetable. Look. Check the menu for Friday, will you. See if you can think up something a bit unusual. Has to sound French. Yes. Good idea. And talk to Martha. No. I'll do that when I arrive. OK? And, Mathew, I do need you to come to the wig shop with me. Oh, and thank you."

She put the telephone back on its cradle and stood there, staring out of the tall window for some time, wrapping the black night around herself.

*  *  *

The London train rattled along. The windows of her compartment were streaked with ancient rain, and opaque with dirt. The chance of love was slipping away, like the unseen countryside streaming past. She had lost so much – Marvin, Eveline, her steady civil service job. Two people loved and disappointed. A serious job started but discarded. What was left? Auriol, who might never forgive her. Arthur, the strange perceptive playwright who had sent her back to her mother. The Poet, who was going to give poetry readings at the brasserie. The brasserie itself.

Marvin didn't die because Lydia failed to be there for the pigeons' wedding. It just happened that he had this impossible illness. Eveline didn't die because Lydia disappointed her, though it sometimes seemed like that.

She lit a cigarette. There were five stubs spilling out of the ashtray. She let the smoke rise through her wrecked thoughts. Poor Flora had had a very hard time. It wasn't her fault that she had loved someone who was taken away by war. That she hadn't had anything to fall back on. Her mother had been afflicted by despair all those years, not nymphomania. Lydia thought about how she had been scared of throwing herself into Marvin's arms, scared that passion, once ignited, would envelop her, pursue her in and out of office meetings and at bus stops and along dark streets at night. If she turned out to have an uncontrollable appetite for sex, it would not be inherited. It would be her own. She lay back against the rough fabric of the seat and blew smoke rings up to the ceiling, the burden of Flora floating away in the cigarette smoke.

Lydia wanted to stop thinking, to see something, to see out of the window. She used her scarf to clean a patch of glass and there were primroses littering the soot-covered banks of the railway cuttings and pale green catkins bending in the wind. Shoots of spring grass coloured the lower ridges of the Lakeland hills, and passing Shap she thought perhaps she caught a glimpse of the rooftops of High Fell Farm and the row of pigeon lofts stretching boldly up the ridge behind it.

* * *

Nothing had changed. There was the blue velvet curtain, the familiar little Matisse-like chairs, the pale wood floor that she'd insisted on
putting down over the flagstones, the frames of the mirrors painted
racing green by Mathew. And there was Martha, backlit by coloured
bottles, running a cloth along the bar.

"Oh, Lydia," said Martha, flinging her arms round her. "It's not
been the same without you. Are you all right?"

"I can't talk about me. Not yet. But what's going on with you,
Martha? You look tired."

"Problems at the other place – them blokes I told you about.
Blackmailing me to come back. Later. Not now."

"I should be here to look after you, Martha. Just wait. I'm sorting
it all out. As soon as we've dealt with this dinner."

Something *had* changed. The brasserie seemed to have settled into
itself while she was away. It felt less temporary.

"Something's different, Martha. What is it? Or is it me?"

"The pictures on the wall over there. That Arthur put them up
himself. Said it shows that we take trouble with the detail. Which we
haven't, have we, so far? *They're* different, they are. Pretty and give me
the shivers at the same time."

"Where's Arthur?" Lydia walked over to the pictures, running her
eye along them, all four of them, snake-like roots and sprouting leaves.
Deformed and beautiful. The Bat Plant. The Bleeding Tooth Fungus.
The White Egret Flower. The Mandrake Root.

"That journalist that's coming. Your stuck-up cousin's friend. The
one you asked to leave. Mathew said we must get new plates to impress
him." Martha laughed at the memory, looking young and pixie-like
again. "But he's bringing someone serious. One of them blokes who
write about 'Swinging London'. For that magazine."

"The *Sunday Times*?"

"That's the one. The one where they all swan around on expenses
with fashion photographers. We have to be well prepared."

"My money's on you, Martha."

"No, Lydia. This time it's up to you to reel them in. Lordy, Lordy. What *have* you done to your hair?"

* * *

Dave Perry turned up. It was the first time she'd seen him since the funeral. Lydia didn't know whether to be pleased or horrified.

"You have to give it a name, Lydia. A name in lights has to involve a name. 'The Brasserie' is like 'The Corner Caff'. What *have* you done to your hair?"

Lydia was wearing a shoulder-length wig, not quite the pond-dark colour of her own hair, a bit too auburn, a bit too like her mother and grandmother, she thought. But it was the best they could find.

"Take it off at once," said Dave. "You should have gone to my friend Vidal, 'the man with the magic comb'. He'd love you. You could have started a new fashion. I suppose it's too late for that now. But really, this won't do. It's not you at all. You look like one of those pert little dolly-bird TV researchers. Don't cry." He put his arms round her. He'd never touched her before. "I'm only horrible to you because Marvin loved you more than he loved me."

Lydia wondered who loved Dave, really loved him, and what about his family? She must find out sometime. You could run away from your family, but you couldn't escape them altogether.

"Martha," Dave said, as though he owned the place, "can you get me the kitchen scissors? Lydia, get on this bar stool."

"I'd tell you to get them yourself, Mr David Perry, if we had more time," said Martha. "And we've got a name for the brasserie, I'll have you know, and Mathew's out the back there now, painting a sign."

"Sit still, Lydia. What is it then, Martha? What've you dreamt up?"

"Ha ha. It's called The Mandrake."

"The picture..." said Lydia.

"Good sound to it," said Dave. "But what's the connection?"

"I thought you'd know," said Martha, "with your encyclopaedic knowledge of drugs and things."

Dave Perry combed Lydia's hair forward over her forehead and cut a slanting fringe.

"A mandrake, my dear, is a plant with narcotic properties," Dave intoned. "With a root thought to resemble the human form and to shriek when plucked. It's said to be an aphrodisiac, a soporific and an anaesthetic. Murderous and magical."

"Just the ticket, don't you think?" said Martha.

All this had happened while Lydia had been away on the Solway Firth. They seemed to have a new confidence and authority, all of them. Lydia could hand over the whole operation to Trevor and Martha, and go back to the Solway Firth and her grief.

"'The mandrake is a Mediterranean plant. Legend has it that it springs from the blood and semen of a hanged man and when pulled from the ground it lets out a monstrous scream and kills all within earshot…','" intoned Lydia from memory. "Whoever thought that was a good idea?"

"Our friend, Mr Playwright Shortcross, of course…" said Martha.

"Does he want you to drug your customers? I'm up for that," said Dave. "For fuck's sake, Lydia, keep still."

"The pictures belonged to my grandmother." Lydia pointed to the row of drawings. "She hated them because they were so strange. But she kept them because the person who did them was a famous botanist and some relation. She put them in the front hall where no one would notice them, she said, because they were all too busy looking at themselves in the mirror by the front door. I love them and they remind me of her. Where is Arthur, anyway?"

"He's somewhere around. He's been worrying about you."

"The Greeks called the mandrake root 'the love apple of the ancients'. Hang on. I haven't finished with you. Sit *still*, Lydia, will you."

"You look amazing, Lydia," said Martha. "Look at yourself in all the mirrors."

* * *

They discussed the menu for the journalists. They decided that it must impress them with its cool cosmopolitanism and originality. Lydia wanted it to be as French as possible.

"We'll keep coq au vin on the menu," said Trevor. "To satisfy the regulars. And some fish. Fish on Fridays. What, though? Sole is so Wilton Place."

"Cockles and mussels," suggested Martha.

"Moules marinières."

"Quenelles de brochet," said Dave.

"*Too* sophisticated. How'd we get pike at short notice anyway? Think simple."

It was late. They were huddled round the radiator under the window, the table strewn with coffee cups and cigarette ends. Dave was still here.

Lydia remembered the trout in a little hill village in France. Memories of Marvin kept wrapping themselves round her heart like the tentacles of an octopus.

"Trout and almonds? Sea trout."

Trevor approved. "But they have to be river fresh."

"We'll get them from the River Esk in Cumberland. A consignment off the night train…" Her mother might be involved.

"Very simple. Grilled. With sage and almonds. And a lot of butter. Why not?" Trevor grinned. "I like it."

"Good. At least sea trout is right pink. I hate that whiteness of fish," said Martha. "Friday convent school lunches. Slimy and white."

"The only thing that stops me converting to Catholicism, Martha," said Dave. "Pallid fish on a Friday."

"Dave, honestly…"

"We need a new starter too. Something unexpected," said Martha. "That people will talk about. It doesn't matter if it's disgusting."

"Something shocking and disgusting. Anybody?"

"I once had garlic soup in the Pyrenees."

"Whenever were you in the Pyrenees, Trevor?" said Dave. "I didn't know they let you out of the kitchen."

"I went to Biarritz with Joel and we walked into the Pyrenees."

"Where is Joel anyway? We need him to come."

Lydia was grateful for their liveliness. "But we've got to get on. There's only two days to go. I think garlic soup is a brilliant idea. If they aren't brave enough to try it, we can taunt them with it."

"Don't worry," said Martha, "I will recommend it most strongly. And most times I get my way with the customers."

Everyone laughed. Few dared to disobey Martha.

There would be mushrooms à la greque as well. Just in case.

"You can be part of Friday's team, Dave, if you like? We could do with help behind the bar. In case, you know, Didier decides not to turn up."

"Will I be paid? I'm running out of bread, man."

# Chapter 33

The tables were filling up. Lydia breathed more calmly. Martha tripped about, lilting footsteps, greeting and recommending. All over again, Lydia watched in wonder as she took the orders without a pad, perfect recall replacing literacy. She was reminded of Marvin, his dyslexic determination, bent over the paperwork of farming. The sense of loss took her breath away. She stood behind the bar with Dave, watching. She insisted that he stayed behind the bar.

The Poet edged through the velvet curtains, uneasy in a crumpled jacket, and limped over to Arthur's table.

"Who's that?" asked Dave. "With Arthur Shortcross."

"I didn't know you knew Arthur."

"One of those 'Angry Young Men'. The real thing, though. Proper working-class background. Invited to all the cool parties. *Thirteen Years* was raw, man. Good songs in it too."

She hadn't seen *Thirteen Years*, although it had been on at the Playhouse in Oxford. But Dave had seen it somewhere. Dave always managed to surprise her.

"There. Over there. The tall sandy-haired bloke who's sitting with him."

"Oh, him. Maelrubha MacKenzie – the Poet, who does those basement readings."

"For Christ's sake. The Poet. The Philanderer. They're real people, you know. You can't call them all by their professions."

"Since when was philandering a profession, Dave? I'm determined to find out what his real job is. But he's cagey. The Poet is an old friend of mine, my only respectable family friend. He's my mother's godson. He loves her one hundred per cent."

"All roads lead back to your mother, Lydia."

"Not any more, Dave. I've just taken my first steps away from her. So drop the subject. OK? I'll introduce you to the Poet later. Concentrate on the liqueurs now. That's your orders and I'm in charge here. Sell as many as you can. Poire William. Curaçao. Armagnac. They often order liqueurs on a Friday. Work finished for the week."

"You've really grown up, little Lydia."

"Shut up, Dave, and get on with the job."

Lydia wondered whether the Philanderer would come. He preferred Mondays, when there was less risk of being seen. But sometimes he came on Friday lunchtime. She wanted him to be here, with his "someone important in the higher reaches of government" appearance, and a glamorous "doing a bit of modelling" girlfriend. She didn't want him to be exposed, supposing he had a wife and children somewhere out in the Home Counties, but then again, what wonderful publicity it would be. She imagined being questioned by the *Daily Express*, giving away a few morsels – "Oh yes, he's a regular of ours and yes, he always sits at the same table in the corner". Would she really do that? Did she care enough about the success of The Mandrake to compromise her principles?

Cousin Griselda had booked a table for four. She leant over the bar and kissed Dave Perry, slowly and with evident delight. Ha. That's how Dave had known that something was up at the brasserie. Could there really be something between Griselda and Dave? Should Henry Sturridge be worried? Lydia had spent too much of her life being worried. Henry Sturridge could look after himself.

Gingham tablecloths like the French Club, shining wine glasses, huge pale-grey dinner plates Trevor had picked up in Portobello Road. Deliberately mismatched glasses. Cool.

The journalists arrived.

"Will you accept my apologies?" said Jamie Cyrus, bowing to Lydia in an exaggerated way. "I underestimated you last time. And my friend was really rude."

He was fat and slightly sweaty, jovial and slightly anxious this time. Lydia could always spot anxiety.

"You're very welcome. We reserved that table for you but Griselda is a step ahead. Over here. Martha will bring you the menu."

He introduced his companion, the *Sunday Times* magazine person, who kissed Lydia's hand. "My respects," he said. "People keep telling me to come here."

He was short and slight and sleek-haired and hungry-looking and dressed in a handmade suit. Adam Faith without the guitar, Lydia thought. He strutted between the tables as though his entitlement came through his masculinity. His small stature offset by a large penis and oversized expense account. Lydia disliked him at once, feeling quite well-disposed towards Jamie.

Martha persuaded them to try the garlic soup and both ordered trout. Lydia breathed a sigh of relief. No demands for something outside the menu. Not yet at least. She left them to Martha.

The old lady who came on Mondays sidled up to her, asking whether it was a waste of a table to give her one. Lydia told her it was an honour to have her any day and especially today. She raised the tone. And would she please try the trout? Small, roundish, grey hair in a wispy sort of bun, and dressed to be unremarkable; you might have failed to notice her on a crowded pavement. But seated firmly at the little corner table, she looked like the queen of the proceedings, eyes sparkling, and filled with curiosity.

There was a rush of a youngish crowd and Lydia missed the arrival of the faithful Philanderer. She laughed at that idea. But there he was, sitting at his usual table, once again with the actress who had accosted Auriol a few months ago. Where was Auriol? She'd like her to be here today. She wanted to thank her ... for what exactly? For looking after the farm and for loving Marvin so much. Where was she? Was it true that she had been arrested?

Today it was Lydia who went over to the Philanderer's table to take their order. Martha was concentrating on the journalists.

With a languid gesture, he asked her: "Who is the small blond man at the table in the middle?"

She told him he was from the *Sunday Times*. She thought it proper to warn him.

He laid a caressing hand on her arm. "Do me a favour, would you, Lydia?" He knew her name, but none of them knew his. "See if you can find out his name for me."

She wasn't sure if that was acceptable. "We're quite busy today, but I'll do what I can."

He looked up at her sharply. He wasn't used to restaurant staff treating him with anything other than obsequiousness. He spread a bit of pâté on a piece of French bread and put it suggestively into the actress's mouth. Presumably garlic soup would interfere with their after-lunch plans.

Something was out of order. It was Dave. He was there behind the bar, where he should be, looking perfect in his French philosopher black polo-neck sweater. A couple of hard men were leaning on the bar. Why were they there? This wasn't a pub. The bar was for show, not for customers who obviously weren't going to pay for a meal. It wasn't there to lounge against at lunchtime and make trouble. Perhaps they were waiting for a table. But they didn't look as though they wanted lunch. She moved towards them and they were gone.

"Who were they, Dave? Those two who just left."

"Them. They were just asking their way."

She knew he was lying. "But you served them something? I saw you. I don't want to encourage people to prop up the bar."

"Got it, beautiful boss lady."

The journalists pulled out a chair and asked her if she would answer some questions.

They talked about the food, the French influence. "Too few genuine brasseries in London. We need more."

Lydia began to warm to the *Sunday Times* bloke.

"I didn't catch your name," she said, fluttering her eyelashes just a little. "I'd like to read your stuff."

He simpered.

"Freddie Mulholland, at your service. Nice touch, the garlic soup. May I call you Lydia? And tell me, what sort of people do you want to attract as customers?"

"Well. Not the West End set, slumming it in Notting Hill. I don't want the braying of posh voices. People who think they own the place."

"That's me out then," said Griselda cheerfully.

"Oh, Griselda, you're welcome any time. You know you are." Lydia meant that nowadays. Griselda was turning out to be human after all. "Fridays are usually quite busy, Freddie, but Mondays, it's a different group altogether. Do you know the magazine 'The New Generation'? They have their editorial meetings here on Mondays."

"So you're a proper little leftie at heart, are you?"

Not that patronising line. But she must keep up the flirting.

"Actually, I just want an interesting mix. People who don't fit the conventional mould."

"Who's that man over in the corner, there? With the actress, Maria Montecelli," asked Freddie.

"They come quite often." Perhaps she shouldn't have said that. But she was determined he should think that the brasserie, The Mandrake, was successful.

"I can only see the back of his head but he looks vaguely familiar. What's his name?"

"I don't know his name, I'm afraid. He always pays in cash."

"Ways and means, Lydia. Does he hang up his coat? I'll go to the Gents and have a good look at him and his pockets."

Clandestine meals were riskier in cold weather, she noted, because you have to hang up your coat.

The Poet was waving at her.

"The garlic soup was a triumph, Lydia. Well done. Very grown-up meal."

"And the trout," said Arthur. "But the bouillabaisse is still my favourite."

"Come back on Monday at lunchtime, then. We can talk. I'd like to hear how you're doing with my grandfather's letters."

"Any time, Lydia." She picked up a tremor of urgency, but there was no time to think about that. Freddie Mulholland, the *Sunday Times* journalist, scraped back his chair and leapt to his feet with a shriek.

Lydia rushed over to their table.

Hardly able to speak for laughter, Jamie Cyrus explained.

"Calm down, everybody. It's all OK. Freddie here bet me he could identify blindfold any liqueur served in this bar. I had a word with the waitress and asked her to bring him a glass of the most expensive one she could find."

He'd smelt it and sipped it and looked puzzled. Eventually he realised he'd lost the bet and asked to see the bottle.

"And then I saw this. And I'd been *drinking* it…"

"The Marc de Viper," she laughed.

There in a curvaceous bell-shaped bottle, coiled in pale liquid, was a whole viper, staring out at the restaurant critic with its sapphire-blue eyes.

"I've never come across that before. Marc de Viper. I must say it's delicious. Where does it come from?"

"It's very rare. I'm afraid I can't reveal my suppliers."

Actually, it had been in the brasserie when she'd inherited it. She'd forgotten all about it. Well done, Martha.

"Lydia." Trevor marched over to her between the tables. Everyone looked up, forks, coffee cups, cigarettes poised at their lips. "I think you should come over to the bar. There's a man with a knife."

He had huge shoulders and a crew cut. A kitchen knife lay on the bar.

"Can I help you?" asked Lydia.

"I'm not moving an inch till this fucker give ova the stuff he's been selling. This is my patch. I tell you I'll kill him if he don't."

* * *

The journalists paid their bill and left. The Philanderer slipped out through the back door without waiting for his, but handed Trevor a pile of used pound notes. More than the cost of the meal, as he must have known. Hush money. "Wages of sin" maybe.

Arthur and the Poet lingered.

"Better than any theatre," said Arthur.

Mathew, Trevor and Martha joined them, little glasses of Marc de Viper still scattered over the table among the ashtrays. Martha kicked off her shoes. Dave Perry leant with his elbows on the bar, his expression impossible to decipher.

"How could you do that to me, Dave? Deal drugs in front of those journalists."

Lydia put money into the jukebox, as she always did when she was upset or angry. Better than taking a bite out of someone, she thought. *Take These Chains from My Heart* filled the room. She had colour in her cheeks, a high, hectic colour. Grief inside, a torture that left no visible bruising.

"A friend of Lucky Gordon's, Lydia. Big Phil. Really hard core. No choice. Had to play it cool."

Dave sounded almost contrite.

"It wasn't me he was looking for anyway. It was Didier. Wouldn't believe I wasn't him. It didn't help that those two blokes had come in earlier to sell me something. It's the area, Lydia. You have to get used to it. There's a lot of it about."

Lydia wanted to trust Dave, but she had no idea whether she could. It was one of those cases where only time would tell.

He started rolling a spliff.

Lydia laid her head on her arms on the table, the haircut sliding over one eye.

"Come on," Dave insisted, "the journalists loved it. It won't do you any harm."

"We'll be closed down, Dave. Just when we're doing so well. I can't believe you did that."

"Think how Marvin would have enjoyed it, Lydia. It would have given him so much pleasure. It was his mission to stop you being serious."

Lydia smiled.

"Perhaps he is still hovering over us," she said, "not yet ready to depart. All this conjured up by his spirit – the journalists, Big Phil and the knife on the counter, the Philanderer unmasked with his mistress, and even the Marc de Viper." She put her head back down on her arms. "Oh, Dave, I miss him so."

# Chapter 34

Arthur went to the brasserie the next day, although it was Saturday. There was no one there except Lydia, just as he'd hoped. She looked exhausted, dark shadows under her beautiful eyes.

He'd held her, almost insensible, in the chapel after Marvin's coffin had disappeared into the flames. He'd taken charge of her, wrapped her in a blanket and delivered her to a young red-haired woman on a wind-blown pig farm – to Flora, her mother, unaware how neatly he was reversing the way Eveline had taken Lydia away from her ten years earlier.

Now he longed to be able to hold her again.

"Did you see this, Lydia? Freddie Mulholland has written something about the brasserie already. Here, look. He seems to write for the *Evening News* as well as the *Sunday Times*."

He showed her a paragraph in the gossip column:

"Swinging Hornbeam Road. Have you discovered it yet? Stray a few hundred yards off trendy Portobello Road, and you will find the aptly named Mandrake, a magical and dangerous French-style brasserie run by twenty-one-year-old, black-haired, Vidal-cut, long-legged, short-skirted Lydia Renfrew, whose cousin is the delectable Griselda Ashfield. A delicious destination hideaway for pin-striped high-ups and their actress mistresses and dodgy dealers doing business over the bar in plain sight. Open weekdays, lunch and evening. Excitement guaranteed. And that's not all. Interesting, well-cooked French dishes, a halfway decent wine list and immaculate service. Reservations recommended."

Lydia read it through several times without saying anything.

"It's OK, Lydia," he insisted. "No publicity is bad publicity. As they say at the advertising agency."

He wanted to take her hand.

"Except when the police close it down. Don't patronise me, Mr Playwright, I may be naïve, but the reference to drugs won't do us any good. And I bet we've scared the Philanderer away."

"Your grandmother used to call me 'Mr Playwright', Lydia. People will flock here. If only to see the scene of the crime."

"It's all very well for *you*. Why should you care?"

Oh, Lydia. If only you knew.

"The telephone never stops ringing. The wrong sort of people keep turning up at the door asking for Lucky Gordon and Christine Keeler. But I'm so grateful to you, Arthur, for getting rid of Big Phil yesterday. Thank heavens you were here. Even Dave was frightened."

"I've had a bit of practice in Burnley, Lydia. Violence was all we had to amuse us."

"But he was so huge…"

"Speed," he said. "That's the secret."

She examined his hands on the table, his pale, ink-stained fingers. He could see that she was wondering how he could threaten anyone. How could she know that he would lay down his life to protect her? And how much easier to write that in a script than to say it out loud.

"I keep having to say thank you to you, don't I? You arranged for my mother to come to Marvin's funeral. And to take me home. My childhood home, I mean. That was … a good thing to do."

"She's had a hard time, Flora."

He realised he knew that before she did. She was really looking at him now, wondering about him.

"How can I thank you, Arthur?"

"I wouldn't mind a glass of the liqueur with the snake in it. If you pressed me."

"Marc de Viper for breakfast. What an inspired idea. Perfect lift to the spirits. We'll both have some. There's just enough left."

The snake was curled up at the bottom of the bottle, barely covered. It seemed cruel somehow, to steal away its remaining liquid. Its wide-open sapphire eyes looked lifelike and alarmed.

He held the bottle up to the light and studied it. "What happens to it now? Can you refill the bottle with ordinary brandy?"

"I was wondering that myself. Metaphor for something. But I think we should try. We may need some again, don't you think? It's so nice that you're a friend of the Poet."

"He's my only friend at Martel and Tillotson, the advertising agency. The only modest, grown-up person there."

"Why are you doing advertising? How do you have time? And read Lionel's letters? And write plays?"

Arthur didn't answer straight away. He studied the bottle, as though the answer to her question was in the eyes of a viper marinated in brandy.

"Perhaps I should try the world of advertising myself," she said. "I'll be looking for a new job if the police close us down."

"You have to fight on. For Eveline's sake. She must have left you the brasserie for a reason. Whatever she might have thought about the drug dealers, she would have liked the drama."

He shifted in the little pine chair. If he let himself look into Lydia's eyes he would be undone.

"Lydia. I've got to tell you something."

"Oh, good. Something scandalous? In the papers upstairs? Take my mind off the police."

"No. It's not like that. It's time I told you the truth."

She tipped the last of the Viper into her glass, the snake sliding towards the neck of the bottle as though it might follow the dregs of liqueur. He watched, fascinated. He drained his own glass. There was nothing like a shot of the Viper with your morning coffee.

"Do playwrights deal in the truth? I thought all dialogue was meant to be lies. Oh, Arthur, do you mind, I think I've had enough of facing up to the truth lately."

Her distress upset him. He reached across the table and took her hands. How slight and bony they were. How pronounced her knuckles. He turned them over and saw the blisters.

"That's pig farming for you. It's hard work." He was glad to hear her laugh.

"When I met your grandmother, I couldn't write," he said. "I hadn't been able to write a word for more than a year. I thought I would never write again."

Lydia sat up and looked at him.

"It's called writer's block." It still made him shiver just to say the words. "Eveline saved me from despair. She made me feel interesting. And she entrusted me with her hopes and fears. And so she changed my life." He paused. "An old lady from a completely different background, wanting to talk to me, spend time with me and go to the theatre with me. She was trying to understand what modern playwrights are trying to convey. To understand the changes around her through the theatre, through something she loved."

"I thought she wanted to shut out new ideas."

"No, that's not right. She was frightened of them. If only there had been more time, she might have come round to…" To what? To Marvin? He paused again, looking at Lydia's hands in his. "I came to love her. I loved her… like… Not a grandmother. My own grandmother smelt of cabbage soup. She brought a litany of complaints into our house and offloaded them on us. The other one, Nana, Dad's mother, I loved her. But she was just a photograph in a lacy collar."

Somehow he found himself telling her about the deaths of his mother and father, his powerlessness in the face of pain and random hospital treatment, the shock of the stroke on the kitchen floor.

She clasped his fingers.

"No. Eveline wasn't like a grandmother to me. It's odd to say it, but she was more like a muse. A beautiful muse."

Lydia fought back tears. "It's so sad. There was so much I didn't say to Eveline."

He nodded. Much later he would tell Lydia how he had taken Eveline in his arms when he realised she was dying. How it was more than he'd managed with his own mother. How many things are learnt too late.

A mere couple of feet between them, the air filled with agitation and tumult.

"Eveline blasted her way through my writer's block, like one of those drain cleaners. She begged me, with tears in her eyes. What she really wanted me to do was to write a play about her family, make it all end well." He turned Lydia's hands palm upwards and looked at them as though he could see her destiny. He saw Lydia's violet eyes light up.

"A new play. And that's what you've been doing up there."

"Lionel's letters were only a cover story. Going through those papers. All Eveline wanted, as she felt death creeping up on her, was to see *you* settled happily. You and Griselda. But mainly you. She felt powerless. She felt out of her depth in the changing world and she desperately wanted to stop you frittering away your beauty and talent. That's how she put it."

"Oh dear. I can hear her saying that. It's so sad."

"She didn't expect you to be like her. But she wanted to save you from a life like your mother's."

"And look at me, Arthur. I've turned out just like my mother. My spirit broken from losing my lover."

"Your spirit isn't broken. Don't you see how clever Eveline was? She left you the brasserie. A challenge she knew you wouldn't reject."

"Then the story will have a sad ending if the police close us down."

Arthur got to his feet. He had to pull this off.

"Listen to me, Lydia Renfrew, Eveline loved you. Make The Mandrake the most interesting place in London. For her. You can make it into anything you want it to be. Create it. Like a play. Or a painting. Women will come to eat on their own, lovers will outwit gossip columnists and the authors of underground political journals will compose their articles. The Poet will read his poems from the gallery. A place where people will fall in love, sit and write poetry, and plan to change the world. It may go down in history. You have to do that."

"And will the avant-garde playwright come here to dream up his next play?"

"In that whispering flat, that's what I've really been doing. That's what I'm trying to tell you – don't you see – he already has."

Lydia held on to his hands and looked into his eyes.

"I've done it, Lydia. It's finished. And it's being put on at the Majestic. My first play was about mill owners and trades unions, and the second about criminals and rock musicians. Forget the third. Men. Men. Men. This one is about women. About time I focused on women, don't you think? It's dedicated to Eveline. And, Lydia? I really want *you* to be with me on the opening night."

# Acknowledgements

First of all thank you to the Faber Academy Writing your Novel course in 2018, where I started writing this novel and which took me out of a Camden garret and turned me into someone determined to be a writer. Thank you to wonderful tutor, Joanna Briscoe, and to all 14 members of that Faber group – talented, friendly, funny, outrageous and mainly millennial. Thank you to Katie Bond for putting me in touch with editor Victoria Millar who significantly improved the story.

Thank you Christopher Tugendhat for recommending publishers whitefox and to John Bond and George Edgeller there who have been encouraging, effective and easy to work with. Thank you Katie Bond, a second time, for a rigorous and scintillating transformation of my understanding of PR and to Gina Rozner for her expert and enjoyable professional advice. Thank you Tony Bryne for teaching me about pigeons and to ex-brother-in-law Bill Garnett for the world of advertising in the mid-sixties. Thank you Kate Gavron for editorial advice and font and covers and spines and pricing. And Anthony Barnett, Anne Chisholm and Rachel Johnson for their kind endorsements.

To all who helped me in various ways including Margaret Atwood, Unna Marie Blundell, Zrinla Bralo, Jon Cook, Jennifer Coles, Chris Crowcroft, Stanley Johnson, Patricia Lankester, Eleanor Mills, Christina Noble, Miranda Seymour, Catriona Stewart and Michael Stopford.

Thank you very much to my children, Achara, Luke and Theo Tait, for their long-running support and to my grandchildren for their curiosity, and to my stepdaughter Becky Hardie for generous and wise advice at every stage. Thank you most of all to my husband, Jeremy, for his loyal and perceptive support through dark days and sleepless nights.